# KEEPING
## *Tabs*

# BEVERLEY
# COURTNEY

First edition October 2020

Published by Quilisma Books
www.beverleycourtney.com

Everything you need is already within you. The beauty of life
is that your destiny lies always in your hands.

Pablo Picasso

# 1

The noise was ear-splitting. An almost indescribable mixture of squawks, laughter, shrieks, shouts, general chatter, with the odd scrape and crash of a chair on the hard floor. Forty children between about 5 and 15, were ready and waiting for the rehearsal to begin. The room was full of movement. The younger children were zooming about chasing each other, the older girls chattering in small groups. The older boys were affecting indifference to the girls while they actually tried to get their attention - largely by pushing and joshing each other. Their breaking voices added depth to the general hubbub.

Peering through the diamond-shaped glass pane in the door and glancing round the room, Tabitha could see clusters of parents - mostly, but not exclusively, mothers - chatting happily, catching up on the week, the occasional burst of laughter giving a peak to the noise levels.

She allowed herself to gaze warmly on this scene. She loved all the children - yes, even Kieran, who had tried everyone's patience for a while till he decided he wanted to join in. She was also fond of the parents, who were a loyal band who truly appreciated what Tabitha did for their children - for their whole family, in fact - and repaid her work by supporting her with their time and their energy, first helping with rehearsals, then helping to fill the hall for performances. She felt a surge of pride as she stood watching, appreciating their devotion. Some had been there since she'd first started, and were now bringing their third or fourth child!

She could spot the new parents immediately. They looked stiff and uneasy as they witnessed the mayhem - a little uncomfortable, unsure, wondering if bringing their precious child to this madhouse had been a good idea, while the "old lags" worked their magic to draw them into their groups. They did their best to involve them in their conversations, chat about their children, get them to join in. But it was uphill. Either they saw the results or they didn't. And if they didn't, they weren't there long.

Tabitha smiled to herself. Actually practically no one ever left unless they were moving far away from the area. Once they saw how much their child loved her drama school, and - more importantly - they started seeing the results in their daily lives at home, they stayed.

Involving some of the parents in the school was one of Tabitha's brainwaves. She needed "minders" for when something went wrong, a child got sick or injured or upset, someone to be able to take the child to hospital if necessary. And she thought at the start that having them there would help with the "discipline" of the group. But she soon found that she didn't need any help there. The children were gripped by what she asked them to do, and - in fact - would do anything to please her.

Her little school, which had started with a handful of young children, children who were now the teenagers looking suave and at home, the girls with their long hair and gangly legs, and the boys with the broken voices, had grown far beyond anything Tabitha had anticipated. She had never guessed how popular her school would become locally. She had so many doubts about her ability, from being so undermined at home, belittled. But there were now sometimes as many as fifty children at rehearsals. As many of the parents chose to stay and watch, this made for a full and noisy hall and a busy session.

Tabitha's approach to rehearsals was very different from what people would expect - the noise and excitement was encouraged, indeed nurtured. It wasn't meant to be at all like school. It took new parents a while to accept that their child was not being turned into a hooligan - rather that the creative side of their mind was being opened up.

This was the most important part of Tabitha's life. A place where she was valued, supported - loved, in fact. A place where she could be truly herself, without fear of folks' opinions. In truth, she knew she could do this, and she could do it well. She didn't have ambitions - any ambitions had long ago been crushed, at home.

Then, she thought, it was *one* of the most important parts of her life ... For a blissful moment her mind went back to her lazy afternoon in Jamie's arms, smiling up at her lover's warm gaze – time with someone who loved her just for herself ... Then her thoughts leapt forward to the invigorating and restorative dog walk in the fields she'd enjoy after the rehearsal. Those walks were her escape hatch, to fields, woods, and the wonders of nature: the open views across the fields, the majestic trees in the copses and hedgerows, the wildlife she saw - hares, deer, birds, the stalwarts of the farmyard, the wind causing the grass to sparkle and shine in the spring sunshine; the tiny flowers growing at the foot of the hedge, the brash stalks of last summer's docks, the perfect flat rosette of a large thistle; the sheep calling their lambs, the sound of the cattle peacefully cudding; the wrens in the hedge, the seagulls following the plough, and the glorious v-shaped skeins of hundreds of chattering geese heading home for the night. The landscape fed her soul.

And she'd set off as soon as she got home.

Home to Angus.

With a deep breath, she prevented the lurch in her stomach turning into the sick helpless feeling she got at the thought of her husband.

She realised that a couple of small children were quietly waiting behind her. She smiled at them, saying "Hi Annie, hello Jasmine, did you come together from school today?" She breathed in, held her head high, pushed open the hall door for the two girls to scamper in, and entered the hall.

The noise was so much greater and more immediate once she stepped inside! She was immediately greeted by a gaggle of small boys who grabbed her hands, all shouting at once in their excitement. Two of the youngsters were shoving each other to take her bag to carry it. "Now Luke! Let Matthew carry my bag this time. I don't want you to pull it in half! I'd love you to go and make sure the table is ready." Luke raced ahead proudly, while Matthew walked beside Tabitha with her heavy bag, crammed with scripts, attendance sheets and all the rest. "Do you always have to carry bricks in your bag?" he asked in his slow, ponderous voice, as he held the handles up under his chin, using his legs to bounce the bag forward as he walked. Tabitha laughed in reply.

The noise of the room! Tabitha smiled fondly at them all, then nodded to Sally, her indefatigable helper, who was organising chairs and supervising the tending of a bruised knee and its sniffling owner. The girl who was comforting the child was Jennie, one of those teenagers who'd been in the School for ever. She was dealing with the anguished child gently and calmly and with such a caring manner - the older girls were brilliant at mothering the little ones.

It was a family atmosphere that Tabitha had taken great care to foster in the group as it grew. She had no time for factions or fights. Shooting Stars worked because everyone was on the same mission - to put on plays that they all enjoyed. To dwell for a while in another world, one without cares.

Sally was one parent who had been outstanding from the start. Her daughter Maisie was shy and really not very gifted at drama at all, but attending the school had helped to bring her out of her shell. It was a joy to Tabitha to watch the transformation in the children. From bossy to co-operative, from shy to confident, from awkward to accomplished. It was the change she effected in the children which was in fact more rewarding to her than even the success of the surprisingly polished productions. It was the change that she wished she herself had experienced as a child and which she was now passionate about bringing to as many children in her small town as she could reach.

This close family feel in the school included even the most gauche and untalented of the children, the trickiest parents. Sally was a marvel at resolving problems. And she had the opportunity to spring into action right at that moment. One of the new parents was heading towards Tabitha with a steely expression, apparently determined to give Tabitha a piece of her mind about the chaos in the room.

"Mrs. Morpeth?" she said firmly as she homed in on her target. Tabitha felt her heart-rate going up, but just at that moment, Sally skillfully intercepted the parent and listened attentively to her protests, allowing Tabitha to continue across the room, in her pre-rehearsal bubble of focus.

".. but I really think .." "I suppose you know best ..." "Alright, I'll give it a try, just for today ..."

Tabitha could hear shreds of the conversation - just the booming voice of the new parent in fact, as Sally was speaking much more quietly - while she detached and centred her mind again.

Not for the first time, she blessed the day Sally's quiet daughter Maisie had joined Shooting Stars and brought her mother with her. Sally managed somehow to approach an issue so that the complainer ended up apologising and thanking her for everything she did and offering to join in and help. She had great gifts!

Right on cue, the new parent was saying, in a much calmer voice, "Yes, of course I can help with the chairs ..."

Tabitha smiled and nodded to the groups of parents as she followed the small boys across to the chair and table put out ready for her. Gauche little Maisie was weaving her way carefully through the moving gaggles of children carrying a glass of water. Most of it remained in the glass, which was deposited in a wet puddle on the table.

"Thank you, Maisie!" said Tabitha. "That's so thoughtful of you. You look after me!"

Maisie was dumbstruck, but gazed up at her teacher as if her heart would burst.

The older children were already gravitating towards the stage and getting into rows. Some of the younger children, especially the young boys, were still racing around chasing each other until one of the mothers came and touched her son on his shoulder and nodded meaningfully towards the stage, at which he stopped his whooping, clapped his hand over his mouth, and clattered up the steps noisily, hotly pursued by his fellows. So by the time Tabitha was ready for the rehearsal to start, there was already a largely silent mass of squirming, expectant, children waiting for her.

Tabitha clapped her hands quietly and the whole room was instantly quiet. The last couple of children rushed to their places on the stage, the old wooden floor giving up its particular woody scent with all the feet on it, and the parents took their seats with eager anticipation. The noise of thundering feet on the wooden steps and the scraping of the chairs on the floor subsided. The electricity of forty children in a room still vibrated, and Tabitha was about to channel it into some warm-up exercises. As ever, the children's eyes shone with anticipation, because they knew just what was coming. Apart from the wriggling of the younger children, they were all still and attentive.

"Let's start with *breathing*," said Tabitha. "How far should the breath go into your body?"

"*As far as it will go!*" chorused the children in unison with an enthusiastic stamp at the end - the impact on the old stage of so many feet making a huge percussive sound. Each child placed hands on tummy so they could feel the breath going right down "as far as it would go", so they could support the sound they needed to project. After a variety of slow, fast, and deep breathing, Tabitha launched them into some vocal exercises - a mixture of singing and humming, declaiming and chanting.

This is where the new parents were always bowled over. Tabitha could see out of the corner of her eye that the new parent Sally had been pacifying was sitting on the edge of her chair, watching intently, mouth open with amazement at the sheer volume of sound the children made, their clear voices singing together with precision. What had been a rabble a few minutes earlier, was now a machine producing a loud penetrating sound. The newcomer's own child, Philip, was joining in as best he could with the group he was already feeling a part of. Tabitha was channelling the energy and excitement that had looked like chaos a few moments before into the focus on producing the sound and the projection that she wanted.

Each child was totally focussed on her, as they carefully used their bodies to make the quality of sound Tabitha was asking for, without forcing, without straining or pushing, without hunching up their shoulders or becoming stiff and rigid. Just allowing the great sound to come out of them. The warm-up finished with singing some fast tongue-twisters:

"Peter Piper picked a peck of pickled peppers - a peck of pickled peppers Peter Piper picked," they chanted in a fair rhythm. Tabitha started them slowly then repeated it, gathering speed, till most of the smaller children gave up and collapsed laughing.

They moved quickly into "Round the rugged rock the ragged rascal ran," with an emphasis on bringing the sound forward in their mouths and not swallowing it, then finished with "She sells seashells on the seashore - the shells she sells are seashells I'm sure!" As always these resulted in much laughter and delight.

"Now here's something new for you!" The children waited in absolute silence, round-eyed, to hear what new fun they were going to have.

"I want this half of the stage," Tabitha waved her arm to indicate who she meant, "to start, with Round the rugged rock. THEN," she added with a dramatic pause, "this side will repeat it, only *faster!*"

The children in the middle of the stage jumped and shuffled towards one side or the other – wherever their friends were – and waited eagerly to start.

"Remember, I want to *hear* every single word!" said Tabitha, as she stepped forward from her table and got one side of the stage going. The older children worked hard to enunciate clearly, keep the rhythm, and go faster than their friends in the other section. They got into it physically too, and the stage became very animated. Inevitably it all ended in disarray, and everyone was laughing, all the children, and most of the parents too. Even Philip's mother was now relaxing and joining in with the fun, nodding with a smile to the "older" parent Sally had strategically placed her beside.

After a few minutes of this, Tabitha - completely engrossed in her work - called for Act II, Scene 3 to stay on the stage. All the other children scrambled off the stage and sat on the floor or chairs, with rapt attention. There was no need for discipline in this school. The children "disciplined" themselves. They had a thirst for learning, desperate to be up on that stage.

Even the shyest or most awkward new child could find expression. Tabitha had watched young Philip copying his neighbours - his new friends - and making an effort in the warm-up. Some, like Sally's Maisie, took weeks and weeks before they would utter a word which wasn't a mumble. Some had been so conditioned by school to keep quiet and not rock the boat that they were afraid of being themselves. Here was a place where they were *encouraged* to be themselves.

Tabitha had created a school which gave children everything she felt she hadn't had in her own life. The children were her. This was her way to help the Tabitha of old, to reach out a hand to the introverted and suppressed child she had been. To show children that everyone could be the best they could be, no matter their circumstances, gifts or lack of them.

When the rehearsal was finished, the children were tired and fulfilled. All of them had had a turn at doing something - plays with lots of crowd scenes were always an essential choice. Sometimes this meant Tabitha would improvise and adapt the material to enlarge the cast, and she happily remembered a Christmas play which had had at least seven shepherds and a huge flock of small, wriggly, "sheep"!

Now Tabitha came back to the moment and dealt with queries, laughed, smiled, acknowledged all the thanks and greetings, and started packing up her things.

"Yes, I think Jason did brilliantly too!" "Of course, see you next week!" "Bye, Cynthia!" "Mind you get those lines learnt, Cassidy!" "Bye, bye-bye ..."

Her work finished, she relaxed and was able to chat to the parents and laugh with the children. Some of the parents just wanted to be sure to say thank you, others had questions to ask about their child's progress. They crowded round her, eager to get their goodbye acknowledged before retrieving their child from the melee and heading home.

Johnny's mother was worrying as usual, "Do you think he'll ever be any good?" she asked confidentially, so Johnny wouldn't hear. She needn't have worried, as Johnny was at that moment across the room playing chase rowdily with his friends.

"He's great, Eileen, really! Just you watch how he'll come on. Give him time."

"I have to tell you, Tabitha," laughed one of the keener parents, moving into the space left by Eileen, "I was running through Jason's lines with him the other day, and he said 'Bring the sound forward, Mum, I can barely hear you.' I had to laugh!"

Tabitha laughed too, recognising her exact words from a previous rehearsal. "I love that!" she said, as Jason's mother added more seriously, "He's doing better at school too. Holding his own. He used to be afraid of making mistakes, you know? I'm so pleased to see him getting braver, and I'm sure you've had a lot to do with it."

She reached out and squeezed Tabitha's hand as she scrunched her lips together to prevent tears. Tabitha returned the gesture warmly, placing her own hand over hers.

"Thank you, Tabitha dear!" chipped in another mother, "it's just amazing what you can do with this bunch of street-urchins!"

Tabitha gave her a beaming smile in response. She knew that she was glowing outwardly as well as inside. She tossed back her dark hair, loose today, as she turned to find another eager parent.

"Are you going to want some sewing help with the costumes, Tabitha? I'm pretty good with the machine ..."

"That's wonderful, Beatrice! Do chat to Sally - she's organising everything. The sewing group could always do with some extra needles - and biscuits!"

Owen, who was the boy currently experiencing a crush on Tabitha, gazed adoringly at her with a lovestruck expression while he waited his turn. Tabitha was patient and kind speaking to him - she knew his crush would pass and she always tried to head him off to join the others his age.

"Well, Owen," she said, "You really looked the part of the handsome young man today - you'll be snapped up by one of the girls at this rate!"

Owen blushed, smiled, and darted off to catch Jennie and Amy as they reached the door.

"Mummy says you're to come and see her again," recited Daphne, standing squarely in front of Tabitha.

"I'd love to!" said Tabitha, resting a hand on Daphne's shoulder. "Tell her I'll drop round very soon - this week." It was true it had been a while since she'd had one of her coffee-and-set-the-world-to-rights sessions with her dear friend and near neighbour, Maureen. She would have to make time for this.

"Yes, Celia," Tabitha turned to a rather tubby eleven-year-old who was yearning to be noticed, "you *will* be getting a bigger part in the next production. I've been watching you - you're doing great! No more talking into your chin - we all heard you loud and clear!"

Celia positively bounced away, grinning widely, chin jutting upwards, while pretending that she hadn't been waiting at all.

Sally waded through the throng round Tabitha to say hello and goodbye - it was the first chance she'd had. But before she could do more than catch Tabitha's eye, a couple of the other mothers came over together, with their children at foot, still playing their parts and laughing. Sally mouthed to her, "talk to you tomorrow" as she left her to it.

"Tabitha, you're a marvel!" said Angela. "The way you get this rabble to concentrate is *amazing!*"

"You should do this professionally," chimed in Linda, the other mother, then blushed and stammered in confusion. "I mean I know we pay a little for this, but I mean - you should be *famous!*"

Tabitha smiled and reached toward Linda's hand briefly to reassure her. "I know what you mean, don't worry Linda," she said. "But I could never be famous. I'm ... just me. I love what I do, but I'm sure there are plenty of people who are better than me."

"Well, we think you're the greatest!" rejoined Angela, whose young son Thomas appeared beside her chanting, "You're the greatest, you're the greatest!" before running back to Sharon, who had tucked her skirt into her knickers and was attempting a cartwheel.

"And *I* think you should be famous," said Linda stolidly. "I can't thank you enough for what you've done for my Sharon. But actually I'm happy that you're content with just us here. We'd hate to lose you!"

Tabitha noticed Sally smiling secretly at the two women. She knew Sally felt she was her discovery, and was happy with this level of reflected fame. And she wondered if she'd ever be able to develop the School as she'd really love to - impossible at the moment, of course.

And after locking up and bidding Sally good night, she drove home, reflecting on this exchange. Yes, she loved Shooting Stars. It was what gave the rest of her life meaning. She was still glowing from the rehearsal, where she was immersed, truly herself. It was what gave her her place in life. Instead of being exhausted after all she'd put into the session, she felt invigorated, energised! She had thought that being a wife and mother would be her place, and that that would be sufficient reward. But being a wife to Angus was so hard – and now she knew there was no hope of any children.

Her euphoria of the day began to ebb away, the nearer she got to home. She was beginning to realise that she used the school as an escape valve for her situation. The thought hit her amidships - she was hiding in her school to avoid facing the realities of her messy and tangled existence.

First there had been her stolen time with Jamie. Bliss. Another escape? Jamie always promised her so much, and she knew he did truly love her. But it was a fantasy. He'd never leave his wife and kids - nor could Tabitha want him to, except in their dreamland time together. She could never take a father from his children. No happiness could be built on that.

She avoided the thought of how Angus would be this evening. Time enough to find out when she got home. She thought instead of the greeting she would get from her dogs. She loved these two uncomplicated creatures so much! They and their predecessors had been her solace down the years. Walking in the fields and woods with them was always wonderful. It allowed her soul to breathe, to rest, to know what was important to her. And these dogs were important! Though they were dogs and she didn't mistake them for children, they were in a way the children she didn't have. They were the warmth in her cold home. But for them she may have given up on life long ago.

And so she could no longer avoid thinking of Angus.

How would he be today? Would he be angry? Again. Would he have been drinking? Again. Would he be lurking in his study and not be anything at all? Would he perhaps feel good and be like he used to be, solicitous and attentive, enquiring after her day, sitting her down, making her a coffee …?

Tabitha shook her head sadly. Those times seemed so long ago. Before they were married he swore to her daily how much he loved her, how he wanted her happiness. But things seemed irrevocably different now.

She drove past Paddy's woods and the big 50-acre field where she found such escape from her life at home, opening her window to inhale the earthy smell. She saw the lights on in Maureen's warm and always-noisy house. And as she crunched onto the gravel of her drive, drawing up beside Angus's car, she could hear the excited welcome barking of Esme and Luigi - the simple devotion she could always rely on.

She turned off the engine and paused for a moment before getting out. She took a deep breath - transitioning from the pleasure of her school to the friction of her home - gathered her bags, got out of the car and headed for the kitchen door. As she put her hand on the handle she got a very different feeling from when she had opened the door at Shooting Stars just a couple of hours ago. She felt suddenly weary. She knew exactly what to expect from her dogs, but what version of Angus would she get this evening?

# 2

It wasn't the sort of day for a bombshell. What sort of day would be a day for a bombshell? Not a day when she had been drowsy in her lover's arms, then invigorated and absorbed by her work, before returning home to her husband.

So she came through the door fulfilled, tired. And unsuspecting. The flurry of wagging tails and soggy teddy bears as her dogs greeted her in their accustomed ecstatic fashion brought a soft smile to her face. She peeled off her gloves and started to unzip her coat, wondering why there were no lights on. Angus was doubtless in his room writing as usual. Time to make a coffee and play with the dogs before yet another painful confrontation.

Then she saw him.

He was there in the darkest part of the kitchen, leaning against the range, holding onto it to steady himself.

"Where have you been?" he demanded, in a slow, thick, voice.

Tabitha's heart sank as the dogs' joy waned and they crept back to their beds.

"Where have you been?" he said again.

He had been drinking. This was bad. It could only be bad. He'd always enjoyed a drink, but over the last couple of years it had become compulsive with him. And it always led to a bad mood, and more demands.

"Rehearsals," she replied evenly.

"Who with?" Tabitha's heart sinks. This is an echo of the last time he got jealous and possessive over her. What had sparked it this time?

Tabitha brushed her hand across her face. She could smell Jamie. For a moment she fled back to the early afternoon, his easy presence, his comforting presence.

"The usual crowd. You know we're working on the new production." Tabitha wondered who it was he had singled out to be jealous over. Last time this happened he decided it was Gerard, the stage manager at School for Scoundrels. Crazy idea! Tabitha was very fond of Gerard, who was besotted with his wife and family and talked of little else. But she regarded him as a friend, no more. As she hotly denied any such thing, he had looked knowingly at her and said, "I see, so it's the guy in charge. Edward, isn't it?" She gave up. No one saw her as a "love interest", least of all Angus. Except, that is, for Jamie.

"You're always working on a new production. It's never-ending, these new productions. Well, I have a new production now." He gripped the rail on the range as he swayed. "I've been invited on a lecture-tour. America. Important. They want me to be a guest lecturer at one of the top Universities. It's a permanent move. So you need to shelve your new 'production' and support me." He said with a flourish. Then he added, *sotto voce*, "And stop wasting your time with this drama nonsense."

Last time Angus had said that, it was three years ago. He always hated her having fun with her work, her friends. He had friends. But he didn't like Tabitha having friends. He was jealous of all of them, and worked to alienate them, one by one. She had been in a small theatre company, the School for Scoundrels. It didn't pay that well - what acting did? - but she had loved it. It was the sort of place where everyone doubled up as something else. So the male lead was also in charge of the props. The stage manager often had small parts to play. And Tabitha, who was content with small roles, could help the Director, do the make-up, research the costumes, live and breathe the theatre.

It was then that Angus had demanded she spend more time at home. Being on tour for a few weeks, leaving him to mind "those goddam dogs", having to fend for himself - burning the saucepans and killing the house plants: since when had he become so inept, this man who had lived independently for so many years before marrying her? - was the last straw for him. He made it clear that she had to leave the company, convinced that she must be "carrying on" with Gerard.

It had broken her heart, but she'd felt she had no choice. She didn't earn enough to live on. She'd chosen to marry Angus. She had to accept what living with him meant. For Tabitha her integrity was all-important. And she had vowed to stay with this man through thick and thin. How could she have foreseen that fitting in with her husband's wishes would be so crippling?

Tabitha looked at him now, his strong aquiline features that she could now make out in the gloom of the kitchen. She had once thought him so handsome. And she had to steady herself too. She held onto the back of the chair she had been going to toss her coat onto, just a couple of happy moments ago. Her friendly kitchen had become bleak and dark. She felt sick. What had she ever done but support him? She had given up so much. Damn her integrity! Damn her old-fashioned ideas about marriage! Angus was making yet more demands on her. And this one was shattering. A bombshell indeed. She felt the blood drain from her face, her lips cold.

For a moment her heart skipped a beat. Was Angus planning to go on his own, leaving her to look after the house while he was away? She felt a sudden rush of freedom sweep over her. As a young girl she had experienced this same feeling when her beloved old dog Simon had reached the end of his life. He was ill and in pain, and the vet said the kindest thing to do was put him to sleep. Tabitha was distraught. She hated seeing Simon suffer, but couldn't bear to lose the only constant friend she'd had her entire life. He had been the same age as her. She'd never known life without him and feared facing a future alone. But good sense prevailed and Simon breathed his last in her arms in the vet's surgery. It was only when his face relaxed as his head sagged that she realised it was herself she'd been thinking of. It was *her* loss and grief she had considered, and not the release the old dog deserved. Only a few days later she felt that rush of freedom, that lightness of heart that her old friend was no longer suffering. She hadn't understood till then how badly his pain had affected her. As now, she seemed trapped in a complex and painful situation – so much worse than she had allowed herself to countenance – and this shaft of light that had momentarily penetrated the gloom accentuated the misery of her life with Angus up to now.

"Well …" she began, lamely. What could she say? Whatever could she do?

She was not surprised by her husband's announcement that he was making plans without mentioning them to her. He was so secretive about everything. She was used to being the last person to know. But that didn't mitigate the hurt she felt at his latest - totally self-centred - demands. She was shocked into silence. She put her hand to her face again, just to smell Jamie once more, just for reassurance that there was someone who still cared for her. Jamie, who had enabled her difficult marriage by providing what was lacking in it.

"That's a great step for you," she said, trying hard to keep her voice even and hoping not to annoy him. "When do they want you to go?"

"Autumn term." Angus replied

Five months away! Five months to her life being turned upside down! She wanted to sit on that chair, stop her legs wobbling. But her home felt suddenly alien to her. And now – another bombshell.

"And it's 'us'. You'll be accompanying me – you're my wife, remember? We'll need to let the house. Probably sell it. There's a lot to do. But I have to finish the book, plan out the lecture series. So you'll have to deal with all the practical details of the move. I'll be far too busy. You'll have to contribute." He shifted his position, grasping the range more heavily.

Go away? Impossible! She couldn't possibly let the children down. And then there was Jamie.

She felt ready to cry. Out of frustration. Out of anger. Out of fear. Who was this man? How could this be the man who said he loved her, cared about her, wanted her to flourish as the green bay tree?

It had seemed so much the right thing to do, to marry Angus. He had taken such an interest in her, encouraged her in her ideas, given her the support that she felt had always been lacking in her life since she lost her father. He seemed to think she was worth cultivating, educating. It was hard to believe now, but he had actually encouraged her to go to Drama School, to pursue the life she'd always yearned for, but which had always been frowned upon by her family and teachers.

Had she loved him? He had always shied away from any physical expression of his love for her. She had thought – in her utter naivete – that it was for honourable reasons. He said that sex before marriage was wrong. But the marriage had come, and he was still unable to show her any physical affection. Since Jamie arrived back in her life, she realized she had never really loved Angus. She had been flattered by the attentions of this older, striking-looking, successful, man, and – with her total conviction that she was not the kind of person people loved – had accepted him as her last chance at marriage and motherhood.

And for a while it had seemed a good choice. She loved moving in the Bohemian circles he inhabited. She met people she would never have met otherwise – people with famous names, who knew other famous people, and who spoke to her as an equal. Strangely, the more she became immersed in this unconventional life, the more she noticed that Angus clung to convention and routine in the rest of his life – as if holding on to that allowed him to keep a grip on the world. She learnt too, to appear capable and deliberate in her actions. She made out that it was her devotion to the theatre that stood in the way of having a family, and never ever hinted that her husband was in any way at fault. So she took the blame for him – even then.

Tabitha had been coasting as her marriage went out of control and she focussed on the things she could affect. She'd been letting things run, hoping somehow to make the best of things. Head in the sand, as her mother would have said. She couldn't have a fulfilling marriage with this person who seemed to operate only on the intellectual side, and fell headlong for Jamie who appeared to offer her everything she felt was lacking in her life - joy, fun, affection. She'd been unable to devote all her energies to serving Angus – she itched to create things of her own, not serve someone else who was doing all the creating - and had started a small children's drama school in the town. Which grew. And grew.

Prevented from having the family she'd always wanted - a physical impossibility in her celibate marriage - she loved working with these children: she had so much to give them! Though it didn't involve travelling away, she spent a lot of time on it. A real perfectionist, she wanted to do the best she could for these fresh-faced, open-minded youngsters. With a small band of volunteers she produced her regular stream of high-quality productions on a shoe-string. So there was now a new batch of people for Angus to be jealous of. But this time she did her best to keep them separate from her home life. Having tried to involve Angus with her drama company colleagues, which only seemed to spark his possessiveness, she had not made the same mistake again.

She planned the rehearsal schedules, worked on the business of the drama school with her helpers. She could fit in those precious moments of joy with Jamie. She could do Angus's bidding and organise his life for him (why did he become more helpless as he became more successful?). But now he'd dropped his bombshell. And there were bits of her life spattered everywhere.

How could she leave? How could she stay? The children. The dogs! Her lover. Her one-sided marriage. Her head was spinning. Her integrity, her loyalty to her marriage, her unfathomed talents, all tangled and whirled together. One moment she could see nothing but walls and difficulties, the next moment, paths opened up in front of her - possible directions.

Jamie! After so many years apart they had not long found each other again - each filling a need for the other. Tabitha's need - for human contact, warmth, affection, physical love - could not be satisfied in her life with her husband. If she stayed behind when Angus left, the Jamie route suddenly became possible.

But was the impossibility the only reason she had always held back? She had never given herself the luxury of imagining life with Jamie, though it was something that he fantasised about endlessly. It had always been an impossibility. At first it was his young family. She could never have taken him away from them. She could not enjoy happiness at the expense of them. And now they were grown and he proclaimed himself free from his dull wife, Tabitha was not free. So only now, in these moments of impending change, did she allow herself to consider it a possibility. But her enthusiasm was strangely lacking! Oh my goodness, Tabitha thought, I had no idea: this has to be thought through very carefully.

There was so much she suddenly had to consider! Everything she'd been keeping under careful control, in different segments of her life, was now there in front of her - demanding to be addressed. It had been a juggling act, with her struggling to keep all the balls in the air, with occasional heart-stopping slips. But now the whole delicate structure was collapsing. Along with her husband's mental disintegration she could see everything was changing. Everything. There was no more coasting time.

She realised Angus was speaking again. Speaking slowly so that he didn't stumble over his words. While he propped himself on the range, he still managed to appear belligerent, chin jutting forward. So much dislike in that face, that she had once thought noble.

"Well?" says Angus, speaking to her as if he despised her, just as her old headmistress Miss Wiseman had done so many years ago when she had dismissed Tabitha's life-plans so coldly and brusquely, "What do you have to say?"

Tabitha could no longer stand being in the same room as Angus - this new, nasty, Angus. She looked to her dogs, keeping their heads down, motionless in their beds. They seemed to be the only constant in her life - the only thing she could rely on. She zipped up her coat and snatched up her gloves again. "C'mon dogs!" she called to them as she turned back towards the dark shape of her angry husband.

"I'm going out."

Resisting the temptation to slam the door behind her, she headed for the fields where she could be alone with her thoughts, where she could walk and walk, breathe in the cool fresh air, enjoy the beauty of her dogs and their freedom together, the wildness of it all. And attempt to make sense of everything whirling about her head.

Tabitha had always gone along with what her husband wanted, feeling that she had to be the good wife and fit in with him. She was shocked - and exhilarated! - to find herself questioning this. Something was making her feel that now she must take hold of her life and - for once - make some decisions based on what *she* wanted. This was as far as she would be pushed. She would go no further. She felt a new energy surge through her.

As she headed for the 50-acre, she suddenly realised she had choices. She'd had choices all along, but had never seen them. And this was such a fundamental shift for her that she needed to be alone and – as was her wont – analyse everything that was happening and how she could shape her future. As Angus would tease her in happier days, "Though the mills of God grind slowly, yet they grind exceeding small."

# 3

Tabitha clambered over the five-bar gate while the dogs scooted under it. Even in her distress she took care to climb the hinge side so as not to distort Tom's gate. Her thoughtfulness imbued everything she did. But even in that moment, perched atop the gate, the damp scent of the grass filling her senses, she questioned how that perfectionism was helping her - indeed, if it were helping her at all! Maybe it was time to cast it aside, think for herself, not try to make the best of something, but rip it apart and make something completely new.

"You can't make a silk purse out of a pig's ear," her mother used to say when purchasing expensive fabric for a new dress.

She turned away from the direction of the house and started walking with a determined air. Though it had been dark for some time this March evening, she knew Tom's field intimately, and had no fear of the dark. The dogs were jubilant at an outing at any time, and busied themselves snuffling in the hedgerow before they started their routine of dashing about chasing each other. She never failed to find their simple pleasure soothing.

The pungent scent of the grass and the early spring flowers under her feet rose up to her and anchored her in the hidden landscape.

But she was in shock. Angus's ultimatum had come completely out of the blue. He'd always been secretive, but this takes the biscuit, she thought. Deciding to take her to another country - without a word to her - how self-centred had he become?

He never used to be like this. When they first met he was solicitous, generous, caring. He would guide her elbow when they walked; he would offer her the best seat; he'd help her with her coat; laugh at her jokes … Where had that all gone? There's no sign of that any more! It was as if his failure to consummate the marriage caused him to withdraw into himself so that he was only able to find fault in her. An attempt to shift the blame to her? She was beginning, just beginning, to see that maybe it wasn't just her extreme unattractiveness that was the cause of their marital problems. Maybe there were two sides to this story?

He had been the perfect gentleman - especially when meeting her parents. They were dismayed that Tabitha should choose an artist rather than a solicitor or businessman like her father and brother, and darkly disapproved the fact that he was so much older than her. It was only fifteen years, Tabitha had protested, but ultimately Angus's manner had charmed them. Tabitha was already twenty-three years old and they were beginning to wonder if she'd be left on the shelf for ever.

He had clearly fallen in love with her, and told her so - "I fear I'm falling in love with you," he had said, with a puppy-dog expression which made him appear very vulnerable. Tabitha - who had never experienced anyone being in love with her, ever (her sexual encounters had been just that, encounters, a bit of exploration) - had felt guilty that she had generated such strong feelings in him. She felt responsible - to blame. When at last she had the power to affect someone else she shied away from it. But she thought this must be the real thing because he was the first man who had ever wanted her company and her thoughts, without wanting her body.

Although she'd met Angus at the impressionable age of nineteen, for years he'd shown no interest in popping the question. As she had got more involved with him, taking his advice on flat-hunting, work - even following his encouragement and going belatedly to drama school - she had begun to wonder if she was heading up a blind alley. People took them to be a couple who were simply not bothered with marriage. But marriage - and family - were something that bothered Tabitha a lot!

She had never let on to others at that time, but there was no sexual relationship at all in their relationship. Tabitha - in her innocence - had put it down to Angus's religious upbringing. She thought there must be some kind of logical reason. But Angus kept a lot of himself secret, and she had just assumed that everything would work out ok once she completed her studies at drama college, that he would eventually suggest they should share a house, and get married while they were about it. And marriage would mean children. And so it had happened, with an air of inevitability - of sliding down a groove and landing at the obvious conclusion. It had coincided with the lease on her flat coming up for renewal, and Angus's location being far more convenient. So they kind of drifted into sharing a house.

And when he had at last asked her to marry him, she felt that a new world was about to open up to her. A world where she could show her value by the ring on her finger. She could justify her place by her new handle of "Mrs.". She shook her head sadly as she walked now, thinking how deluded she had been. How misled by her parents' indoctrination, her upbringing, the popular idea that single people were lacking, and needed a partner to justify their existence, to complete them.

But things were not how they seemed. Angus had hinted that sex before marriage was wrong, to explain the lack of it. What she hadn't bargained for was sex *within* marriage being wrong too!

Esme, her younger dog, ran up to her and presented her with an Alder cone from near the ditch, jogging her thoughts back to the present. Puzzled at Tabitha's mood, she was trying to interact with her the only way she knew. Tabitha smiled and tossed the cone a few times, realising that she was getting cold and stiff. And tired. She sighed.

It wasn't just the sex she missed. It was the physical contact - the hugs, the cuddles, the hand-holding - that had made her feel accepted by previous boyfriends, and which was provided so lavishly by Jamie. With Angus there was none of this. And it hurt. It gave her a physical pain when she wanted contact and he shied away from her. She cursed her innocence! She had never met a man before who had not been interested in sex. She had had no idea that this lack of interest was even a possibility, no idea that there was such a thing as sexual dysfunction - still had no idea: she didn't read popular magazines, nor take an interest in real-life dramas on television. So she had entered all unsuspecting upon this marriage. And it was a small hop from this revelation to her feeling that it must, just must, be her fault.

Why else would a man not want her? They slept in the same bed, albeit swaddled in pyjamas and nightgown, like a Victorian couple. But there was no warmth there. Perhaps Angus had married her because he was sorry for her. He pitied her. Because no one else would ever want her!

She'd tried - how she'd tried! - to interest and arouse her diffident husband. But her shyness prevented anything really daring. She longed for the physical relationship to complement the undoubtedly good intellectual relationship. She wondered why he had wanted to marry a woman who was clearly so unattractive - repulsive, in fact. His intellectual connection to her had been very strong and she had concluded she should value that and not find fault over such a small thing as sex.

But it wasn't a small thing! Apart from anything else it meant she could never have the children she desired more and more as the years went by.

And they certainly did have common interests. Angus being an artist - a writer - meant that he was sympathetic to all the things she loved: mainly music and the theatre. She loved meeting his arty friends and listening to their stories long into the night when they visited. They all had their own partners, some had children, and Tabitha just hoped that this would one day be her lot. This was what people did, wasn't it?

Tabitha wiped a tear from her cold cheek. Esme was bouncing around Luigi joyfully. She was now taunting Luigi with her Alder cone, daring him to chase her. But the old dog had had enough chasing for one day, and just mooched along behind Tabitha.

Tabitha remembered the last time - the final time - she had tried to start something with her husband. She'd come home - from a winter walk with Riffle and Sparks, the dogs she had had back then before Luigi - with wet hair, rosy cheeks, and cold fingers. She had dried the dogs and settled them in their beds, then dived for the kettle to make a warming coffee while she dried herself.

"Here - I'll do that for you," Angus had said, emerging from his study.

"Oh thanks! I'll hang up these wet things," she'd said, heading for the row of coat-hooks under the stairs. "What are you up to today?" she called from the hallway, trying to find a way to hang her coat so that it wouldn't make everything else wet, and beginning to towel her hair.

"Oh, just writing," he said, declining to give her any more information. Why did he act like someone who'd signed the Official Secrets Act in regard to his own work? Couldn't he let her in a little more?

"I've been thinking," said Tabitha, having spent her walk, as usual, deep in thought. "I'm fed up with "resting" more than working. I got on so well with that little bit of teaching I did at College."

"You're good at teaching," he interjected.

She turned and looked full at him, with surprise. "Well, I thought I might do some more. Work out some sort of program that would help people express themselves. Children, maybe?" She breathed the "child" word carefully.

"You should. You'd be good at it. I'd like to see you fulfilling yourself." He gave her a smile, a smile of camaraderie - of affection. She reached out to him. This was the warmest he'd been in months. Perhaps now may be the moment? She leant forward and kissed his cheek, his neck, her breathing speeding up.

He put one arm round her. Then the other. Faces touched, breath fluttered on cheeks, bodies closed - then BAM! he let go and ran, *ran*, from the room.

Tabitha couldn't breathe. Her heart, her humiliation, rose up to choke her. Her throat hurt. The pain was intolerable. She rubbed her hands over her face, looked at the dogs - one was peacefully snoozing, the other watching her move about the room - then made for the kettle to make that coffee for herself.

Carry on as normal? Was that what she must do? No. This was it. This was the nearest they had got to intimacy - ever. She must resign herself to being so unlovely that she was unlovable. Yes - Angus was fond of her and liked her company. But no more. She had all the duties and responsibility of marriage, with none of the advantages.

There seemed only one thing to do, and that was to immerse herself in her new plan. She could divert all her sexual energy into enthusiasm to help the children. She couldn't have her own children - she realised now she could never have her own children - and that still provoked that ache in her heart. But she could work with other people's children.

She wasn't good enough to be like the rest of the human race. Perhaps she never had been. She had been told often enough by her mother that she wasn't up to scratch. It was clear that William was the darling of the family, and she came a poor second. And her hopes and desires had always been dashed and derided by her school teachers. She had to do what she could now to fulfil herself in some way.

That had been the moment she realised that her unattractiveness - so often hinted at by her glamorous mother - meant that she should think herself lucky to have got a husband at all. She had to put behind her all thoughts of a warm relationship - and babies - and focus her thoughts elsewhere.

And this was where she was when Jamie had breezed into her life. It was not in the script! But he happened, and brought her much joy ... as well as the inevitable anguish that would come with any illicit affair. Looking back, she could see that she was vulnerable to someone having this huge attraction for her. Someone who thought it normal and natural to stroke her hand, kiss her cheek, fondle her hair, give her shoulders a friendly squeeze to underline a comment (just as her father used to do, telling her how proud he was of his Tabby). And how she rejoiced in this. Jamie was always ready to compliment her, to tell her how much he loved her, how he wished he'd met her earlier, before his marriage.

"Oh Tabitha, where were you fourteen years ago?" he had wailed one night.

She should have felt guilty about Jamie. But she couldn't. She had all the burdens of marriage, she felt, with none of the privileges and perks. She felt entitled to satisfy this neglected part of her life. So she never felt too guilty about her relationship with him. It was as if she spent time with certain friends who enjoyed playing chess, or tennis. It was a legitimate way to satisfy a need in her - a deep need which she was entitled to have. She hated lying, but felt herself forced into the situation by her uncaring husband, who neglected his duties in this area - even though it was understandable, given her plainness.

For someone who upheld the sanctity of marriage to such a degree, her position here would appear strange. But she was of the firm conviction that physical contact between partners was right - why, even her parents had publicly expressed affection occasionally! - and therefore her relationship with Jamie was right too. The fact that Jamie was married with a young family somehow failed to impinge upon these feelings. It was his choice to love her. Maybe he did it for different reasons from her - while she had no children to cherish, he had four to wear him down. And she could never take a father away from his children. That would be totally wrong, totally unacceptable, totally unimaginable.

She was caught in conflict. Undoubtedly she and Jamie loved each other. Her feelings about his commitment to his marriage and family - and, to be fair, deep down these feelings were shared by Jamie - meant that it was only ever going to be an adventure. And if he should risk so much to spend time with her - and clearly found her beautiful and desirable - maybe she wasn't quite as ugly and unattractive as she thought? Or was it just fate that the one man in the world who was able to love her had stumbled into her life too late?

"I love you so much - I just want to hold you and protect you: I'm such a romantic!" he'd said one day, pressing his forehead to hers and peering at her from beneath his eyebrows.

"I'm not," she'd said. "I've suppressed it all over the years. Don't expect - then you're not disappointed."

Sweeping her up in his arms with a flourish, he'd said, "Then I'll have to teach you to be romantic again." And so he had. He was always giving her presents, though they were little things - insignificant, undetectable, of themselves. A wild flower one day, which he'd tuck into her hair over her ear, as she blushed and smiled at him, still not believing anyone could genuinely love her like this. A torn-out cartoon from a newspaper which had made him smile and think of her, a ribbon for her hair which he'd enjoy tying round it. Once, back then when they were first in love, he had given her a postcard of a dog which looked just like Sparks. But he didn't write on it.

The two men were so different! Jamie lighthearted and comical; Angus serious and reflective. Jamie passionate and devoted; Angus reticent and private. They each filled a need in Tabitha. Would that one of them could have been the whole deal!

As the dogs started to slow down and amble round the field with her, she realised it was getting colder and she had been thinking for a good while - and getting no further. She was going round in ever smaller circles, feeling a victim of circumstance.

She redoubled her efforts to focus on the problem at hand. Did she want to go to America with Angus?

No! She'd have to leave Jamie!

No! She'd have to close her school!

No! She'd become once more an appendage of Angus, instead of an individual in her own right.

No! Luigi was really too old to make such a journey.

And no! She'd have to start all over again, in a foreign culture.

But what were the alternatives? If she didn't go with Angus, she was effectively ending her marriage. This was a dreadful thought! She stopped so abruptly that Luigi bumped into the back of her leg. Her marriage - uninspiring as it was - was hugely important to her. She wasn't going to be one of those selfish women who left when the going got hard. She had taken vows. She couldn't just abandon her husband. It was wrong! Breaking a solemn vow was - just wrong!

But hadn't she already? By spending time with Jamie - over the years?

She had ended that affair the first time after a couple of years. But when they ran into each other again fifteen years later, they were instantly back together: they found each other irresistible. And this time round they hadn't dissembled. They accepted that they loved each other passionately. They didn't concern themselves with the rights and wrongs, just revelled in their closeness. And now Jamie was urging her to leave her unsatisfactory husband and be with him. She started slowly to walk on again.

She had her life divided up into compartments. There was her life with her husband, the respected author. There was her secret joy with Jamie, her happy-go-lucky lover. There was her work with the children in her drama school - immensely satisfying and endlessly fascinating. Whatever would those children's parents make of her strange and unconventional life? Perhaps they'd put it down to the artistic temperament, something foreign to so many, more prosaic, people.

These compartments were now threatening to burst open and spill over into each other. Angus's proposal would affect all the threads of her life - with devastating effect.

She had managed to keep them all running alongside each other - no mean feat of organisation, she realised! - and now she was going to be forced to start making some decisions. She could no longer coast along. Something big was happening. And she had to ensure she came out of it intact.

The wind was getting up and her head was beginning to ache. But still she trudged round the field with her now-subdued dogs. And still she worried it all around in her mind. She was tired. She was going in mental as well as physical circles.

The lack of a full relationship with Angus was bad enough. But it had got worse. He had become jealous of her finding any pleasure except in his service. He resented her few friends, and surreptitiously but effectively alienated them. He would emerge from his study if she were on the phone, and start clucking and complaining about the length of time she'd been talking. He came from an age where you paid for phone calls by the minute, and completely failed to appreciate that this was no longer so and you could talk as long as you liked. It was just his ingrained meanness coming to the fore. If she were listening to a radio programme while cooking, he'd walk into the room, turn off the radio, and go out again, leaving her open-mouthed and causing her to leave floury marks on the knobs as she turned it back on again to continue listening to her programme.

When she wanted to fix extra rehearsals for Shooting Stars, Angus would find pressing reasons why her chosen days were unacceptable. Any thought of developing the school further came up against firm resistance. She felt blocked at every turn.

He kept her continually short of money, while preventing her from developing her career and any meaningful chance of earning money of her own. She had tried a number of things, knitting garments for designers, a brief foray into network marketing, trying to write stories for women's magazines, even addressing envelopes. None of them worked. With a sudden jolt she saw that his solicitousness when she came back from rehearsals at the

School for Scoundrels - waiting up for her to get home then asking her all about her evening - was part of this control.

He liked to know where she was and when, and with whom. And gradually he'd alienated these people from her - on occasion actually taking the phone from her hand, saying "goodbye," and hanging up the receiver, cutting off the call from her friend, and leaving Tabitha aghast. He controlled all the household expenses, the utilities, the payments, giving her just enough to pay for the food and fuel and not a penny more, and complained about her profligacy. But he had little understanding of the real cost of things, and overlooked the magic Tabitha performed with his small allocation for grocery shopping. He felt that once you'd bought something it should last for ever, and she only managed to get a couple of windows replaced when Gary, Maureen's husband, had pointed out that they were so rotten they were dangerous. That was when people still visited the house. She had no money for clothes or haircuts or anything of that kind. She frequented charity shops and let her hair grow, having to plait it and tie back the awkward straight hairs which insisted on escaping bondage, the rats' tails, as her mother with her fair curly hair had called them.

She remembered how her mother would rail against the bad fortune that gave Tabitha straight dark hair instead of her brother's luscious blonde curls. Everything about William was better.

It was funny, she mused, how Jamie loved to thread his fingers through her dark, straight, silky, hair, stroking it down over her shoulders and breasts. *There* was someone who loved her for herself and her dark brown hair.

She looked down at old Luigi, who was beginning to plod stiffly along behind her. She realised that she was exhausted. She had been churning everything round in her mind and the only conclusion she had come to was the inescapable one that things could not go on as they were. Perhaps the offer of Angus's post was timely. At last something was going to have to happen. She had tried and tried … and yet she should never have let things get as bad as they had.

She was not the type to make trouble. So when Angus pushed her a little she would acquiesce. Then he pushed again and she would acquiesce further.

So it had gone on, for years now, until she looked around her and found herself in a lonely and desolate place. This was not where she should be! Putting up with stuff she shouldn't have to, continually going along with things she didn't like or choose, just in order to keep life calm, to avoid one of Angus's outbursts and his accusations of her selfishness … it just couldn't go on.

It was time she took control and started doing her own pushing. What she had been avoiding all these years now had to be faced. Was she strong enough? Yes! She had to be! Her mind was made up. She had to make some decisions that put herself first. But now was not the time to tell Angus, of that she was sure.

As she headed toward the five-bar gate again, she knew that she had to play for time while she considered the enormity of what would happen. She would not be forced into an early answer. He could wait. And so, firmly resolved in her very first decision, she went back to the house. She'd give Angus some dinner and take herself off to bed.

# 4

It was a very subdued Tabitha who returned to the house. She ministered first to the animals - put the hens to bed, collected the eggs, fed the dogs, then started Angus's dinner. It seemed such a long, long time since she had lain in Jamie's arms, without a care in the world. Now cares were heaped upon her, weighing her down, turning her physical tiredness into mental exhaustion. She'd thought she was tired after the rehearsal - a "good" tired - but that paled in comparison with how she now felt.

She resolved to stop thinking about the problem, as she was done with it for now. She turned her thoughts instead to the children's rehearsal scheduled for a couple of days out. There was a lot to work on, and after starting the dinner she spent a happy twenty minutes planning how it would go, nibbling at a bit of food as she worked. Channelling the children's wild enthusiasm into the controlled energy she wanted them to bring to the performance was a fine skill that she had developed over the years, and she was proud of it. So it was easy to immerse herself in this work.

She had to remember to ring Sally the next day to check up on some details. They were nearing the date of their next production, so planning had to be tightened up to get everything done in time. You never knew where you were with children. A bout of Mumps in the school, or just seasonal sniffles, could severely interfere with a rehearsal schedule. And some of the parents were quite cavalier about taking their child out for a holiday, or a visit to relatives. Take Jennie for instance. Gifted, certainly, but with almost no support from her parents, who saw Tabitha's school as a time out for them to indulge their own hobbies. She had to think what she could do to help Jennie - whose parents never would, that was for sure. She had spent time in the past worrying about this. But she didn't have the contacts she needed to make the difference she yearned to make with children like Jennie. Jennie would probably do well at the National Drama School, but Tabitha saw little hope of her parents subscribing to this idea - especially if it were going to hit their pockets. So this one went onto the back burner again.

The key students, though, were committed, as were their families. Some of them would bring large numbers of neighbours and extended family to the show, turning the event into a big party, vying in a friendly contest with some of the other parents to see who could pack the hall. Some of them organised post-performance parties at their home for all their guests, turning it into a big social occasion. Tabitha sat back and thought about the dedication given to her by so many of her children. Their loyalty was superb.

And perhaps, she thought, it was a reflection of her loyalty to them. She never let them down, never missed or rescheduled a rehearsal. She was always ready to listen to any problems a child may be having. And more than once she'd been able - very tactfully - to alert a parent about an issue the child seemed to be having at school. When it came to performance, all feelings were on show! A troubled child would be unable to conceal their anxiety, especially one who usually took part with abandon.

She sat back in her chair and reflected that it was her pesky loyalty that had landed her in her present predicament! She was unfailingly loyal to Angus. She never complained about him to anyone - certainly not to his friends, and not even her own, only, friend, Maureen. Even with Jamie she forebore to complain, instead rejoicing in the pleasure and lightness of his company. She saw that this loyalty, this refusal to acknowledge Angus's faults publicly - even though by being so unattractive she was equally at fault - was actually a cover-up. It enabled her to cover up what was really going on - sweep it under the carpet, pretend it wasn't happening. By keeping herself busy, she didn't have time to stop and analyse it all.

But now she was going to have to. And she had a sneaking feeling that her friend Maureen knew a lot more than she ever let on. She looked forward to seeing her again. Reliable Maureen! Always there for her, despite having a busy family life herself. She'd shamefully neglected her friend recently, what with one thing and another. But she'd promised Daphne she'd call her mother this week. She couldn't go tomorrow, but by the end of the week she'd definitely drop in.

So she focussed on thinking about the things she *could* control - her school rehearsal and her visit to her friend. Everything else was whirling out of control, and for tonight, she'd let it. She'd had enough. She was all in.

When the food was ready, she wrenched herself back to the present, put her head round Angus's study door and said, "Your dinner's on the table."

"Ah, good," he said. "I wondered if you'd decided to skip dinner."

"I've had some and I'm off to bed. I'm very tired."

"Well, if you will walk for hours in the dark … When are you going to get started on the America plan? There's a lot for you to do."

"Can we talk about this another time?" Tabitha put her hand to her head. "I need time to work this all out."

"What's there to work out? It's just a question of getting things organised - putting the house on the market, and so on."

"I'm not going to discuss this now," Tabitha said firmly, surprising herself into the bargain. "Please lock up when you're done."

She turned to the dogs who followed her up the stairs to the bedroom. They crawled straight under the bed to their sleeping places. Sliding into the cool sheets and feeling the pillow on her still-hot cheek, Tabitha realised how very upset she had been.

She was not going to start all over again with worrying! So she firmly closed her eyes and as so often, was fast asleep long before Angus came up to bed.

In the small hours she awoke again. She lay on her back, staring unseeing at the ceiling of the darkened room. Beside her was the mound of her husband's back. He always faced away from her. He was snoring and twitching his feet from time to time.

She dropped a hand down to the dog under the bed and touched his soft head, hearing a sleepy flip-flip from his tail in response. Thank heavens she'd stood up to him over dogs in the bedroom. Once they stayed under the bed he allowed it.

She carried on staring up, wide awake, unhappy, not knowing how she got herself into this predicament, and with little idea of how to get herself out of it.

# 5

It was the next day when she met up with Jamie for another of their snatched hours. That's why she couldn't accommodate a visit to Maureen till later in the week. She had a certain amount of freedom, but she'd always been careful to farm it strategically.

They were walking along a towpath by the canal, with that particular blend of still water and the musty brickwork of the tunnels, that always made her think of the Navvies who had built them, all laboriously by hand. It was quiet and they were alone apart from the occasional dogwalker, who would acknowledge her as a fellow spirit once they saw she had her dogs with her. The path would be full of homegoing schoolchildren a bit later. But for now they had it virtually to themselves.

"Off you go, dogs," said Jamie when the path was completely empty, "I want to kiss your mother." Tabitha laughed as she received his kiss. She knew the dogs would never be far from her.

It was a beautiful spring day. Trees were blossoming and the wild flowers along the path coming into bloom - the young cow parsley already giving off a heady scent. The dogs snuffled happily in the undergrowth. They were her official excuse for being there - a walk in a different place: something Angus struggled to comprehend, but he let it go. While Jamie enjoyed the dogs, he was a bit traditional in his approach, and he was quick to dismiss them when he'd rather have Tabitha to himself. So she insisted on bringing them with her whenever she could. He knew better than to raise his hand to them, but he had raised his voice in the past. She hoped that eventually Jamie would see how her way of being with her dogs was much more effective (and enjoyable) than his way. At the very least it might enhance his interactions with his own children, understanding them better without need for old-fashioned approaches.

While there was no doubt that he loved his children dearly, many years ago Tabitha had seen him strike one of his young sons. He had called the boy over to him, asked him to turn round, then gave him a kick on the bum. It wasn't the physical assault which had upset Tabitha so much - it was more a tap than a kick - it was the fact that the boy had complied with two requests without question and still got punished. That thought occasionally revisited her and choked her with its unfairness, its wrongness. She had no evidence that Jamie had ever done such a thing since. The chill of her shock and disapproval at the time must have sunk in.

So now, while her dogs sniffed and scampered around them, she and Jamie walked together, chatting happily, able to hold hands when nobody was about. He was telling funny stories about the others at work.

"So he measured twice and cut once - but still managed to cut the wrong bit!" As they laughed, Jamie put an arm round her shoulder and hugged her to him, "Love your laugh, Tabitha," he murmured as they walked.

As a carpenter Jamie had found himself doing a lot of work for theatre companies. In fact, that's how Tabitha had met him, when he was making scenery and props for the School for Scoundrels, the company Angus had forced her to leave. It was only after she'd left - with Angus's accusations of her playing around ringing in her ears - that she realised how she missed Jamie, what a fun part of her life he had become at the sessions. And it was only after she'd left the company that they started their intimate relationship. Angus had been so wrong at the time!

That had been so long ago. It was that first time she and Jamie had been together. So much had happened in the interim, splitting up, then meeting up again years later and taking up exactly where they'd left off. It was as if they'd been resisting the inevitable for so many years, and just gave up the resistance once they met again. Now, after a few months the fresh feeling still remained. Tabitha still loved him every bit as much as she ever had.

They didn't always make love when they met. That would be sleazy in Tabitha's mind, and Jamie readily agreed. He reckoned that time spent together without sex was important to make their relationship normal, and lasting. So they'd meet in a cafe or for a walk, and just enjoy each other's company, regaling each other with tales from their lives. Jamie still had this rosy idea that they would one day be together, though the *how* of it happening never seemed to trouble him too much. Tabitha realised again with a start that this was something that in theory they could now do. But she had a feeling deep down, that it could never, would never, happen.

Why? And why was she not telling Jamie all about Angus's bombshell? She pondered on, indecisive.

After a while, they fell into step and into silence.

"There's something you're not telling me," said Jamie. "What is it, Tabs?"

"Oh," she said, blushing a little, "I had a headache this morning, and you know how they make me a bit cloth-headed for a day or two after."

Jamie turned to face her, placing his big warm hands on her shoulders, fixing his clear blue eyes on hers. "If there's anything, you will say, won't you," he stated firmly.

At that moment a moorhen skittered off the water and flew straight past them, giving Tabitha the distraction she needed.

"Being here with you and the dogs, in this fresh sunny air, is doing wonders for my head," she smiled at him, took his hand again and kept walking, Jamie entwining their fingers as he so loved to do. Would that what she had said were so! In truth she was in turmoil inside – a headache would honestly be preferable!

Why did she not want to confide in Jamie? Angus's bombshell was going to affect him massively, whatever happened. So why the reticence? Did she not trust him? No, she felt comfortable and trusting in his presence. That wasn't it.

She had to work out what *she* felt first, before even mentioning it to Jamie. She had to make these decisions for herself - no more letting others decide for her, dictate her life. And she seemed no further ahead there! As she saw it, she'd arrived at a fork in the road in her marriage. She had to make a decision there before she could look at the ramifications for all the other parts of her life. But they were all so wound up in each other that it was proving hard to disentangle them in her mind. She unwound her fingers from Jamie's and bent to admire the pretty clump of pink Herb Robert at the side of the path, seeing with delight some delicate Cowslips lurking beneath the swaying taller plant.

Did she want to stay married to Angus? This was the big question. And every time she looked at it, her head began to hurt. She'd married forever. "Till death us do part." She had always considered her word the most valuable thing. Her integrity. She felt a grating, searing pain whenever she thought about ending this marriage.

Failure? Yes, definitely! A failure on her part. Her inability to inspire love and passion in her husband was clearly her fault. But it was also her fault that she allowed him to bully her into positions she didn't want to be in. Losing her friends, limiting her interests, preventing her from doing what she wanted in life. The only friend she still had was Jamie, because she'd kept him completely secret. And Maureen, who was way too strong a character to pay any heed to "Angus's nonsense". The others, from her school days, drama school, the theatre group, had scattered to the four winds. She didn't have anyone left from back then. Anyone who really knew her.

But blaming was no use. It was unimportant now whose fault it was. "That's another fine mess you've gotten us into," she smiled to herself. It was how she was going to get *out* of the fine mess that counted.

She thought for a moment of the friends she used to have. Drama school friends, colleagues from the School for Scoundrels - even further back, the schoolfriends she'd got on with so well, back in those troubled days at school when she felt so misunderstood, Yvonne, Veronica, and Clare too, had been the ones to keep her cheerful and looking forward. Angus had managed to alienate all of them, one by one, keeping Tabitha a kind of prisoner. She wondered where those friends were now. Making a terrific success of their lives, she felt quite sure.

Esme's nose butted into her thoughts. Curious to see what she'd found, both dogs had come to join in the exploration, and took advantage of her face being at their level to lick her face enthusiastically.

She laughed as she stood up and smiled at Jamie, who, she realised, was watching her with a thoughtful expression. He stooped to pick up a stick and tossed it into the grass at the side of the path for Luigi to find.

"Here ya go, Luigi!" he said, as he feinted a huge throw before tossing it in another direction entirely.

She thought to herself how she had schooled him well that the dangerous stick should always land before the dog could get it. Some of what she did rubbed off after all, she reflected. As Luigi sniffed out the stick and brought it back he took it to Jamie rather than to her. Wise Luigi knew well that Jamie could throw far faster and farther than Tabitha could, and adding a bit of a chase to the game made it more fun for the old dog, who was hopping stiffly on all four legs as Jamie built the suspense - winding up for a massive throw into the deep grass. She loved watching her lover play with her dogs and she relaxed and laughed to see the fun. Such a contrast ... at home they were always considered a nuisance, in the way, things to be endured, put up with. No fun there.

Luigi had always loved hunting with his nose, and this was one thing he was just as good at as he grew older. Luigi growing older ... everything changed. That was life. And there was no getting away from the fact that things were now changing for Tabitha.

Which way was she going to jump, that was the question.

# 6

The noise was even greater than usual as Tabitha arrived at the next rehearsal. As they got closer to the performance, the children's excitement grew. And, until the rehearsal began, excitement meant noise! As usual before entering, she looked through the glass in the door, an expansiveness filling her heart as she saw what she had created.

The mothers were a-buzz with conversation. Linda and Angela, two of her most loyal parents (though goodness knows their kids were only average at best - they still loved Shooting Stars and wild horses wouldn't drag them away) were engaging Elizabeth, the slightly frosty new parent from last week. She was clearly warming to being included, as her son Philip dashed about with the other boys. "She'll do fine," thought Tabitha to herself with a smile.

There was an older man who she didn't recognise. He smiled in a friendly way to Linda who gave him a cheery welcome. "Must be someone's Dad or Grandad," thought Tabitha, though she noticed he looked a bit different from the other fathers - something flamboyant about his dress. She knew Sally would have greeted him on arrival, so she had no worries about whether he should be there - something they had learned to be careful about with so many children in their care. Sally was right now busy checking the register and answering queries.

Sally had seen how valuable the school was for her daughter. She knew it would take time and a lot of encouragement to bring Maisie out of her shell, so she decided in Sally-fashion to jump in and get involved herself, and had brought her super organisational abilities to the fray with gusto. Since giving up her work as a personal assistant in order to devote herself to her children, she'd found sorting socks and planning menus to be insufficient challenges to absorb her. So she'd welcomed the opportunity to bring her skills to bear at the school. To her, spreadsheets and planning were a snap, while to Tabitha it was all a confusing headache. She was really becoming indispensable, thought Tabitha. And Sally exactly knew that at rehearsals, all Tabitha's energy was focused on the session: she liked to stay in her bubble of focus till after the session. Discussions were always reserved for their planning meetings, rehearsals being kept for action.

"You've got it all planned out!" Tabitha had said at their last planning meeting, when Sally had produced a magnificent set of rows and columns, with colour-coding to make it all easier to read. She appreciated having the charts, but she neither would nor could ever have made them herself!

"You're a genius with the kids," replied Sally, "and I just do what I'm good at. That's why we work so well together, Tabitha!"

She felt differently towards Sally now. There had been a time when she'd rather resented this pushy parent, who seemed to her to be muscling in. But as she had let go of some of the more menial tasks which Sally had taken over with enthusiasm - sometimes deputing them to another parent or bunch of kids - she realised how very valuable Sally was. She got all the parents who were willing to help, working in their own zone of expertise, so she had make-up groups, costume sewers, props procurers, and so on. She was happy to take over a lot of the donkey work in running Shooting Stars - she loved all the things that Tabitha found to be sheer drudgery! Tabitha felt she didn't deserve such devotion, but she was very glad she had it.

There was a pile of paperwork now on Sally's table - probably some of her beloved spreadsheets! - clearly she'd been hard at work on the new business plan she had been proposing, to make the School financially secure. "Hopeless idea," thought Tabitha to herself, who had never had any ambitions to make money from the school. She really didn't find business easy to understand. Thank heavens for Sally, who did!

As she waded through a flock of excited children all clamouring for her attention, Tabitha laughed and smiled at them, as ever delighted and amazed that she could inspire such devotion.

"Hello Kieran!" she said to the back of a small boy who was flying past her, waving his hand cheerily over his head. "Yes, that's right, Scene IV tonight," she said to Sharon, not cartwheeling this time, but bouncing with excitement as she clutched her friend Emily's hand. "Hallo, good to see you back again," to Jonathan, who had been away ill, again. Tabitha wasn't sure if he had some serious medical problem or just a careful mother, but he still looked frail. "Mind yourself!" - this last to a group of small boys whistling past, Philip in the thick of them, and Kieran racing behind. And she smiled at Jennie, who looked across at her from the group of older girls, some of whom were actually studying their lines.

She made quick, slightly distracted, greetings to the parents then headed to the table set up for her in front of the stage, to start the rehearsal. As she stepped up to it a silence fell over the room. Tabitha's ability to control an apparently uncontrollable group always brought an envious smile to the lips of the watching parents. Always impressed with herself by the effect she had on this outwardly chaotic bunch, she wondered for a moment why she could never get this kind of attention from her husband. She shivered the thought away and quickly got to work.

She never tried to shut the children down to control them, with "Stop thats" and "Don'ts" and "Tabitha, I'm waiting …" (she remembered that as being one of Miss Wiseman's catchphrases way back in the day, at school). She was far better getting them to temper their own enthusiasm so they could channel it into rivetting performances. It had taken a while at the beginning. She'd started off following the conventional wisdom of trying to get them to be still and comply, which only resulted in lacklustre and self-conscious performance, and also a drop-off in numbers attending the rehearsals. The children were bored by what they saw as an extension of school.

Once she realised her mistake, she changed her approach entirely. It had come to her as a shaft of light one day when she was teaching one of her dogs a new trick. She was following the directions she'd found, but Luigi had gazed up at her, with no idea what she wanted. She suddenly realised that she had to make the game exciting - that as teacher she was only there to guide and facilitate, and the learner had to *want* to learn in order for true learning to take place. Once she started a game with him, the trick emerged easily. Now Luigi enjoyed "taking a bow", and her School had benefited hugely from this revelation.

She enjoyed and encouraged the noise and mayhem that always happened when the children - freed from the confines and disciplines of school - arrived for practice. She put up with things that their schoolteachers would never have tolerated, knowing that she could turn them in a moment and put their excitement and enthusiasm to good use. Even the shyest of children began to open up and engage wholeheartedly with the work. And she got a very high rate of attendance and compliance with extra rehearsals and learning of lines.

She knew, also, that the children needed to feel free and warm up their voices if they were to declaim their lines and sing their songs out clearly. Relaxation, deep breathing, and opening up were the order of the day, not tension and keeping still as they had had to do all day in school.

And so the rehearsal began, with the warm-ups. Elizabeth, the parent who had been new last week, and who had been a bit shocked at the apparent lack of discipline in the group - as the children shrieked, laughed, and ran around - had been confounded when Tabitha actually started working with them, and the power and clarity and sheer volume of the voices of such young children unified in their work had completely astonished her. The fact that she was back again - possibly nagged silly and bullied to come by her son Philip - meant that she was beginning to see what Tabitha was about, and how it had actually started to change her family dynamic at home as well. Though she had not yet heard this from Elizabeth, Tabitha knew that home-life changed for many of the parents once they saw what happened at Shooting Stars.

All eyes were on Tabitha as she directed, encouraged, enthused, and excitedly praised, her charges. The time flew by. Children were able to speak out their lines with feeling and intent. There was no awkwardness of "going wrong" in front of the other children - who were extraordinarily supportive.

Tabitha remembered the very first time Jennie had had a solo part. She had stammered and fluffed her line, then was about to burst into tears when several of the other girls jumped forward beside her and said her line with her. She had been thrilled by the children's response, and vowed she would never let a child feel that lost again.

Maisie, Sally's daughter, had been in Shooting Stars for ages, but her shyness had always prevented her from doing very much, love it though she did. But Tabitha had decided that the time was now right, that she'd be able to make the leap. It was a risk! She hadn't worked out what she'd do about this very important line if Maisie failed - the fall-out didn't bear thinking about! So she gave Maisie an encouraging, secret, smile as she stepped forward, ramrod straight, to deliver her one, very important line. There was a hush on the stage - all the children held their breath, and some crossed their fingers and gritted their teeth, looking conspiratorially at each other.

"So we've changed our minds and decided to invite you to join our team," declaimed Maisie in a stentorian voice, projecting clearly to her mother who had put herself at the back of the hall in readiness.

The whole room burst into spontaneous applause and was echoed by cheering from the stage. Maisie looked pink and enthralled as some of her friends clapped her excitedly on the back as she stepped back to them, smiling and breathing out a great sigh of relief. Tabitha smiled with deep pleasure at Maisie who she could see was now craning her neck to catch a glimpse of her mother. She followed her gaze and saw the older man she'd seen earlier, smiling and clapping vigorously - was he a family friend of Sally's, she wondered? Then with a nod she encouraged all those on stage to continue, urgently swallowing the lump in her own throat. She knew just what this achievement would mean to Sally.

Tabitha found this work totally absorbing, totally fulfilling. She focussed on each individual child, striving to get them to take their next step into self-expression, all the while keeping a clear view of the overall picture she wanted to create and the purpose of the production. She knew that every child's part was important, and a weakness anywhere affected the strength of the whole. She felt lighthearted and liberated from her worries of the last few days. She allowed herself to accept that this was what she should be doing - this was her calling, the way to self-fulfilment.

Some of the older children, who'd been with her from the start, were astoundingly good. Jennie was one who Tabitha now thought could make a career on the stage. She was turning sixteen - approaching the age limit for the group - and would be leaving soon. Jennie's parents were not that supportive, seeing the drama school as a form of cheap childminder rather than something worthwhile in its own right. They showed little interest in any of their children's achievements, and had broken Jennie's heart by being "too busy" to attend the last performance where she had played a major role. Tabitha was determined to help her, and had been mulling over the possibility of getting her further in her career, maybe a scholarship at one of the drama schools? She berated herself inwardly for not planning this sooner. Jennie was in the very first intake of Shooting Stars. This problem was going to arise for more and more children as they got older. But Tabitha was out of touch with her drama colleagues and erstwhile friends. Angus had seen to that very effectively. She could see no way she could effectively promote her better students.

Jennie excelled this evening. She took possession of the stage. All eyes were on her - the scenery could have collapsed behind her and "the play would have gone on". She was gripping. And her girlishness that Tabitha had known all these years was actually turning into the beginnings of beauty. Her looks were unusual, with her jet-black, dead straight, hair, and her long but distinguished-looking nose, and she carried herself with the confidence born of realising her gifts. She was clearly poised to take hold of her life. If only her parents could see these gifts! Of course, they were never there …

At the end of the rehearsal the children were released to their excited noise again. Tabitha saw Sally approaching her anxiously. While she continued chatting to the wriggling and bouncing children round her who were still in a state of high excitement, she wondered what Sally had in mind.

"Yes, you were absolutely brilliant, Jane," said Tabitha to a child who then grabbed her friend's hand and ran off giggling.

"Kieran - I loved your 'old man' - really convincing!" Kieran shrugged and tried to hide his pleasure, giving a crooked smile as he turned to push one of his friends.

One of the quietest children in the whole school planted herself in front of Tabitha, who had to think for a moment to recall the child's name. "Philomena?" she said quietly. As if she were repeating lines she had learnt, Philomena blurted out, "I love Shooting Stars. I would die if I couldn't come any more. It's the *best* thing *ever*." Before Tabitha could respond, she turned and ran back into the hubbub of children and parents.

"Jennie - amazing," she tossed to her protegée, over the heads of some of the other girls as they headed towards the street. Jennie smiled back as she turned towards the door.

Sally was by now agitated and rosy-cheeked. Tabitha saw that she had that older man with her, who she'd wondered about during the rehearsal. With a flourish, Sally introduced him.

"Tabitha, this is Timothy Baker," she said with a voice full of meaning.

Tabitha quickly received some of the younger children's thanks before turning to shake Timothy's hand.

She knew him, of course, by repute. Timothy Baker was the new Head of the National Drama School, and had made some notable changes there which had caused a lot of discussion - for and against - in the drama world. And this was exactly the person she could ask for advice about Jennie's future!

"Welcome to our little school," said Tabitha, as she shook Timothy's outstretched hand. "I had no idea you were here - are you a relative of one of the children? We're a long way from your usual stamping-ground."

"I'm absolutely delighted to be here," responded Timothy warmly and expansively in his rich Shakespearian voice. "No, I don't have a personal connection with your school, but word gets around, you know. People are talking about what you're achieving here." Tabitha felt her mouth drop open in surprise. People talking about her? People noticing *her*?

"So I thought I'd come and take a look for myself at what they're so excited about."

"Really?" Tabitha answered quietly and rather lamely. She honestly couldn't imagine that anyone could take an interest in what she did. For so long she'd felt her work - though important to her! - was not of any import to anyone else. Was this desperate insufficiency she got from Angus wearing her down all the time? No, it was more than that. It was a feeling of inadequacy - of failure - that seemed ever-present in her, and which Angus plugged into and stirred, rather than encouraging her as she might have expected a husband to do. Once he'd egged her on to go to drama school - and found that instead of satisfying that craving it simply made it stronger - he'd done no more encouraging.

"Yes. Really." Timothy smiled at her anxiousness. "And I haven't enjoyed myself as much for a long time!"

"Oh!" breathed Tabitha with relief. She noticed that Sally was still standing with them, witnessing this exchange with bated breath, her eyes darting from one to the other in excited expectation.

"I absolutely love how you get the best out of this bunch of provincial children. They clearly don't come from the usual route of pushy families and inflated egos which we see a lot of in the city. They're natural and charming - and very, very good."

Tabitha managed to shut her gaping mouth and smile, but before she could say anything, Timothy went on, "I've got something I'd like to discuss with you. Could you call in at the NDS and see me? I really think you may be the answer to a dilemma I've had." He handed her his card. "Ring up and we'll fix a time. Don't delay," he added, as he gave her and Sally - who was still listening agog - a little bow, turned on his heels and left the building, demonstrating to everyone how an exit should be made.

"Wow, Tabitha!" said Sally, bright-eyed with excitement, hurrying forwards to be the first to speak to her, "You've hit the big time!"

"Oh no," said Tabitha, lowering her eyes and blushing. "He probably just wants some help with something - and he seems to think I may be able to give him that help. I don't think it's anything to get excited about - but I can see a way that it could really help some of our top students."

"Nonsense, Tabs," rejoined Sally, "Don't always think of other people - put yourself first for once. You've been *talent-spotted!* I just hope you won't forget us when your name's in lights!"

Sally's words had the ring of truth, Tabitha realised. She *had* been talent-spotted! She'd been shy and dismissive when Angela and Linda had said something along these lines the previous week … she'd never expected this. She'd started her school as an outlet for her acting gifts when Angus had insisted on her leaving the School for Scoundrels, the small touring company.

She'd so loved that group! It seemed to have been a period of undiluted fun for her, a magical world where time stopped. Angus was always uncomfortable about her obvious enjoyment of this activity which didn't involve him. But staying away from home when they were touring, leaving him to mind the dogs ("bloody dogs"), leaving him to imagine dark doings, was the straw that had broken the camel's back. That's when he'd insisted, in a cold, quiet, voice that brooked no argument, that she leave the company. She was upset, frustrated, bordering on angry … but she felt she had no choice but to obey her husband.

She felt a taste of bitterness rise up in her at the thought of that episode, which was quickly overtaken by the sweet taste of what she'd achieved with her school as a result. She had started doing this completely as a way to feed the drama beast within. But then it had become a mission, when she saw how deeply it affected the individual children. Jennie herself had been gauche and clumsy when she first arrived. She'd affected disinterest in the work ("Whatever.." she'd shrug and turn away) - but gradually Tabitha had won her over, and drawn out her natural talent. The ugly duckling really had become a swan on stage.

The thought that word of what she achieved was getting around, that she was doing something special enough to get the notice of the National Drama School, suddenly ripped through her - this was something she could do! She'd never seen moneymaking as an aim of her school. She was happy to be allowed to do the work, and the subscriptions were just enough to cover the expenses, more or less. But if people really valued her work, perhaps this was a way she could actually earn enough money to survive - on her own?

Perhaps she could get some sort of fee as an advisor at the NDS? Perhaps she could get Shooting Stars on a better financial footing and actually earn some income from it?

She glowed inwardly at this astonishing thought. One of the worries that had constantly revisited her over the last couple of days since Angus had dropped his bombshell - which she had as yet mentioned to not one soul - was how on earth she could support herself if she were to leave him. That very thought still made her stomach lurch. Maybe, just maybe, here was the hint of a way.

She realised Sally was still chattering at her with excitement. She was always suggesting that the school should become self-sustaining in some way.

"Tabitha! I can't believe it! This may be the way to get the school bigger - better - more secure! Your Mr. Baker may be the answer!"

Somehow in the short space of time since the rehearsal finished, the chairs had all miraculously found their way back into stacks, and the floor had been swept of all the scraps of sweet papers, empty water bottles and hair bands which the children always managed to forget, and the hall had become empty and quiet. Sally could achieve organisational things even without being there! Maybe a couple of the parents had helped out, seeing Sally occupied?

"Sally, I really don't know what to think," replied Tabitha. "I wonder what he wants to see me about?" Her head was spinning with possibilities.

"I wonder … Anyway, see you tomorrow with your new plans," she smiled at her friend as she headed to the door.

As she made her way to her car, Tabitha thought about Timothy's words. First thing tomorrow she'd be ringing the NDS to take him up on his invitation and satisfy her burning curiosity about what he wanted from her. The future suddenly looked a lot brighter, and she suddenly felt a lot stronger. She was worth something! She could do this!

# 7

It was only a few days later that Tabitha mounted the stone staircase at the entrance to the National Drama School to visit Timothy. Of course she had visited the School before. She had been at a provincial drama school for her own training, but trips to the National School were always popular with the students. Planted, as it was, in the centre of the city, with all the other arts represented nearby - the music college and concert hall, the massive art galleries, the museum, not to mention the theatres! - A visit was a huge and enduring experience for someone "from the sticks".

But this time, as she climbed the stone steps, she felt different. This time she had a purpose, as an individual rather than as part of an anonymous group peering and pointing. She still couldn't quite grasp what had happened. Timothy Baker turning up at her little school was beyond anything she could have imagined or wished for! In fact, she'd never sought recognition from anyone else in the business because she thought herself so insignificant, that no one would value what she was doing. Angus made sure to keep her feeling this way. Why? Did he just want a servant, not a wife - an equal? But clearly some people thought she was worthwhile. Perhaps she'd have to revise that opinion now? She dismissed thoughts of her home life from her mind and focussed on what she did well, what she was seeing now as something that she had a gift for - just a small gift, she thought, drifting back to her feelings of insufficiency.

She gave her name to the lady at Reception and took a seat to wait in the grand hallway. She gazed at the framed photographs covering the walls, of productions past, and the smiling portraits of one time students who had become household names. She was thinking of how she could broach the subject of Jennie - see if there was a possibility of her moving on to the NDS. As she watched the flamboyant students in their exotic and colourful garb coming and going through the myriad of swing doors leading off the hall - hearing them posturing and acting in every fibre of their being while they studied the noticeboards for mention of themselves - she wondered, yet again, what Timothy could possibly want with her. What had she to offer that he might need? Maybe someone else wanted to start a school like hers and he wanted to refer them to her for advice. That was probably it. Hmm. He could have just passed on her name. And how did he know about her anyway? Tabitha guessed it must have come from one of the many actors she'd worked with down the years. Or stage managers. Or scene-shifters. Or a parent, perhaps?

Her ruminations were interrupted by a girl dressed in a carefully-judged compromise between artiness and professionalism, who bounced down the staircase of the once-splendid mansion to greet her.

"Tabitha Morpeth? Mr. Baker will see you now."

The girl led the way up the broad sweep of stairs again, her soft shoes making barely a sound on the stone steps, Tabitha creeping mouse-like behind her. Halfway up was a huge stained-glass window - a pre-Raphaelite scene of noblemen and women in mediaeval garb in a marble hall with cypresses to be seen in the sun beyond the pillars and archways. As Tabitha gazed at the window she heard her guide knock on a large and solid-looking mahogany door equipped with beautiful brass fittings, at the head of the staircase, and hurried up to join her.

Timothy rose as Tabitha entered the room. She remembered enough of her acting training to make sure it was an entrance, and not an apologetic slink through the door, as he came to greet her with outstretched hand and a broad welcoming smile. Showing her to a seat and requesting coffee for his guest from his departing assistant - "Some coffee, please, Janey my dear," he returned to his chair behind the large desk and smiled avuncularly at her.

"I've heard so many good things about you, Tabitha. Tell me a little about yourself," he said.

Tabitha was sure he could have found out her history and qualifications if he'd wished. So rather than give him a potted biography, she told him instead about her hopes, her disappointments, and her desires.

"I've always been gripped by the theatre," she began, and went on to tell him how she had forever found the theatre fascinating, but that parents and school had dismissed such a notion.

"'Ridiculous idea.' was all my headmistress had to say about what I so wanted to do!" Timothy nodded sympathetically. It was something he was always coming up against. Contrary to popular perception, all theatricals were not extroverts. He knew that a lot of people were lost because their dreams were squashed at an early age. That would have included him had it not been for his English teacher who saw the spark early on, and encouraged him all the way to drama school, in the teeth of his family expectations for him to enter law and take silk - though that was another type of acting, to be sure. And this was the principal reason for his dedication to his students now.

She told him how she had struggled to find anything else as interesting as drama; how much time she had spent "in the gods" at theatre productions wherever she could find them. She told of her joy when her new husband encouraged her to follow her passion and apply to drama school, and how she had instantly taken him up on his suggestion.

"I couldn't believe my luck when he suggested that!" She warmed to her narrative, and went on to tell Timothy of the touring company - the School for Scoundrels - which had thrilled and absorbed her for a few years while she did every job possible to do with productions - from assisting the director, to wardrobe mistress, to prompter, to actual acting - though she added that her skills did not really lie in that direction. Timothy nodded understanding again - he knew the company well, knew its ethos and its easy-going and appealing approach, knew how it could grab people and never let them go.

She glossed over, with a bit of hesitation, trying hard to suppress her blushes (she always assumed that the person she was talking to knew everything about her - so knew that that was where she had met Jamie and what had happened between them since), when and why she left the School for Scoundrels, and how - faced with a future with no drama outlet - she started her own children's school.

"Shooting Stars! I loved it from the first minute, when the first handful of wide-eyed young children and their anxious parents put their trust in me and joined us."

And here she became animated and excited. She explained the transformations she witnessed in the children in her care - how they blossomed and developed as rounded people before her eyes. How it was much more than just putting on a play - she was turning these awkward children into youngsters who could believe in themselves, who would be able to pursue their own dreams regardless of others' opinions.

"We were all close to tears when Maisie said her line that day you visited! Did you feel the support for her, the love, the enthusiasm, the fellow-feeling?"

Her passion and warmth came through clearly, and Timothy smiled and said "Indeed I did! I didn't know the history, of course, but I guessed at it."

At last she came to a stop. She looked out of the huge sash windows at the busy street below. After a brief pause she turned back and added, "I feel that if I'd had an opportunity like that when I was that age, I would have benefitted enormously. I think it would have given me the confidence to have made different life choices - um, maybe start my school sooner," she ended, rather lamely.

Timothy finished his coffee and replaced his mug on the desk carefully before saying, "I think that your diffidence is part of your charm."

Tabitha blushed: this one she couldn't suppress. She smoothed her skirt over her knees, just to occupy her hands. Should she go straight into asking about Jennie, or was he going to reveal why he'd invited her here?

"Gifts like yours," he continued, "are rare. So many people in the theatre can be self-absorbed and see the whole venture as an ego-trip. That can work alright when teaching new students who are old enough to make their own decisions. But to be able to work with children, to keep their attention, focus them on your task, and - yes, inspire them - is really an unusual talent."

Tabitha wasn't sure whether to continue gazing at him in stupefaction or to twiddle the bracelet on her wrist in her confusion. She decided that twiddling the bracelet would be annoying, and placed her hands carefully in her lap, focussing her gaze on Timothy, hoping she didn't look too moon-faced, and hoping she came across as capable and not as gauche as she actually felt in his presence.

"As you know, our students come here after leaving school, so they're in their late teens by the time they get here. There are, of course, lots of stage schools around - but most of them seem to cater for Variety rather than serious acting. Singing, dancing, that kind of thing. I feel that we're losing a lot of genuine talent by not capturing their hearts and minds early enough. You don't have to be flamboyant to be effective in the theatre - you're not, and look at me with my grey suit and grey hair!"

Tabitha smiled at him, warmly yet apprehensively.

"So what I would like to do is to start a Junior Academy here at the NDS, to cater for children from age six up to when they're old enough to come to the main school. Exactly the age group you're working with, in fact."

"And you'd like to grill me for what does and doesn't work?" Tabitha smiled shyly.

"Oh no," said Timothy, causing her to colour again. "No, no, no, my dear Tabitha. I'd like you to run it."

# 8

Tabitha was dumbfounded. This she had not expected! She struggled to get her thoughts in order. She was being invited to run the Junior Academy at the National Drama School. It was unbelievable! But just too late. Her heart thumped down into her stomach. She was going to have to leave the country, her school ... and everything, and follow her husband. But how could she leave this opportunity behind? Could she ever forgive herself? She'd achieved little in her first nearly forty years of life. How could she pass this up? The enormity of breaking up her marriage dominated her thinking.

But maybe? Just maybe? .. it was fortuitous. What did they say about one door opening as another closed? One of the big reasons for her indecision over the whole affair was her worry about how she could possibly support herself if she were to leave Angus, or - to be more accurate, as it was Angus who was doing the moving - if Angus were to leave her. She was still reeling from the shock of it all, and the discovery of her feelings about her life. How inadequate she felt, how she had been marking time, lapsing into a kind of learned helplessness while the winds of change buffeted her.

Now, perhaps, a miracle had happened. The perfect, unbelievable, opportunity had fallen in her lap. It was an amazing coincidence - that the way for her to survive was being presented to her out of the blue. Was someone up there watching out for her? Was this a sign that she should grab it with both hands? Her stomach lurched again. She had made wedding vows, she couldn't weaken and just leave when she felt like it ... Though of one thing she felt sure: even if Angus were not planning to leave the country, he would find a way to kill this project.

Her mind rushed on. This was such a great *honour* being offered her. This would be a coveted post - and she was being given it on a plate! Surely Timothy would have to look into candidates for the post far more deeply? She realised he was watching her, his fingers steepled to his mouth, as her face went from pink, to red, to a kind of sickly pallor.

So she offered Timothy a face of utter confusion - which caused him to smile gently to himself as he lowered his hands. "Me?" was all she was able to muster, albeit in a tiny voice.

"Yes. You." said Timothy firmly.

"But won't there be a selection process? You don't know me!"

Tabitha knew that all posts like this had to be seen to be awarded fairly. Wherever public funds were involved, selection processes had to be squeaky-clean. Furthermore, she had seldom done very well in auditions, which were really the only things she'd ever applied for. Surely there were lots of fences for her to fall at before she might be appointed? She was in total disbelief.

There *had* been a time when she was bolder, had more confidence. She remembered when she applied for Drama School, and then for the School for Scoundrels. She'd been young, fresh, full of hope, and she'd felt sure she'd get in, to both. Now she felt so unsure. Her confidence had fizzled out over the years. There was only one thing she absolutely knew she was good at, and that was Shooting Stars. The one place she didn't let Angus in. And that was what Timothy was basing his offer on - her ability at her own school. "Buck up Tabitha!" she thought to herself. "This amazing chance has just landed in your lap - time to stand tall and know you can do this!"

"You are forgetting, young Tabitha," Timothy went on in his most fatherly fashion - looking quite the distinguished figure he undoubtedly was in his field - interrupting her reverie, "that I know everyone in this business. Some by repute, most by personal contact. I've been looking into your work carefully over the last few weeks, and taking advice from those whose opinions I respect. Yes," he said, noticing the deepening look of astonishment on Tabitha's face, "you are talked about."

He smiled and poured some more coffee for both of them from the tray

Janey had put on his massive desk. "Visiting your rehearsal this week was just the confirmation I needed to have. I had to watch you working personally. Yes, there will be detractors. There always are. So that's why I needed to come and check you out for myself."

Blow after blow! People talked about her? Her? And some were detractors. Tabitha wondered who, and which was which! Trust her to go straight to the naysayers. She thought instead of those who had recommended her. Who might Timothy know who had worked with her? She scrambled about in her head for some rationality. She realised he was waiting for a response.

"I ... it's a great honour," said Tabitha. "When are you envisaging this Academy opening its doors?"

"September - it'll have to fit in with the school year."

"September," mused Tabitha. A few weeks ago that month just signalled the resumption of her school rehearsals after the long summer break. This year, though, it had taken on a very different hue. September was when Angus would be setting sail for his new life in America. And so far he still thought she would be going with him. She was coming to the conclusion - more strongly by the moment - that this was not going to happen. She'd been pushed as far as she would tolerate. The worm had turned! She was not going to be pushed an inch further. Actually contemplating the end of her marriage was something she found very hard to do. So she was thinking along divergent and inconsequential lines at the moment. On the one hand she was not going to America. On the other hand she was not doing anything as momentous as leaving her husband. On the third hand she was entertaining the idea of a new career! It would take time for these threads of thought to tie together and make any real sense.

While Angus clearly saw himself as the senior partner in their relationship, that his work was infinitely more important than hers (besides which, he was a man), Tabitha realised that just perhaps, her time had come. Didn't this invitation of Timothy's prove it? She was going to do what *she* wanted to do, and if that meant losing her husband while following her passion, then so be it. She had been thinking of doing that even before she could see any means of supporting herself. Now, with the prospect of paid work, it was full steam ahead! So much was suddenly happening in her life. As the years had gone on and she felt more and more ground down, she had settled into a rut where she seemed unable to look out at the rest of the world. Now everything was changing! This was an opportunity she absolutely could not miss.

She started to think constructively about this project. Then - with a gasp of dismay - she said, "The sessions will be at weekends, right? That's exactly when my school sessions are. Oh no ..."

"We are hemmed in by the hours that the children can attend. Not just that our hours don't clash with school time - many different schools across the city - but ensuring that the children are not overstretched and end up exhausted. So, yes, Saturday would be the day."

Tabitha felt her exhilaration beginning to ebb away. She couldn't do this. Never mind doubting her ability to do the work - she couldn't abandon Shooting Stars. The whole thing was a fantasy, not for her after all. She felt her heart sinking.

"I had envisaged the younger children in the morning, and the older ones in the afternoon," Timothy went on, "with some weekday evening sessions in the run-up to a performance."

Tabitha's dismay deepened. How could she have thought this was for her? How could she have thought, even for a moment, that this was her answer?

Timothy was still explaining: "Of course you could have private pupils on weekdays too. As a staff member you could use the facilities for private lessons. All the teachers do - to be honest it's the only way some of them can make ends meet."

Tabitha got a mental grip and started to try and work this out in her head. There had to be a way! She had to open her mind and see what could be done. Could "her" children possibly move to a weekday evening? Could she start training someone to do some of the work at her school? Would she be able to focus on two schools at once? There was so much to consider. What looked like a wonderful opportunity was filled with difficulties when she began to look more closely at it. She was passionately devoted to her students and would hate to disappoint them. They gave her such loyalty ...

Timothy got up and looked out of the large Georgian windows at the Square below. "But we're only an hour or so from your school. Perhaps some of your students would like to transfer to the Academy? It would be helpful anyway to have some experienced children in the group - not all raw beginners."

Tabitha took this all in. She had to stop thinking impossibilities and start thinking possibilities. This was her big chance! Perhaps it would be her only chance, and it had come as salvation just at the right moment. It was also a great opportunity for some of her more gifted students. Jennie could come here to the NDS! There had to be a way to work this all out so that everybody benefitted.

"That would be marvellous!" she enthused. "There are some children there who've been with me a long while and I'd hate to just abandon them. I couldn't."

She thought of Jennie, and the younger ones who were also showing promise. She thought again that perhaps this could be the way to get them into the NDS set-up? A golden opportunity for them … She wondered how the children - not to mention their parents - would respond to this idea .. then realised she was looking too far ahead, "meeting trouble halfway" as her dear friend Maureen would say.

"But you know, Timothy - I have to go away and think this over. There's so much to think about and work out. Is that ok? It's such a wonderful opportunity - I can't quite get my head round it! But," she added hurriedly, "I'm amazed! I can't believe you've asked me. And I am really, really, interested in seeing how this can work out - for everybody. The children at my school … I need to make sure they're looked after. Just, please, don't ask anyone else!" she laughed, "I'm really bowled over …"

"Of course! It's a big step, and the planning we'll have to do over the next six months will take up a lot of time. But you go away and discuss it with your own people and come back to me. How does this day next week sound? Does that give you long enough?"

"Yes - this day next week I'll be back to you here with my answer. And whatever happens, I'd love to give you the benefit of my experience at making this type of school work. I'd be happy to share that with you!" Tabitha was still struggling with the thought that she could be of value. She had been ploughing her own furrow for so long that she found it hard to accept that she was rated by her colleagues, her fellow professionals in the field. So, she found herself downplaying herself and the value of her contribution yet again. How much had Angus closing down her world affected this? It was beginning to dawn on her that she was more capable than she had ever given herself credit for. Look at Timothy's offer!

As she descended the large staircase again, now noisy with excited students switching classes, her legs were a little unsteady. She was grateful for the ornate mahogany banister rail she clung to. Her head felt hot and heavy with all that was spinning around in it. Her school. Her future. Her home. Her dogs. Her husband. Her lover! Her whole life. How different she felt from the Tabitha who had ascended those stairs only a little while ago!

She began to see more clearly that sorting out her marital affairs and where she could live was absolutely a priority. She had been resisting the practicalities of her situation. Like Luigi burying his quivering head under a pillow when there was a thunderstorm, and hoping it would go away.

The time had come for some hard decisions to be made. It couldn't be put off any longer, and Timothy's offer had crystallised this in her mind. She couldn't mention all her personal upheavals to Timothy as yet. But she was doing that thing again, of thinking everyone knew everything about her. Like a seven-year-old who is baffled that his parents seem to know exactly what he's been up to! She didn't need to involve Timothy in all that, at all.

Angus, the famous writer as he was, hadn't made any announcement about his departure from these shores, so she couldn't tell anyone anyway. As always she instinctively wanted to protect Angus, and this was why she had still told absolutely no one about his bombshell.

And she hadn't even mentioned it to Jamie yet. Why not?

# 9

It was fresh and bright when Tabitha set off down the road with Luigi and Esme to the 50-acre the next day. They sat at the gate patiently waiting for her to release them. She bent to unclip their leads so they could scurry under the gate and start their explorations, then paused when she climbed to the top of the five-bar gate, to admire the view. She'd been so wrapped up in drama and events that she felt she was losing sight of the beauty that she so enjoyed when out with her dogs, the beauty of nature that fed her soul, replenished her. It was something that neither Angus nor Jamie were that bothered with. They didn't seem to need recharging time. But Tabitha needed a retreat, quiet, to get away from the busy world, in order to reconnect with herself and let everything fall into place.

The large field sloped down towards a ditch - sometimes full to the top with water in the winter, and a great place to wash the mud off the dogs, and sometimes dry and revealing its winter catch of twigs, cattle eartags, bits of fencing wire, the odd discarded plastic bottle, and once the surprise of a cracked and stained white flowered china teapot. At the moment it was just between, and still treacherously black and muddy, so she would keep the dogs well away.

Behind the ditch was a bank with mature trees. The trees were showing their sappy new growth, their leaves a bright transparent green. In a couple of months they would become a blowsy dark green, and the flies would come. For now they were reflecting the spring season - the time of change and new growth. How appropriate, thought Tabitha, as she jumped down from the gate. The dogs had given up waiting for her and were doing important sniffing and exploring under the hawthorn hedge bordering the field. She enjoyed the scents from the hedgerow, the heady cow parsley releasing its wondrous smell as the dogs brushed through it, the pineapple weed she trod on round the gateway giving up its exotic scent. She paused to admire some Herb Robert with its little pink flowers turned towards the openness of the field, jostling for airspace with the pretty Red Campion. And she spotted the tiny blue flowers of wild Forget-me-not peeping through the riot of vetch and cleavers. She was pleased that Tom left the hedgerow alone. It was clearly ancient, as could be seen by the great variety of species of tree and hedge. And it was a welcome change for the grazing beasts in the field, where they could choose their own medicine and up their mineral intake.

And beyond the row of trees sparkling in the sunshine, was the hazy shape of the distant hills. Tabitha could never tire of this sight, as the hills lay pale blue waiting for the sun to burn through the mist and expose them in their full beauty, their own fields and hedgerows emerging prosaically to the day.

The joy she felt in the landscape - her dogs a ticket to this world, making her feel as if she belonged and was not an intruder - helped to raise her spirits. She knew she had to work through these multitudinous problems that had suddenly landed on her, but she felt light of heart as she approached them. She set off round the field, and smiled as she thought of her friend Maureen watching over her as she ground out her issues.

A solid clipclop on the road caused her to turn her head and check where her dogs were. As the rider passed the gap of the gate she waved to Tabitha. It was Tom's wife Nell, and she had a black dog trotting along behind her horse. Tabitha waved back with enthusiasm, then allowed herself a few minutes playing with the dogs before relapsing into silence and starting to think. Esme, seeing that there was no more entertainment coming from Tabitha, nudged Luigi and they headed for the hedgerow again.

Tabitha found herself once more going round in mental as well as physical circles. She was frustrated by finding herself pulled in so many directions - where did this guilty sinking feeling come from, she wondered? There's Angus's plan to think about. There's Timothy's wonderful offer. There's her own school which she could never abandon. There's the small matter of money to support her and the dogs if she leaves Angus, not to mention somewhere to live. And what about Jamie?

She couldn't work out what she thought there. For so very long they had lived in a fantasy world. They were like children of the storm - clinging together amidst the beating of the elements. The impossibility of their relationship ever coming to anything meant that they accepted it would never happen and they enjoyed warm and reassuring thoughts about what they had together. At least, that's how Tabitha thought of it. She pulled up with a jolt as she realised that these thoughts were in *her* head. What did Jamie really think?

She turned to make sure Luigi was catching up with her - Esme was racing about ahead as usual, nose to the ground, trying to cover every inch of the 50-acre.

Sometimes she and Jamie would dream, about being Mr. and Mrs. Average, but Tabitha never took these dreams seriously. She was the practical one, and she knew, deep down, it was never going to happen. But Jamie had wanted to marry her from the start.

"I want to marry you," he'd said, all those years ago when they had only just met. They had been sitting on a bench on a big hill overlooking the town, huddled together from love and cold.

She had laughed. "You're already married! And so am I."

Jamie's declaration had shocked Tabitha. She knew she wasn't the sort of person people took seriously. No one had ever taken her seriously. Her wishes to pursue her dramatic interests had been swept away by teachers and family alike, and she had been pushed into a path she had really never chosen. She remembered Miss Wiseman, the overbearing headmistress at her school, simply dismissing everything she'd wanted - dreamt of - in those two thorny words: "Ridiculous idea." That had made such a deep impression on her, disabling her for so long. Even when Angus asked her to marry him, it was for some strange ulterior motive she was only just beginning to fathom. How could Jamie possibly be wanting to marry her when he hardly knew her? Was he being serious? She couldn't say she was the sort of woman "men didn't marry", because she was, at least technically, married. But she was surely the sort of woman men didn't love.

"Yes, but I still want to marry you. I'll get a divorce," Jamie had insisted.

"No you won't. It's a pipe-dream. You have four young children. You know you're just dreaming." Tabitha knew that times must sometimes be hard: coming home from a long day's work - sometimes late in the evening too - to a noisy and demanding household of children, and a wife who had had only their company all day and perhaps harboured the thought that Jamie had it easier, and resented it. But she also knew that Jamie could never leave his children. He appeared the gay gadabout by pursuing a relationship with her, but she knew better. She couldn't have loved him as much if he'd been prepared to sacrifice his children's happiness to his own.

"But what a dream!" he'd said then. "Oh Tabitha! Where were you fourteen years ago?" he cried, as he stroked her cheek and her hair, and gazed into her eyes. He really did mean it! Someone loved her this much! It was such an exhilarating feeling, to be valued - just for herself! Her heart rose up within her, constricting her breath.

But that passion had subsided after several months. It was only after Angus made her leave the touring company, where she and Jamie had first met - he doing some extra joinery and carpentry work, she doing a bit of everything theatrical - that their relationship had begun. She realised once he was gone out of her life how much she'd enjoyed his company, how much she missed his light banter, his ever-cheery smile, the way his mouth turned up at the corners, his thick black hair, his silly jokes. So her possibilities for spending time with him were curtailed dramatically, and it had all become so hard. Having to spend most of her time at home serving Angus meant that she had fewer opportunities to meet up with Jamie. Then her distress when she heard another baby was on the way had rocked her. Angus was abroad leading a writing workshop, so they'd spent a glorious evening together in her own bed, with Jamie making his usual grand statements about his devotion to her, his longing to be with her always. She was basking sleepily in these voluptuous thoughts when he mentioned as he started to dress that he'd be unable to see her again that week as he had to use his time off to go to the hospital for his wife's scan.

"How could you?" she had cried as she realised that all this time he had been continuing his relations with Annette - whom he had sworn was no longer of interest to him save as the mother of his children.

"I have to look after my marriage," he'd mumbled, sitting hunched on her bed with his back to her, sulkily buttoning his shirt.

Tabitha was shocked. Deeply shocked. She'd had no idea she'd been getting proprietorial thoughts about him - thinking he was hers. She suddenly saw herself as the "other woman", doing everything the "other woman" did, feeling the same insecurities. But wasn't that what he was always saying - that she was his, he was hers? He had lied! Or he had at least misled her - or allowed her to be misled by her own assumptions. Or perhaps he'd just misled himself. It was all the same, in the heel of the hunt. While he swore he wanted to leave and be with her, he was still "looking after his marriage". His words were empty. This was just another tawdry affair! She had felt sick. And things unwound fairly quickly after that.

And so she had tried to live without him. She had really tried. She'd find herself staring into the distance when she was out with the dogs. She'd gaze at the inevitability of the unfolding seasons, in distant views and in the denizens of the hedgerow, and weep inwardly for her season having passed. Staring mesmerised at a beautiful sunset - like the ones they had watched from his car - or hearing someone laugh like he did would cause her heart to lurch in her body. She'd suddenly experience the pain of his absence. It was a real physical pain. Over the years it would subside a little, be less visceral. But it was always there. The beautiful thing she had lost. She might hear the opening chords of "their" song. She might see a small boy who reminded her of one of Jamie's little boys, so long ago. They would be nearly grown up now, she knew - late teenage perhaps - but frozen in time in her memory. She might be struggling with a particularly bad batch of depression from Angus, and find herself longing for the easy and loving relationship she had had, all those years ago. Was theirs one of those relationships where you couldn't live without each other, but you couldn't live with each other either?

She had thought it was all over. She wasn't to know then how Jamie would erupt into her life again, so many years later

As she now touched the head of her old faithful friend Luigi, her fingers ruffling the soft hair behind his ears, she reflected that they were *all* grown up now - but frozen in time in her memory.

She was dawdling round the field. She headed for "Luigi's log", and sat on the huge length of trunk from the massive old felled Beech tree lying in a dry ditch. It was Luigi's log because he had loved to jump across the ditch, banking on the log as he went. Sometimes she'd play a game with him - getting him to jump on the log, then either sending him over to the other side of the ditch or asking him to jump back - or just stay there and sit up on his back legs waving his front paws. She hadn't visited this log for a while, as Tom had fenced this area off in a short-lived experiment in strip grazing. Now she saw that the smooth grey trunk was pitted and crumbling. The whole log was much lower in the ground, and bits were disintegrating under her exploring fingers. She sat on the log and started to cry. Tears welled up in her as her chest and throat hurt with the pain of Luigi's lost youth. Luigi was now way too old to be jumping and frolicking on this log, and the log itself was rotting and falling apart. Life moved inexorably on.

And her youth was lost too. Time did not stand still. Tabitha had to move on, before everything around her crumbled and rotted away like the Beech log.

Luigi was getting on; she was getting on. Soon Esme would start looking older. Time was flying by and what was she doing with it? If she stayed in the thrall of Angus - nothing! And what future did she have with Jamie?

And with the clarity of hindsight, Tabitha saw that these were decisions she should have made long ago. Why had she not? Why had she put up with it all for so long?

It was there, buried deep in herself. She had to put a brave face on things. She had to efface herself, fit in with other's desires. Why? Why did she feel like this? She stood for a moment and gazed at the unfolding hills as she thought back to another day which was bright and sunny, this one hot and sultry, one of the endless days of summer which seemed to characterise her childhood. She thought it was probably just the best days she remembered, but she didn't know that this one was even in her memory! It had just unearthed itself, reached down through so many years to remind her. And it was as clear and real as if it were happening right now, immediate - as everything is to a three-year-old. She is back there now, the sand scraping her legs as she sits on the brick surround of the sandpit Daddy had built her.

Bees are buzzing round the scarlet runner bean flowers. Simon dozes on the paving stones by the sandpit. He's stretched out on his side, just in the shade, panting slightly. You can't see where Simon ends and the paving stones begin. I fill my painted metal bucket with my spade, and pour the cool sand over my toes. It's like water. But not.

I look up and see the swing hanging still at the bottom of the garden. I love the swing. I can swing really high and I can swing-jump. William can stand on the swing while it swings but I'm not allowed to. Not until I'm seven like him. Beyond the swing I can see all the houses and gardens stretching up and over the hill. I can hear Malcolm and Roger playing cowboys and Indians in their garden. Boys are so noisy. I'm happy here alone in my sandpit. Except for Simon of course. He's my friend and he's always there.

"Tabitha!" Mummy is calling.

"I'm making sand like water," I reply.

"Can you come here a minute?"

I clamber out of the sandpit and go through the kitchen door. Simon shifts himself and follows, still panting, and slumps down on the cool red quarry tiles, already asleep again. Mummy hoists me up onto the wooden table. I look up at the towels and socks hanging from the laundry dolly strung up over the cooker. There always seems to be washing hanging there. Mummy is always busy cleaning something.

As she brushes the sand off my feet with a damp cloth, she says, "I'm going to make you look pretty!"

I didn't know whether I was pretty already or not. I hadn't thought about it much. Daddy swoops me up in the air when he comes home, presses his mouth to my cheek and says, "How's my beautiful Tabby today?" So *he* thinks I'm pretty. William says that all girls are stupid and useless, so he doesn't think I'm pretty. My mother doesn't think I'm pretty either. She's always poking and prodding at my hair or face, holding out a handkerchief for me to lick, then pressing hard into my cheeks as she scrapes off the dirt or the jam.

It'll be nice to be pretty. Some of the girls at kindergarten are small and don't get into trouble like I do. Maybe that's because they're pretty and I'm not. Amanda laughed at my shoes because they were so big next to hers. I know my mother is pretty because she has that way of holding her head which shows she knows she is.

"Miss Ooitt says I'm too big."

"Yes, you're tall like your father. You look a lot older than three. And you sound older too - you're a right little chatterbox! And not many three-year-olds can read like you can. But don't mind Miss Hewitt - she's no oil painting herself."

"What's an oil painting?"

"It's a picture of someone pretty." She picks up a hairbrush. "And I'm going to make you as pretty as a picture!"

She starts to drag the brush through my hair, showering sand onto the table and my bare legs. "We're going to visit Grandma tomorrow, and she can't see you looking like this."

Having my hair brushed seems to happen all the time. Or at least every day. So I don't mind. But after brushing my hair and twisting my head this way and that, Mummy turns to the stove where she's cooking something.

"Keep still!" I hear a crumply papery noise near my ear, then a hot tightening as my hair is pulled and something hot is burning my head.

"Ow," I yowl, reaching up with my hands to pull the thing off.

"Don't touch it! You'll get burnt," she pushes my hands down to my lap. "Hold this," she says, putting a stiff piece of paper into my hand.

I begin to snivel.

"And stop crying. You have to suffer to look beautiful - you'll learn that in time."

I carry on sniffing and snivelling as she snatches the paper out of my hand. There's another crackly noise followed by a sharp pain pulling more of my hair next to the first thing pulling. Then she gives me another piece of paper while she turns back to the stove and uses the wooden laundry tongs to pick up another iron from the steaming pan, ready to clamp it onto my head.

My mother chatters as she crimps my hair into waves with the hot irons. "I don't know where you get this dead straight brown hair from. And those brown eyes. William has lovely blond curls and blue eyes. You're a girl. You should have pretty blonde curls and blue eyes too."

William doesn't seem to get poked with hankies or have the hair scraped back off his face. He doesn't seem to get into trouble either.

"I think you're a changeling," Mummy goes on. "Someone came into the nursing home when you were born and switched babies. There was another baby there who had fair hair. I think they took my baby and gave me you."

My mother often tells me this story of The Changeling. She did so well having William. I'm a bit of a let-down. It's hard to be the wrong thing. I'm the wrong child and too big and can't please her. I can't even have the right hair. My brother makes her happy all the time. He doesn't even have to try. He's just right already. Maybe if I look pretty Mummy will like me more? Maybe I'll be more like William and not be odd, not the changeling.

If you start out wrong you have to be put right. And putting my hair right hurts. I suppose that's because I'm not pretty and I'm too big. I feel the pain working its way across my head. The hot iron touches the top of my ear and I start crying again. Simon pads across the tiled floor and pushes his damp nose against my dangling feet. He gives my sandy toes a lick. I'd like to be back in the garden with Simon. He doesn't mind what my hair is like. He has black hair and he's alright. Maybe dogs don't have to be pretty. But I think he is.

It seems to go on forever, but eventually it's over. My head feels very odd. Mummy leans back and smiles and pats my hair saying, "Your hair looks really pretty now! Grandma will be pleased. We'll do it again for Daddy on Saturday. He never sees you in the week, so it'll be nice for him to see he has a pretty daughter."

She lifts me down from the table and I run out to the sandpit and jump into it, scraping my foot on the metal spade. I don't actually feel very different. I mean I don't feel prettier. My head is sore and the air feels different on my head. Inside I feel the same. But a bit empty. Maybe it's because it's nearly tea-time. Or maybe it's because I'm just not enough. Will I always have to hurt so that people will like me?

As I start swirling the sand with my toes again, a curly bit of hair keeps falling over my face. I push it away with the back of my hand and get sand in my eyes. The tears wash it out again.

Still sitting on the log, Tabitha was stunned. This episode had come to her like a vision. It had clearly been inside her all these years but only now showed itself because of the turmoil she was going through, all these whywhywhy questions she was demanding of herself.

Is that why I think I'm lucky to get the scraps that others leave? she asked herself. Was this feeling of unworthiness instilled in her all along? This went some way to stop beating herself up over her inability to make a decision. She didn't feel she had the right to an opinion. Wasn't this how her life had played out so far? Always fitting in with other people, not feeling strong enough to be herself?

Is that why I went into a loveless marriage, then fell for someone who could give me what I thought I needed?

It was fifteen years later that Jamie and she crossed paths again - quite by chance - when she stopped at a garage for fuel. As she had headed to the shop to pay, there was Jamie, changing a tyre on his truck. She had bumped into him on a couple of occasions, but he always had one of his children with him. This was the first time she'd happened upon him on his own, without the social brakes on. As soon as they set eyes on each other it was clear that their feelings were just as strong as they had ever been the first time round. While the sensible thing would have been to say "Good morning" and pass on their way, sense had gone out the window again. The pull was so strong.

"Well if it isn't Tabitha Morpeth!" laughed Jamie, as if he'd just bumped into any old friend.

"And how are you doing, Jamie?" Tabitha responded deliberately, folding her arms in front of her to steady her heart. "You haven't changed one iota in all these years." She admired once more his thick black hair flopping over his forehead, the way his mouth curved up at the edges in a permanent smile, and noticed the lengths of timber in the back of the truck. "Still busy being a carpenter?"

"Sure, and what else would I do?" he smiled back at her. They spoke normal words to each other, but those words carried a million hidden messages. "I stick to what I know." His look was meaningful. "We need to catch up. Coffee?"

Tabitha knew she should simply say no thanks and go. But instead she heard herself saying, "Yes, we must," and knew she was slipping down the slope again.

Jamie took a step closer to her.

"In all those years, not a single day has gone by without me thinking of you," Jamie said, looking straight into her eyes - her soul.

Tabitha's heart lurched. She was desperate to reach out to him. It was that pain again - the pain of wanting him and him not being there. Only now he was there. He was right there where ... perhaps he always should have been. This was possibly the most moving thing anyone had ever said to her. Ever. She knew in an instant what she had lost by giving Jamie up all those years ago. Their love had been real. Had it really survived this huge gap? Her fingers brushed his shirt, and Tabitha knew with awful certainty that it was all going to start up again. She felt the warmth rushing back into her body - a warmth that had been missing for so long. Here was the one person who had made her so happy, and at this moment she forgot all the pain and the misunderstandings, the deceits and the tiredness - the sheer exhaustion of keeping their relationship going. They couldn't be together, and they couldn't be apart. They'd proved that. There was an inevitability about their finding each other again - each was magnetic, irresistible, to the other. And so the clandestine meetings began again. The deceptions, the passion, the misgivings, the utter joy.

They were both awe-struck. The fifteen-year gap was as nothing. They hurriedly completed their business at the garage and drove to a quiet cafe nearby. It was straight into conspiratorial mode, little needing to be said. They were back on the hurtling train again.

And yet it was different this time around. It was as if they'd both grown up and were accepting the present state of their lives. She knew - did he not know? - they could never be together, even though Jamie still would talk endlessly about it. But they both found such huge solace in each other that

that alone kept them going. The excitement of their initial exploration had given way to a more accepting relationship. It was steadier, less heady, possibly less hedonistic. Jamie's children were older and becoming independent. Even that baby was now about to leave school. Tabitha's marriage had petrified into its present state, and Jamie was back to his fantasies of them one day being together - for ever. Tabitha, after the initial glorious burst of love, was not sure where her life was going. She buried her anxieties about Angus in her passionate encounters with Jamie - such a release.

They managed to meet frequently. Sometimes they'd slip back into their private world, alone together. And Jamie was just as enthusiastic as he ever had been about how they could make a go of it. As the practical one of the two, Tabitha could not share Jamie's views. It wasn't only their circumstances. She just wasn't at all sure that she would be satisfied with being married to Jamie. And as time went by, Tabitha knew a marriage to Jamie was never going to happen, and she had to face the fact that she had mixed feelings about this.

Esme hopped up onto the log beside her, bringing a small twig to be thrown. Tabitha smiled at her two friends and tossed the little stick onto the ground in front of her, saying, "Here you go, dogs!" Esme dived on it but, bored once it had stopped moving, was quite content to relinquish it to Luigi, who just loved sticks, and carried it proudly, head up, as they walked on, away from Luigi's log, Tabitha's tears now dry.

At the moment she had a marriage which was, at its best, intellectually stimulating - but devoid of physical affection. And with Jamie she had fun and passion - the intense and delicious feeling of being loved - but there was not the same intellectual connection she had with Angus. She seemed to have two halves of a marriage - if only she could have combined both of them into one! For just a moment she felt envious of those who appeared to have both.

She had been wandering too far into impossibility.

She snapped back to the present - the thrilling present! She hadn't given a thought today about Timothy's offer. She really didn't need to - it was perfection. She felt a strong need to run this new project by a friend - someone who would perhaps understand how valuable it was to her, and who may see what she might be missing. So she resolved that she would talk to Jamie about it, and give him the chance to get involved with her future, to show that he genuinely cared - while still avoiding mention of Angus and his bombshell. She couldn't tell him about that yet. It would complicate everything.

Was she testing him, she wondered? And what did she hope to gain? Could she really rely on Jamie as a good friend, or was it impossible to imagine, without their physical relationship? But she needed him to understand the momentousness of Timothy's invitation. She needed to know he understood what drove her. He had to see how important it was for her!

Tabitha's thoughts were violently interrupted by a yelp from the hedgerow. She ran to Luigi, who had caught his leg in a bramble in the ditch and was struggling to get free, yelping as the thorns dug into his lower leg and paw.

"Ok buddy, it's ok," she murmured as she snatched her penknife from her pocket and hacked the briar away. She called Luigi up to the top of the bank and asked him to lie down so she could check his paw. Esme came to join this inspection, and eagerly started licking the blood from a nasty rip in Luigi's pad. A bit of pressure ensured that it stopped bleeding, but he wasn't happy about putting any weight on it.

So Tabitha hoisted her old pet up in her arms and started trudging back across the field to the gate.

She reflected as she walked, shifting the heavy dog from one side to the other as her arms tired, that there was nothing she wouldn't do for this dog. That was the unconditional love she shared with her dogs. Their fidelity and devotion was so simple, so straightforward. There was nothing they wouldn't do for her. And that's not how it was with her menfolk. They seemed unprepared to do anything for her that didn't suit them.

She had been so caught up in working through the issues with Jamie - and the vision of how her feelings of insufficiency had all begun - that she hadn't thought things through as she'd planned to do. But she saw that in fact she had reached at least one decision. She knew she had to strike out on her own, act with integrity. It was time she fulfilled her early - gifted - promise, and made her mark on the world

"If I leave Angus" was shockingly just beginning to become "*When* I leave Angus". Tabitha didn't see how she could go back to the way things were. She did not want to leave her little school and the country she knew and loved in order to follow Angus's star. That decision seemed to be making itself, in the teeth of her indecision.

She remembered something she had read from St. Francis of Assisi (always a popular saint with her in her childhood as he seemed to be the only one who actually rated animals). He was talking of faith - religious faith in his case - and he said: "You stand on the edge of the abyss and you jump."

Tabitha was going to stand on the edge of her abyss and she was going to launch herself into it! She didn't know what lay ahead, but she was going to find out.

# 10

It was later that day that Tabitha threw herself down into the armchair in front of the range in Maureen's kitchen with a big sigh. So much introspection over the last few days had driven her to seek her friend's company and her gentle understanding. She knew where she was with Maureen. She knew that the truth would be faced and confronted and knocked into shape with Maureen's down-to-earth approach. And she knew there'd be no blame or shame.

She picked up the sheaf of hotel brochures and catering lists from the footstool and put her feet up on it, leant back, closed her eyes, and let out another long sigh. She glanced at the brochures before setting them on the cluttered table beside her. Evidently Maureen's Silver Wedding party plans were moving on apace. While Tabitha was not generally a fan of parties, she had been roped into this one at its inception, and was happy to be involved with her friend's big day.

"Now there's a person who needs a cup of tea, if ever I saw one," said Maureen, lifting the lid on the range and moving the kettle across to the hotplate.

"You read my mind," murmured Tabitha as she wriggled her shoulders to relax into the back of the chair. Tabitha met Maureen when she and Angus first moved to the little hamlet. Maureen came to welcome them when the house was full of packing cases, and brought some freshly baked scones, plus butter, a knife, and plates. She had known that finding a plate would be nearly impossible, despite not having moved house herself in over twenty years.

Maureen was nothing if not thorough. What a lovely welcome she gave them! And Tabitha had had an easy friendship with her ever since. Maureen had not had the benefit of Tabitha's education - leaving the village school at fifteen, as soon as she was allowed - but she had learnt so much more than Tabitha ever had in the School of Life.

"I've seen you over the last number of weeks, walking round and round that field. You'll walk the legs off yourself before you work whatever it is out of your system."

Tabitha was an intensely private person and she appreciated the fact that Maureen never asked or tried to wheedle out answers. She was skilled in making openings, offering her the chance to speak if she wished.

Although it had never been discussed openly, Tabitha knew that Maureen had a pretty good idea about what was going on in her home. While Angus was always polite and friendly towards her, he recognised Maureen's power and wisely stayed out of her hair. She was one friend that he had never tried to meddle with or remove from Tabitha's life. Tabitha also knew that Maureen knew about Jamie. It had never been discussed either, but she knew that she knew. Even Jamie knew she knew. When Tabitha had dropped round to Maureen's one evening after work and introduced her colleague Jamie, she had struggled to keep her hands off him, and had been quite unable to keep even her eyes off him, and this she felt sure Maureen would not have missed. But Tabitha knew things about Maureen and Gary too, and the two friends felt quite safe with each other's secrets.

"You know how you always say that 'Woman was made for man's use and benefit?'" asked Tabitha.

Maureen smiled as she picked up the kettle and poured the steaming water into the teapot. "That's what they'd like to think," she murmured. She and Tabitha had had many a hot drink in front of the range at one house or the other, questioning why women seemed to have drawn the short straw.

"Well, I'm thinking you're right." She was beginning to feel tired of both the men in her life. Tired and used. And as far as she could see, men definitely did like to think that. She felt she was being used and abused by both Angus and Jamie, and the thought was creeping around the edge of her mind that a stronger woman would abandon both of them before they abandoned her. She sat up abruptly as she felt she was at last beginning to understand that it was up to her to steer her life, to make her own decisions.

She took the mug of tea from Maureen and put it on the table beside her chair - Gary's chair, if truth be told - while Maureen relaxed into her own chair opposite her.

"Not that woman should be," Tabitha continued, after her first sip of tea - too hot yet for a full glug. "I mean, I always thought men and women should have an equal chance at everything in life. Funnily enough it was my father - who seemed so traditional in his views about family - who instilled that in me." She put the mug down again, slowly and carefully to avoid spilling it on the brochures, while she reflected that though her father publicly subscribed to the status quo, when it came to his darling daughter and her opportunities it was another thing altogether! He had always championed her ideas when she was younger. It was only as she became teenage and "marriageable" that he became old-fashioned again. He did have very conflicted feelings about a woman's place, and his daughter's place. "But the fact remains that not only is it not so, that we all have an equal chance, but men really do have the upper hand. When push comes to shove, they reckon it's up to them to make the decisions."

Tabitha was aware that Maureen knew well enough that the lack of children in Tabitha's household - in stark contrast to her own rowdy home, which always seemed to be full to bursting with her four children and their friends - was not what Tabitha wished for, however much she feigned the contrary. You can't keep these sort of things secret, especially when Maureen often had a child to nurse or comfort, and Tabitha showed herself so adept at this, so willing to help. And of course she related so well to the children in her school. And she realised she'd learnt from wise Maureen that you could never really know what was in another person's relationship. You could try guessing, but they'd always surprise you. So she was content to watch Maureen waiting patiently to hear whatever Tabitha wanted to tell her.

"Yes. I've been walking a lot round Tom's field - the dogs are very happy about it all!" Tabitha took a mouthful of her tea and smiled. "It's when I think. You remember when I was working out how to start the school? Round and round and round that field!"

She sat up straighter in the chair and sighed.

"It's Angus." She said, as if that were a total explanation.

"Yes?" prompted Maureen quietly, after a pause. She reminded Tabitha of a priest in the confessional, quietly urging the sins out of the penitent.

"He's been offered a post in America. Wants us to pack up and leave. Wants me to leave the school, and … and everything." She blushed slightly as she looked towards Maureen. She knew that Maureen would interpret "and everything" to include the love of her life - Jamie. But she still was … embarrassed? shy? ashamed? to admit to it out loud. She never had admitted it to anyone. Jamie's men-friends knew and kept their mouths shut. Jamie's wife Annette suspected, but was sensible enough to subscribe to the view that "least said, soonest mended". Tabitha, who had no longer any real friends other than Maureen, had actually never discussed it with anyone. It was yet another secret burden she had to carry around with her. And the burdens were growing heavy.

"But he's just asking you to leave the school, right?" This was Maureen's way of finding out if He Knew.

"Yes. Close the school. And head off with him as his support and … Events Secretary, I think. Ohhh," she said, in exasperation, and flopped back in the chair again.

"And you don't want to go," said Maureen flatly.

"I don't." Tabitha responded, quietly, wondering if she was ever going to open the flood-gates in her mind and see everything washed away.

"It's written all over your face! After everything you've already given up for him. What does he want, blood?"

"I haven't talked to anyone else about it. Just putting this into words shows the enormity of what he's asking. He belittles everything I've worked for … I just feel so small, so insufficient." She felt that stab in her heart again, the knowledge that there was so much more she was born to do, the stab of Timothy's offer, of finding acceptance at last!

She looked out at Maureen's busy garden, the runner bean and pea frames already soaring up between Lily of the Valley, weeds, and lazy beds for the potatoes - a reflection of the busy and chaotic inside of the family house, with its tables and chairs laden with books, toys, magazines, and sewing, the mending basket ever present by Maureen's chair.

She felt it there, buried deep in herself. She had to put a brave face on things. She had to efface herself, fit in with other's desires. Why? Why did she feel like this? And as she looked from the beanpoles in the garden of this family home, and gazed up at the children's clothes airing over the range, she was pulled back in time again. She remembered the revelation she had had earlier, on Luigi's log: where this feeling of insufficiency, of not being good enough without having to change, had been born; how important it was to suffer in order to please other people; how she never seemed to fit in - even in her own family where she was the Changeling! And now she was being offered a place by Timothy where she felt so comfortable, where she really did fit.

Maureen was watching her intently, pity showing in her face.

"No. I really don't want to go." Tabitha looked straight at her friend. "But that's where my husband is going, and I think he wants to make the move permanent."

"I see why you've been wearing a groove in the 50-acre now," said Maureen.

"I always thought that if I made my bed I must lie on it," Tabitha said. "But I'm beginning to wonder just how much I need to give up for that bed. Or even if it's the right bed." And at that moment she knew full well that Jamie's wasn't the right bed either. She glanced up at Maureen, "I know Gary's old-fashioned, but you seem to manage to keep your own spirit?"

"I don't think I ever told you this," Maureen said, as she quietly replaced her mug on the table and leant back in her chair, clasping her hands across her generous body, "but when we were first married, Gary was getting a bit too big for his boots. He was beginning to treat me like a workhorse. I've always thought it's the man's job to bring the coal in because my father always did, but he'd started to stay late in the pub of an evening, so I had to do it if we weren't all to freeze to death. So, one evening when he came back late and expected me to serve his dinner, I did just that. I'd made a beautiful pie and

I set it before him and went out of the room. I was afraid I might start giggling if I stayed there, and spoil his surprise! And can you picture his face when he cut into the pie and found nothing but lumps of coal?"

Tabitha gasped and laughed out loud. "You didn't!" she said. She loved that her friend was courageous enough to find this solution to a problem without confronting it head on. Could she ever do this with Angus? No! And that's one reason she had ended up where she was. She'd never stood up to him. Always pushed along in the direction *he* wanted to go. Whatever he had decreed she had gone along with. She thought she was a free spirit but that was nonsense! She was a captive, a slave. She did whatever she was told.

Why did she do this? Why did she kowtow to Angus over everything? What did she fear? She didn't fear that he'd be violent. And obviously she didn't fear that he would find another woman, as women in general didn't seem to turn him on at all. Or was it only her? She hurried on in her thoughts before slithering down that rabbit hole. Did she fear being abandoned? Was that what it was that kept her in thrall? Did she need the veneer of marriage, a position, the fact that someone had once chosen *her* in order to hold her head up and live her life? Had she such low self-esteem that she was grovellingly grateful to the person who had chosen to marry her?

And yet there were a couple of areas of her life where she could hold her head up very well without her husband. There was her defiance in her affair with Jamie (oh, that word "affair" she thought - it makes it sound so tawdry), and the fact that she had ploughed on with Shooting Stars regardless of all the taunts and jibes she got at home about her nursery-school-cum-childminding service.

And why were these thoughts only now marshalling themselves in her mind? What did it have to take to make her see the reality of the situation? What had happened to her resolve? Hadn't she been about to jump into an abyss? She needed some of Maureen's native courage. She needed to believe in herself.

"And did it work?" she asked now, thinking of the coal pie.

"Course it worked! I've never had to bring the coal in from that day to this. It's true that as soon as the boys were big enough to lift the coal hod he gave the task to them. It was comical to see two small boys heaving it in between them, as much coal on their hands and clothes as in the hod. It was good learning for them, it's true. But as long as I didn't have to do it, I was happy enough. It did give him pause to think. And it made me think too. I realised that he could only make me unhappy if I allowed him to." She unclasped her hands, took a drink of her tea and set the mug down again. "And," she raised her hands in a gesture of 'there we are', "it's been mostly good since." She smiled at her friend.

Tabitha turned Maureen's words over in her mind: that Angus could only make her unhappy if she allowed him to. For all her doubts, Jamie only made her unhappy by his absence. It's true that she gave in to Angus again and again. What had started as an apparently fairly equal relationship had become so one-sided! She'd give in on something he wanted, a little thing, then another little thing - and before she knew it, here she was, way off-course, caught in the weeds as everyone else marched down their paths. Something in her head was wrong. Why did she allow this to happen? She'd always thought herself strong. She did strong things. And yet when it came to her husband she laid herself down on the floor and said, "Please wipe your feet on me." She felt suddenly sickened with herself. She seemed to think that she should be grateful for anyone taking an interest in her. She'd always felt so insignificant. She had accepted Angus almost as soon as he proposed. She couldn't believe it - that someone would want her! And why should she think that? There was nothing wrong with her, even if her mother didn't think her pretty - hadn't Jamie proved that? Despite her mother's influence, she knew she was good enough in Jamie's eyes, without crimping irons! She didn't need this endless pathetic gratitude to anyone who tossed her a bone. She pushed these thoughts from her mind again as she had a sudden thought.

"I think that's my trouble. I've never really stood up to Angus. Except over getting Esme. Do you remember how irritated he was about that? 'Not *more* bloody dogs!' he said." Tabitha smiled ruefully at the memory. "I can stand up for my dogs any day of the week, but I've never stood up for myself."

"Perhaps it's time that changed?" said Maureen quietly, "and there's no time like the present! When I think of everything you've done - not just for

Angus, but for those children in your school. It's amazing what you manage to do with them. Daphne really came out of herself after the first production she took part in. Even the boys enjoyed the play! And that's saying something, as they're part savage. I think you don't realise just what you're able to do."

Tabitha felt stirrings within her. She knew Maureen was right. She did have something unique to offer, and she had a right to express herself too. She was admirable. Hadn't Timothy said as much?

"You'd think with Angus being a writer he'd be more ... I don't know ... in favour of people developing their talents. But it seems to be just *his* that should grow, not mine."

"Well, I would be sorry if you went anywhere. You know how much I enjoy your company. But you have to do what's right for you. And of course, there are other fish in the sea. You have options. Whatever you decide, I'll back you to the hilt. If you do go, I'll miss you terribly." Tabitha appreciated what a huge declaration of love this was from her old friend.

Options. Yes, there were options. And she knew Maureen was not trying to influence her one way or the other. There was Jamie, who Maureen was carefully not mentioning. There was the possibility of developing her school further. And there was the new possibility she hadn't even mentioned to Maureen yet, of working with Timothy - who'd said clearly that he'd welcome someone on the staff with her talent. The post was hers for the taking. It was funny how just sitting quietly with someone you trusted could start to make sense of your problems, thought Tabitha. Maureen was stating the obvious. Yes, I am worth something. I don't just have to fit in with others. It's not as if I haven't tried, all these years, to make my marriage work. There are people who value me. Maureen does. Does Jamie? And why am I more excited at the prospect of working with Timothy than the sudden opening to be with Jamie? She looked across at her friend who passed a tissue box over to her. She hadn't realised she had tears on her cheeks.

"I think," said Tabitha, as she stood up and put her mug on the kitchen counter, "that my next tramp round the field will be spent making some decisions. I'll start doing some sums this evening, and see what's possible."

"If you decide," said Maureen, "I think you'll find that anything is possible."

# 11

And so it was that the very next day, she came to be meeting with Jamie in an out-of-town pub. Tabitha walked into the pub, looking for Jamie at one of the tables in the gloomier, further part of the building - the sort of place they always chose where they could be apart from everyone else, not feel so scrutinised. His face lit up as he saw her, and she felt her own expression respond warmly. He had the coffees set up already. He'd known she'd be there on time, just as promised. She leant against him as she slipped off her jacket, her thigh touched his as she shuffled on to the bench seat next to him. He reached under the table and held her hand, twining his fingers carefully and thoroughly into hers. Tabitha felt her cheeks warm as she gazed at her lover.

"So how's my favourite woman today?" he asked her, his free hand adding a mountain of sugar to his coffee cup.

"I have news!" said Tabitha. "I have something to tell you!" The bustle and noise in the pub subsided for her as she focussed on Jamie's face.

She was going to be careful to keep it low-key. She had a fear that he wouldn't really understand its importance, not realise that this was something she had been unconsciously working towards for so long and which was now landing in her lap. She needed to tell someone who cared, and she wondered if Jamie cared enough. Apart from Maureen, Jamie was the only one of her friends that she had fiercely hung on to. Angus had got rid of the rest of them. Angus was always so secretive - could it be catching? Or could it be that she didn't trust that when she told them, the very people she wanted to understand - they just wouldn't. So she was delaying the moment of her anticipated disappointment.

And she didn't want to tell Maureen yet, either, though she felt sure she would be supportive - even pleased for her. She thought it may muddy the waters, add an extra layer to her decision that she didn't want her to know about yet. She had wanted to know how Maureen felt about "the bombshell". And she had found out. She could tell her about the NDS any time, though soon!

There was a mixture of anticipation and apprehension on Jamie's face. Once before, in a pub, she'd given him news. News that she was ending their relationship. His face told the story of his anxiety.

"Don't look so worried," laughed Tabitha, "it's all good." And she began to outline her tale - about Timothy's visit to her rehearsal, how impressed Sally had been, and about the incredible offer. She filled in who Timothy was and underlined the seriousness of the whole thing. "So you see, I'm actually being asked to run this new Academy! It's an incredible honour - I can't really believe it."

"That's great news," said Jamie, affecting an excitement Tabitha sensed he didn't really feel. "You'll do it very well." Then, turning his spoon over and over in his fingers he said quietly, "But what about Us?"

While she hadn't expected him to be as excited as she was, she was pretty deflated at his response. This was her big breakthrough, the culmination of everything she'd been working for for years … and Jamie just wasn't as excited for her as she felt he should have been. His first thought was about how it would affect him. She had half-thought of telling him her news was a test. He'd failed.

"Us? Why would it change Us?" she asked. "If anything it'll make it easier to see each other when I'm down at the NDS regularly. Can you see this is a fantastic opportunity for me?" she said urgently, squeezing his hand which still held hers under the table.

"Yes, of course." He smiled with a closed mouth, a false smile.

Yes, she could see he was pleased for her. But she wondered if maybe he sensed that she would slip away from him once she had this important position. That a mere carpenter and scene-shifter would not be good enough any more. She needed him to understand the momentousness of Timothy's invitation. She needed to know he understood what drove her. He had to see how important it was for her! Was this why she had never felt they could make a life together as a couple? That she felt he wasn't completely with her?

She was seeing that this was a real turning-point in her life. Not just in her career (she was having a career!) but in her marriage and her relationship with Jamie. She hadn't quite realised how it was going to touch everything. Maybe Jamie saw it as a turning-point too, but in another direction. He treated her news rather as she may have responded if he had told her he was working for a different company that day. Her gut feelings were right. This relationship was going nowhere. It was a dream, a fantasy without backbone. Jamie could never really understand her deepest desires. He was just the wrong person.

She almost felt that she would have got more enthusiasm from Angus! Or at least from the old Angus, before he became the broody and dark person he now was. That old Angus, early in their relationship and even in their marriage, would encourage her in her ideas about making her way in drama. It was, after all, Angus who had encouraged her to go to Drama School all those years ago, when previously she had been prevented by her school and parents. He had urged her to fulfil her artistic desires - and he should know all about those, being a writer himself. But looking back, it seemed he'd only ever seen it as a hobby for her. Something to keep her occupied and out of his hair while he did the real work. But he would certainly understand the importance of this appointment, and the honour - if he could only look at it dispassionately. Of course, Angus now had to be the last person to know.

Tabitha felt guilty too, that she was not telling Jamie the full story. She knew instinctively that this was not the time to mention the whole Angus fiasco. Keeping that secret from him grated with her. She and Jamie had shared so much, down so many years. Of course she had confided things to him about Angus. And now something really important was happening, something that would affect both of them, and she felt unable to tell him.

She lifted his hand, still wrapped round her fingers, and kissed his knuckles, before replacing their hands under the table, out of view. She felt a great sadness, an air of finality about the gesture. And she wasn't sure what exactly had prompted it.

Why was she keeping this to herself? She knew she just didn't trust Jamie at that moment with this new development in her life. She wasn't sure how he'd react, but she feared that he'd see it as the opportunity to pursue his fantasies of leaving his family and marrying her at long last. But she didn't want that! She suddenly saw that that was not what she wanted! All these years their domestic situations had prevented it happening. Now her shackles were about to come off. Were they? Is that what she was deciding? She was accepting this more and more - and she saw that she didn't want another marriage. She didn't want to go from one bondage to another! She needed to try her wings in this new life that was being offered her. She needed to fly solo for a while.

"I really thought you'd see it ..." she said, with a touch of bitterness. She looked away from him, stared into her empty coffee cup.

Her frustration came out in her manner with Jamie, and she could see this hurt him. While *she* knew she was keeping something from him, he didn't, and she saw his puzzlement over her distance. Her own confusion made her frosty.

It was not his fault he was him! It was his lightheartedness, his spontaneity, his lack of endlessly seeing problems ahead which had always so magnetised her. But did it still magnetise her? Yes and no. She would always find him irresistible, love the moments she spent with him, rejoice in their passion. But every day, with shopping, bills, household repairs, car servicing, dealing with his children ... she increasingly found it hard to imagine life with Jamie, and had a sudden pang of sympathy for Annette. But she could hardly blame him now for not being someone else!

And so their unsatisfactory meeting came to an end.

"I am pleased for you, really. Don't shut me out, Tabs!" said Jamie.

Was their relationship really so brittle that this could destroy it? And why was Tabitha not caring? The closer she came to the possibility of being with Jamie, the more she pulled away from it. Were the difficulties she found with her husband a necessary irritant in this relationship? Did she only find solace in Jamie because she could not find it in her marriage? How shallow did this make her feel!

So while she found both of her menfolk falling short in their support of her, she realised that her father's old saw, "if you want something done right you have to do it yourself" was true.

Would that there were someone who could really understand what this meant! Someone who could rejoice with her and be truly happy for her! She felt a strength growing within her. *I* will rejoice, she thought. *I* will admire myself. *I* will be the person I can depend on. The feeling was creeping over her that the only person she could truly rely on was herself.

"I'll text you," was all Tabitha could say.

# 12

Tabitha chewed the end of her pen like a seven-year-old while she worked through all the numbers. The kitchen table was strewn with sheets of paper. She scratched her head and wished that Sally were there to magic it all into order! She'd worked out what she was being offered by the Academy, and she'd added in the tiny amount the Drama School yielded. She'd been scouring the papers to see what rent would cost - she was so out of touch with this! And the sums were not making a lot of sense. Her precious Shooting Stars was really a financial burden. Good sense would tell her to close it entirely. But good sense was not taking account of just how important this school and all its fresh-faced young students were to her. She pushed the papers away, slammed the pen down on the table and leant back in her chair with a sigh, pressing her hands into her face then up into her hair, holding it high above her head before letting it drop and pulling the papers back to her again.

"This has to work ..." she thought. "I have to find a way to make it work." If only her parents had managed to leave something to her. The firm had gone to William, which was only fair as he'd been running it for a number of years. But the family home had been hocked to pay for cruises and holidays to sunny places that her mother had craved once her father retired. So she was on her own. As ever. "I must become more resilient," she said out loud. "Esme. Luigi. Help me do this."

Both dogs wiggled over to her, glad to get some attention. Luigi rested his chin on her leg and gazed at her, while Esme pushed an old sock onto her lap, backing off, tail wagging fast, waiting expectantly with bright eyes.

"Ah, you are such wonderful friends," she said, joining in their simple enthusiasm. "If only I could touch you for a fiver or two!" Esme pushed the damp sock - her currency - further into Tabitha's lap. Suddenly both dogs alerted to a sound outside, and started their noisy barking.

Through the noise she heard the crunch of Angus's car on the gravel drive. She'd had no idea when he was coming home from wherever he had been - Tabitha was never party to his comings and goings. So she jumped up, snatched up all her papers and stuffed them in a folder marked Shooting Stars Production July, and slid it into her workbag.

And she was busy at the sink when he came through the door.

"How's things?" he said, brightly and chattily. This gave Tabitha the hint that this particular conversation may go ok. It always seemed to depend on Angus's mood at the time and how much he'd had to drink, and right now she thought they may be safe. She feared for his mental health at the moment, and she felt utterly responsible for his volatility and unpredictability, not to mention his drinking. Though how she thought this was her fault she couldn't honestly say. Was this feeling of guilt something else she needed to address? And change?

"Just tidying up," she replied, trying to sound as bright as possible while remaining on her guard. "Coffee? Tea?"

"Tea please!" he responded, heading to the cooker and filling the kettle for her, leaving her blinking at him for actually doing something so menial. He sat down at the table and waited for her to complete the task. Esme wandered over to him to sniff his trouser leg and find out where he'd been. She may or may not work it out, but sadly she wouldn't be able to impart this knowledge to Tabitha, who forever remained in the dark. Angus reached down and ruffled the top of her head, saying, "Hello Esme!" She ducked away from his hand, giving him a sidelong glance as she walked away and flumped down in front of the cooker alongside Luigi and his bandaged foot – now healing nicely from the bramble rip - where Tabitha was now dealing with the teapot and cups. He noticed a dog! Whatever was going on, she wondered? Perhaps he was being super-friendly to get her to talk about his plan. She felt rather irritated that he could switch on a good mood to try and get what he wanted.

But she didn't want to give him the opportunity to start questioning her again, so she tried to lead the conversation by asking him about his current book.

"How's the magnum opus?" she asked.

"Ah, it's going ok at the moment," he replied as he leant back in his chair. "I've just been to town to check on some research at the Central Library. I'll get back to processing that in a minute. Thought I'd keep you company for a bit first." He smiled at her. He hadn't smiled at her like that for what seemed an age. Things used to be better - things used to be fun, in the beginning.

She saw his laughing face across the pub table. He had been regaling the group - some of his writer friends - with a funny story about his publisher.

"So he ended up with two manuscripts - neither of them any good!" he had laughed.

They had all nodded knowingly and laughed with him - either because they had experienced similar things with their publishers or because they wanted to make out that they actually had a publisher. It had been a new and exciting world for Tabitha. These arty types, with their long hair, quirky clothes, and disregard for convention, were different from all the people she'd grown up with. They had a different worldview. Only later was she to find out the overweening egos some creatives could have - expecting the world to recognise their greatness and fit in with them, sometimes setting themselves apart in order to appear more gifted than they were.

They liked to be part of Angus's circle - he had been pretty good at controlling people even then, she reflected - and accorded her a special place in the group, a bit like John in Leonardo's Last Supper, enjoying the special place next to Christ. They thought that she must know Angus's intimate thoughts and so they would listen to what she had to say. If only they had known! She didn't know his real thoughts much at all. They could discuss art and literature, but there was no intimacy there, he was such an intensely private person - and no physical contact. The odd fatherly kiss or hug, but nothing further. He would pull away from her, saying, "That's wrong before marriage." She had been a very naive nineteen-year-old. And she interpreted this to mean that he found her attractive and was keeping self-control in challenging circumstances. And that if it was wrong before marriage, this suggested to her that there would be an "after marriage" where things would be very different.

And so she had been led to believe when Angus asked her to marry him, that this would be the beginning of that private and grown-up bonding of two souls as one. Yes, she'd had sexual partners before, but never with that spiritual connection she yearned for. This must be it!

How sadly she had been disappointed, when things carried on just as before. There was a marriage, but still no sex. She had hoped that somehow things would magically change - until that awful moment when she tried to encourage him after her cold, wet, walk, and he had actually run from the room to get away from her. That was when she finally realised how ugly and unattractive she must be to her husband. She was perplexed and puzzled. Had he married her because he was sorry for her? Was it just pity which had turned sour?

She wished things had been different. She so wished she could have made a success of her marriage, not to mention have the children she had always longed for. But it seemed to have been taken out of her hands. She found herself turning away towards the tea-making task - rather than have to smile back.

She passed him his mug, but left hers on the edge of the cooker. If she went and sat down with him right now, she felt sure he'd start questioning her about the arrangements for their emigration: had she researched the journey yet, booked any plane tickets? What about putting the house on the market? What about the dogs? Since he first told her about his bombshell, his ultimatum, she had been managing to avoid putting herself in the firing line again.

"How much longer till you finish this book?" she asked, then realised her mistake.

"I hope to have the first revised draft with Philip before we leave for America," he said, an actual beaming smile on his face.

"You're really looking forward to this new post, aren't you." Tabitha decided to get the focus off her and onto him. Not usually too hard.

"It's what I've wanted for years!"

"Really? I had no idea," responded Tabitha, wondering for a moment about all the other things of which she had no idea. Why didn't her husband ever confide in her?

"Well, I'm sure you'll make a great go of it," she added. "You'll be lionised - the great English author with the quaint accent and strange vocabulary. They won't be able to get enough of you."

"We'll have a wonderful time there," said Angus. He seemed to have forgotten she had yet to give an answer. Perhaps he just assumed that she would naturally comply and there was no further need for discussion. "And you'll need to start getting it all moving pretty soon."

"Just let me get through this next production first. We start the final run-up next week and it's going to be hectic - extra rehearsals, all the things that suddenly come up: sick children, children whose costumes no longer fit because they've had a growth spurt, parents wanting more tickets than their allocation … it goes on."

"Okay, if you must," he tutted. "But don't leave it too late or you'll land yourself with a lot of extra work." Angus got up from the table, tiptoed towards her shyly and planted the tiniest of kisses on her nose. Then, with a smile (again!) he turned and scooped up his mug of tea, and headed to his study.

Tabitha stood there, bemused. With her bare toes she ruffled the hair down Esme's spine where she lay by her on the warm tiles in front of the cooker. Esme groaned and stretched slightly, pushing her back into Tabitha's foot, before subsiding again and instantly returning to sleep.

For a moment Tabitha wished she could lie down there on the floor, and stretch out asleep with Esme and Luigi. Their lives were simple - though it's true Luigi had issues, fear of the unknown, the strange - but they lived in the moment, took each day as it came. If they liked something, they did it. If they didn't like something they didn't do it - they'd avoid it. Like Luigi with strangers - he'd prefer to avoid them entirely. Tabitha smiled to herself at the thought of her picking up Luigi's paw to check over his claws, and him shifting slightly and politely removing it from her hand, as if to say, "No thanks, no paws or claws today, thank you." There wasn't a bad bone in his body - she knew she could do his claws when she needed to. No need to push it when he said No.

She understood her dogs and their uncomplex lives so well. The time she spent with them was refreshing, re-invigorating, rewarding. None of the ups and downs of life with her difficult husband. And none of the passion and doubt she had with Jamie. Yes, she was passionate about looking after her dogs, their welfare always foremost in her mind, but the fervour, the total joy and abandon she had experienced with Jamie ... that was another thing entirely. And something she felt, with a jolt in her heart, that would not now be continuing. She found it so hard to accept that she'd made this decision already. It was done. It was over. And her heart was in pain.

It would be just her, her dogs, and her talents. This was where she felt most valued, most cherished, most effective. She had to become self-reliant, be able to plough her own furrow. Decisions were beginning to be made in her head. She would make a start by settling down to draw up some plans to take to Timothy for her promised appointment in two days' time. That was really exciting! Something that she'd achieved, all by herself. Though she'd certainly value Sally's help tomorrow with the numbers. She straightened up and looked out at the magnificent hills beyond the kitchen window. All this thinking and brooding was getting her nowhere. She needed to be doing.

# 13

The next morning saw lots of activity. Once Angus had left, the hens were let out - Tabitha as ever enjoying watching them scramble for the left-over breakfast toast - and the dogs were walked, Tabitha got out her hidden papers and carried on with her pencil-chewing, getting things ready for Sally's arrival. She was relieved when she arrived with her professional-looking box files and folders, quick-moving, busy, and ready to dive into the work. They negotiated the joyful greetings from the dogs before sitting down at Tabitha's kitchen table, Sally poring over her charts and logs. She was never happier than when she was creating order out of chaos - the ideal administrator, really.

So this morning they happily worked through the registers, made some decisions about who would approach which parent about their child's attendance or lack of it, and started in on the forthcoming production. Organising the fathers to help with building and painting the scenery, and scene shifting at the performance, was Sally's *forte*. They responded so well to her time charts which made it feel like a professional job, and enjoyed the time they spent with one another, happily out of the house and messing about with paints and tools - and usually a crate of beer as well. For some it was a welcome way to contribute to their children's lives without actually having to do hands-on child-rearing.

Tabitha negotiated with the costume shop for the best price possible for those complicated costumes that had to be hired, and got the keener mothers involved in a sewing circle to design and make the simpler costumes - in many sizes and with plentiful seam allowances so that they could be used again and again.

"Here you go - fuel!" said Tabitha after a good hour's work, heading back to the table with refilled mugs and a plate of doughnuts. The warm scents of coffee and sugar characterised their meetings, imbuing the paperwork tasks with a sweetness and flavour they otherwise lacked for Tabitha. She smiled at her able assistant, who did so much for the school, and all for nothing. Neither of them made a bean from it. Tabitha ran it on a shoestring budget, charging the parents just enough to cover the expenses. And Sally's reward was in seeing her shy daughter Maisie blossom in the school. But Tabitha knew she couldn't continue to expect this.

They had these planning meetings regularly every month, sometimes in a coffee shop, sometimes here at Tabitha's home, sometimes at Sally's house - though it could be hard to find the space on her table without moving loads of books and crayons, dollies and plastic cars, uncovering unnamed sticky patches that had to be cleaned off, and with constant phone calls to be fielded. Angus had set off this morning saying only that he'd be back for supper, so Tabitha had switched this meeting back home as they'd have more peace and quiet here.

And Sally had been such a find! Asking for volunteers from the parents had been one of Tabitha's better ideas. Running a school like hers on her own was tricky. Being the creative director as well as the organiser, not to mention the babysitting aspect of managing lots of children from seven to eighteen with all their proclivities for feeling sick, bursting into unexplained tears, or falling off the stage, was difficult to wrap up in one person. She had a rota of parents to deal with all these minor catastrophes, so there were always several on duty at every rehearsal - and everyone else was always welcome to watch. It was ideal for Tabitha to have a flock of mother-hens to cluck over scraped knees and imagined slights. She had a tendency to stick on a plaster and dismiss them with an "Off you go now", and was considered heartless by some of the fussier mothers. But Tabitha's undoubted gifts and the hero-worship of their sons and daughters ensured that they let this pass - puzzling as it was to some of them.

By the time the doughnuts appeared on the table - one immediately finding its way into Sally's mouth - they had already spent a good couple of hours on their current project, the next production.

They pushed the charts aside and tried not to scatter sugar all over them while they munched their prizes. They both felt fulfilled and happy, and it was into this chewy silence that Tabitha outlined to Sally the meeting she'd had with Timothy. She gave her only the barest bones of the plan. She wanted to sound Sally out and see what she thought about the venture, and just suggested that Timothy was offering her some teaching work.

"So you'll close your school?" was Sally's second, dismayed response. Her very first response had been wide-eyed wonder and admiration - "Wow, Tabs! You've arrived!"

"No. I absolutely don't want to close the school," replied Tabitha evenly. "I don't know how it's going to work, but it must be possible to fit it in and carry on. I couldn't bear to disappoint all our children. What would they have in our quiet rural area without Shooting Stars? They love it so much - it's such a joy to see them burst out of their chrysalises."

"Maisie is living proof of that," said Sally, thinking of her once shy and gauche daughter now brave enough to declaim lines on stage. "And that girl Daphne - you're friendly with her Mum, aren't you? She was such a shy plump little thing when she first came. And now she holds her head high, carries herself better. I noticed last week how much more she interacts with the other kids these days ... It would be awful to lose what you've built up." She stared into her coffee mug for a moment. "Actually," she continued carefully, "we've been thinking recently - that's Brendan as well as me. You need to work on the creative side of the business - that's what you're brilliant at. So how about I take over all the admin and organisation side? I could devote more time to it now Maisie's moving up to senior school. I could go into partnership with you, so we could take this all so much further. Obviously there'd have to be an income involved for so much more commitment. We'd have to start charging a proper rate, but I've got this draft plan here ..."

Tabitha was swirling with mixed emotions while Sally chattered on. She tried to restore her relaxed expression, and said, "What do you mean, Sally?"

"Oh, I just think it may be time to get this on a more regular footing. Brendan thinks it should be put on a legal basis, you know - just to avoid anything going wrong in the future."

Tabitha knew she should be happy to have someone as able as Sally, someone she could rely on. But she was surprised to find that Sally and her husband Brendan had already been discussing a takeover, even before Timothy had come to the rehearsal!

As Sally noisily licked the sugar off her fingers, Tabitha dropped her half-eaten doughnut back on her plate where the jam oozed out of it like a broken heart.

"I … don't know." Tabitha struggled to make sense of this sudden attack. Because an attack is what she saw it to be. Brendan and Sally discussing moving in on *her* business - the school she had spent nine years building up all on her own.

Having a business partner had never been in her long-term plan. She liked to be able to control the outfit entirely on her own, without all the hassle of paid staff. But what Sally was suggesting went way beyond even that!

Sally actually wanted to move in on her business. Though Tabitha enjoyed her planning and admin sessions with Sally, she didn't see her as a bosom pal.

In fact, in her usual way, Tabitha had remained a little aloof to her small band of volunteer helpers. Knowing she was not an attractive person - one who did not make friends easily - made her suspicious of Sally's motives. She felt her soul harden within her: this was a blatant attempt to move in on a thriving business and take it away from her!

Nobody could want to partner with her - work with her on a daily basis - unless they could see the prize at the end of it. Even Timothy must have an ulterior motive. Her panic was taking her straight back into her old thinking, the thinking she'd begun to change since Timothy had visited.

Sally was still going on about the way she saw things shaping up, with her running the business day to day, leaving Tabitha free to do her "creative stuff". As Sally listed all the advantages, clearly worked out by Brendan, Tabitha felt cold and alone.

But she steadied herself long enough to realise she was being so narrow-minded! So introspective! She thought of her school as a thriving business - but it wasn't a business at all! It made no money - just about broke even. Sally was suggesting actually turning it into a business, one that could give them legitimate reward for the huge amount of time and effort they put into it. Sally was right. Tabitha was useless at business. She just loved creating! She realised she was at a time of change in her life - huge change! catastrophic change! - and she had to alter her thought processes about absolutely everything. And one of those thoughts was that she was not going to let Angus stifle her beloved School's development any more.

She had to truly accept the fact that perhaps she was not so unattractive? She had worth! Perhaps Sally genuinely wanted to get involved more to *help* her, not to try and take over? With the possible move to the National Drama School, wouldn't she need to have someone as reliable as Sally to keep her own school functioning - or else close it? And far from wanting to run the school all by herself - wasn't she just trying to hang on to control because of some nameless fear about handing some tasks to others?

People were giving - giving her loyalty, friendship, opportunities. All she had to do was open her heart and receive. The floodgates had burst open - and there was no way to close them again. Rather she had to channel the flow as best she could. This required positive planning, not whingeing and crying!

She met Sally's eyes and smiled at her, noting her flushed cheeks and bright expression, the nervousness behind her enthusiasm. And a great realisation hit her. Keeping Sally as an unpaid helper was not in Sally's best interests - never mind Tabitha's! Sally needed this too. Keeping the school going was essential for the children - Tabitha now saw that it was essential for Sally as well. Once her children were more occupied at school, Sally would need to find employment - Tabitha may lose her entirely and then Shooting Stars really was doomed!

She saw that in her hour of need, an answer had jumped up in front of her! Picking up her discarded doughnut and biting into it again, she shuffled her chair round the table.

"Budge up," she said. "Let's have a look at these plans, then."

And so their planning meeting became more animated than ever. More coffee was brewed and more paper and pens needed. They worked out what they needed to achieve, what had to change, what must never change. They compared their school to other children's activities, and realised just how much they were under-charging. They allocated tasks and thought deeply about the ethos of Shooting Stars and how to convey these changes to the loyal parents. By the time they finished they had the outline of a new, vastly-improved, school, empty cups and a doughnut plate with only crumbs of sugar and a smear of jam.

They were tired but excited. "This is a fantastic new chapter, Tabitha – for both of us!" Sally enthused. "Brendan will be so pleased. Honestly, he knows how I love the School and he doesn't want me working in a shop just to fill time."

All too soon it was time for her to go and pick up her children, and as Sally drove off, her many sheets and folders safely stowed in her large workbag, Tabitha looked forward with a happy heart to tomorrow's meeting with Timothy. Everything was incredibly just falling into place! The small income Sally was planning for Shooting Stars would make all the difference to her sums – she would be able to survive!

She cleared up the kitchen, hid her paperwork again, and took the dogs into the garden for a quick game. She realised how much hard work they'd just done: no wonder she felt hungry! Time for some proper sustenance, she thought, as she came back in and opened and closed fridge and cupboard doors, finding not very much. So, settling the dogs down, she headed off into town for some food shopping, snatching up the mail as she left.

# 14

In the Shopping Centre car park, Tabitha picked up the envelope from the pile of junk mail she'd brought with her in the car. It was handwritten - unusual enough these days! And even more unusually, it was addressed to Tabitha Morpeth née Thomasson. What could it be?

Impatiently she ripped open the letter and flipped to the signature on the back page. Clare! Clare O'Sullivan! What a surprise!

Clare had been one of her closer friends at school. She'd never had a really close - best - friend, but there were a few who had been always around and did their best to help each other through those harrowing teenage years - and Clare had been one of them. Always cheerful, always lively, Clare had left early, pregnant, and under a cloud. Tabitha felt her heart warming as she read.

"Hi Tabs, I hope this manages to reach you! I got your married name from Veronica who'd read about it in the papers years ago, and got your address from your husband's agent. Ever resourceful, me!

I'm back in England after many long years in the wilderness, and I'd love to see you. How about we meet up for a coffee? Here's my email address, for more civilised contact."

Well, this was more of her past catching up with her. She smiled at the mention of Veronica too. They'd all been such friends back then, and it had been years since she'd seen her, another victim of Angus's isolation policy. She hoped Clare wasn't now in a state and needing support. She felt all supported out - drained by everything that had happened recently. But she'd be glad to hear Clare's story, and it would be a nice diversion to get away from her present woes and listen to someone else's.

So she was distracted as she did her shopping. She'd just picked up the last items from her list and was heading for the car park when she saw a familiar figure gliding through the Shopping Centre towards her: a tall and willowy girl - a young woman, even - with a fluid gait and head held high. It was Jennie! Young Jennie, Tabitha's star pupil.

Tabitha never ceased to marvel over the transformation in Jennie. She had first come to the school because it fitted perfectly with her mother's bridge evening. It was a way to get the child minded for a few hours. Mrs. Warwicker had little interest in drama or what it could do for her daughter, but it sounded good for her to be able to say to her bridge partners, whose offspring were at martial arts or dance classes, that Jennie was at Drama School.

Jennie's parents were nice enough, and the child had everything she needed and a lot of the things she wanted. But Jennie had surprised everyone by becoming very, very good at the school. She changed from a quiet, rather mousy-looking girl with a resentful attitude and little interest, to an outspoken, forthright young woman once she was onstage. So Tabitha was always passionate in her encouragement of this young talent - if only to give Jennie confidence in her own abilities, in everything she did.

She stopped and greeted Jennie, and with her mind brimful of the excitement of the new developments, offered to buy her an ice cream. Jennie was delighted and they went and chose her treat carefully. "Have whatever you like," Tabitha said, as she saw Jennie biting her lip and hesitating over her choice, worrying about whether it was polite to have the expensive one she really wanted.

Shortly after, they were sitting on the low wall of the little pool and fountain in the town gardens, with Jennie admiring the splendid raspberry and watermelon ice cream she had chosen, licking the melting drips round the edge of the cone.

"I'm glad I ran into you, Jennie," said Tabitha, happy to give the sophisticated teen such a childish pleasure. "I've been wanting to have a chat with you about the next few years. You're ... how old now?"

"Sixteen," replied Jennie, as she contorted herself under her upstretched hand to catch some more drips.

"Sixteen," mused Tabitha. "You'll be making some decisions soon enough about what you hope to do with your life. Have you given this much thought yet?"

"Well, Mum and Dad want me to go to College and study business, so I can get a decent job. I think," she captured another drip and took a big lick of the raspberry side of the ice cream, "I think they just want me to marry someone decent so they can get on with what *they* want to do. Not sure why they had me, really?" She gazed into the distance, her treat temporarily forgotten.

"And what about you? What would *you* like to do, Jennie?" asked Tabitha quietly.

"Oh," Jennie shuffled her feet a bit and stared at them. "I don't know. The only thing I'm really good at is acting. I love it! But you can't make a living at that, Dad says." She returned to her licking again.

"What about all the people you see on television? In films? Don't they make a living out of it?" Tabitha reasoned. "And then there are so many more who just love being involved in drama, productions, the theatre ... You'll find them working backstage, doing the lighting, the sound systems, managing wardrobes, directing, booking actors and locations, writing scripts." She waved her hands around animatedly as she spoke. "There's so many other ways to be involved in this wonderful field, even if you don't make the top spot as an actor!"

"I s'pose," thought Jennie, pausing. "But I don't really know how I could get those jobs." She had licked her way down to the cone now, and chewed thoughtfully, cocking her head to one side.

She's so clear in her body language, thought Tabitha - so expressive!

"Supposing you were able to go to an even bigger drama school than mine? One where you'd meet the sort of people who dish out these jobs? Get to meet the insiders in the business?" asked Tabitha.

Jennie flashed her an excited look - "Oh, I'd love that!" she said enthusiastically, then licked her fingers sadly - "But I can't see Dad and Mum ever agreeing to pay out good money for me to 'mess about acting'." She accentuated the phrase with a different voice - ah, such a natural, thought

Tabitha! "That's why they want me to do some kind of business. Accounts. Whatever."

Watching this fresh-faced young girl, Tabitha found herself whistling back in time to when she was the same age, the same girl almost, with the same dreams and the same obstacles to surmount.

It had been the day of the end-of-year assessments. With one year left in school, the parents were invited in to discuss their child's future academic path with the form teacher. Tabitha had been looking forward to this, as - unlike so many of her classmates - she knew exactly what she wanted to do with her life, and had known for years. She had once thought she wanted to be a vet and work with animals all day long, but her science results were never quite good enough. So she looked to her other favourite subjects - English and Drama. She loved being in the school plays. She was the director one year (she didn't know she'd been chosen by the other children to direct because they didn't want her on stage. Veronica said she turned into someone else when she was acting and it was weird.) It was the most exciting thing, preparing for a performance, then the huge surge of adrenalin as the time arrived and the play began. There was something about the immediacy of the performance that thrilled her.

Thinking about how this was now going to be her future, she had been flushed and excited as she met her mother at the Lodge and showed her to Miss Wiseman's room. Her father wasn't there. Of course. He was never there. He was at work. Always at work. But she was proud of having at least one parent there, and managed to trip nervously only once as they walked the endless polish-smelling corridors of the old-fashioned school.

Miss Wiseman looked stern and forbidding as always as they entered her room. She didn't rise, but had positioned herself with her back to the large window, the dark and huge bookshelves which lined the entire room ensuring that no light bounced onto her face. So Tabitha and her mother were confronted with a dark faceless figure, which quite unnerved Tabitha. A quick glance at her mother showed that she too felt anxious, put at a disadvantage.

They sat down in the chairs in front of the desk, and the faceless figure looked up from her papers saying, by way of introduction, "If Tabitha can apply herself, she may get sufficient grades in her exams to afford her a place at one of the northern universities." Miss Wiseman was not one to waste time with pleasantries. The North - that was the other end of the country! Tabitha felt a homesickness she never knew she had - a dread of being so far from everything familiar to her.

Her mother looked anxious, twisting her hankie round and round in her hands. She had been summoned to enough meetings at school down the years to be nervous about what this strange child of hers had done now. William had never given her this trouble! He had always pursued the Right Subjects at school and university and was destined to join the family building firm and follow in his father's footsteps.

Tabitha listened to the reasons why, in Miss Wiseman's opinion, she was unlikely to be accepted at the premium establishments. Not quite good enough ... falling short of expectations ... unable to grasp the realities ... were some of the reasons she heard the teacher trotting out. At last she could listen no more, and burst out:

"But Miss Wiseman, I don't want to go to university. I told you - I want to go to Drama School."

"Ridiculous idea." Miss Wiseman snorted, dismissing Tabitha's precious dream in two words.

"Quite," added her mother. "There's no future in that. You need a proper qualification so you can work in a nice office where you'll meet the Right Sort of Person."

Her father may not have been there, but he might as well have been. He used to be the one who would come home from work and scoop her up in his arms for a kiss, not minding the paint and sand on her face, or her grubby trousers and shoes. But in the last couple of years he seemed to have changed. He spoke of wanting her to be more "ladylike". He seemed concerned about what she wore when she wasn't in school uniform. He would adopt a worried expression when he spoke to her, unlike when he talked to William - now very tall. He'd clap him firmly on the back and squeeze his shoulders while he gave him a smile and called him "son". They just seemed to hit it off, and now William was finishing college and starting work in the firm, they were becoming as thick as thieves. Tabitha felt quite pushed out. She didn't at all mind that William would inherit the company - that was only right, for she had no interest in it, nor inclination. But it wasn't so long ago that her father had said to her, "Tabby - you want to be careful to mix in the right circle. And from that circle you'll be able to choose a husband."

The faceless figure across the desk was in full flow again, shuffling report papers and exam results as she discussed Tabitha's future with her mother - with no regard at all for what Tabitha wanted herself. "... a reasonable brain but not top-flight ... have to settle for what is appropriate ... expectations ... supervision ... keep her on the right path ... she'll understand when she's older ... foolish idea ..." Her mother nodded, and continued winding the hankie round her fingers.

Tabitha looked past Miss Wiseman's hidden face at the trees beyond the windows. She could hear the birds singing. "Why are you so happy and carefree," she thought, "when I feel imprisoned?" She wanted to be free like them. She wanted to be out of this dark room, away from the disapproval of her "elders and betters". She couldn't understand why they pooh-poohed her idea. But she didn't have the courage to go against them. Perhaps they were right? Perhaps her ideas were nonsense. But they were *her* ideas, and she dearly wished to have the chance to find out for herself! She had felt trapped.

That uncomfortable feeling in her body, of being trapped, brought her back to the present. Jennie was crunching the last of her ice cream cone, and watching some children playing around the ornamental fountain.

"Jennie," said Tabitha decisively. "If this is what you want, then you should go for it. We only have one life. We have to do what we feel is right. You can't let your life be decided for you by others. *You're* the one who has to live this life. *You're* the one who has to take risks, to try to be what you want to be, to make mistakes, perhaps to take the wrong path. It's you who's going to face your life alone. It doesn't matter how many parents or teachers or friends say different. When it comes down to it, it's you. You have to be able to look in the mirror and say, 'Yes! I did what I wanted to do!' Whether you succeed or fail is not important. But you have to try. You have to follow your dreams and get what you want for yourself out of life. You can't be forever fitting in with others. If acting is what you want to do, what you are meant to do, it's in your blood. It's there. And it will come back to haunt you. It will demand fulfilment."

Tabitha stopped abruptly. Jennie was gazing at her face, her mouth falling open with astonishment at seeing her usually controlled teacher so passionate.

"Jennie, you have to follow your star. You have to do what *you* feel is right. And I'll support you every inch of the way."

Tabitha realised that she was speaking to the young Tabitha. That young Tabitha who didn't have the courage of her convictions, who made what she now knew was a disastrous marriage because she felt pushed into justifying her existence on this planet by becoming a wife and mother (ha to that). She had buckled beneath the pressure and lost so many years when she should have been devoting all her energy to what she now saw she was born to do.

Jennie had shut her mouth again, but Tabitha could see that her words - and her passion - had hit home. There was a steely look in the child's eyes. Tabitha had been lost all those years ago, but she now had the chance to rescue another girl from the same fate. Tabitha was beginning to make an impression on the world, do valuable work. How much more could she have contributed if she'd been able to follow her own desires from the start?

Jennie said quietly, her eyes searching Tabitha's face, "Do you really think I can do it? Could I really become an actress?"

"I am going to do my utmost to ensure you get the chance," replied Tabitha firmly. "Don't mention this at home just yet. Don't make any rash decisions ... I'm going to give this some thought." She frowned at her car keys for a moment, then, tossing the car keys up then gripping them in her closed palm, she said, "We can do this!" and jumped up from the wall.

The happy Jennie danced off towards her home, as Tabitha walked with a firm resolve back to her car with her shopping. Now she was really looking forward to her meeting with Timothy in the morning! She knew what her path must be. She had to secure Shooting Stars, develop the Academy with Timothy, and do what she did best.

There were to be no more broken-hearted Tabithas!

# 15

It was a week after her first meeting with Timothy when Tabitha walked with purpose along the pavement of Benjamin Square, headed for the National Drama School. She had made a big decision and couldn't wait to discuss it all with her new colleague. Imagine! "My new colleague, Timothy Baker, the Director of the National Drama School!" She chuckled to herself happily, and strode up the steps and through the mighty doorway, feeling ten feet tall.

This time she ascended the stairs with the stained glass window proudly, her steps ringing on the stone treads: she felt she belonged. At last she felt she belonged somewhere!

Timothy greeted her warmly at the door to his office. Tabitha hoped that her barely-suppressed excitement and flushed cheeks would show him that he'd picked a winner.

"Tell me how you like your coffee," he said as he motioned her to a seat in the great window overlooking the leafy gardens of the Square. "I have a feeling we'll be enjoying many more together?"

"You can see straight through me!" laughed Tabitha. "Yes - I hope this is the beginning of a fruitful co-production! Oh, and white, no sugar," she added, as she got her planner out of her case.

As Timothy turned away to prepare the drinks, Tabitha noticed a secret smile on his face. He brought them over and joined Tabitha in the big bay window, saying in a more confidential voice, "Everyone wants to make a mark. And this idea of the Junior Academy has been brewing in my mind ever since I was appointed a couple of years ago. It's something I'm passionate about, and I knew I had to get it right - to start off with a bang. So you are an answer to prayer, young Tabitha."

Tabitha was amused that Timothy called her "young Tabitha". He wasn't that much older than she was, but he had achieved so much. She supposed that in this field she was still fairly new. She glowed inside. Was this really happening? Yes. It was! And she'd better start growing into her role.

So they got down to solid planning, discussing dates, rehearsal times, possibilities for extra coaching, the scope for assistants later on, how they wanted to approach the advertising and auditioning, the production they wanted to start with ... There was so much to plan, but Timothy's razor-sharp mind and his huge experience in sorting out timetables and productions focussed them on the essentials they had to iron out. Tabitha was really glad of her meeting with Sally the day before. All this wrenching the mind out of the complacency of years and opening up to new opportunities - it was as if she could feel her body crack and growl as she grew!

"I've appointed my chief helper at Shooting Stars as my Admin. We're putting the School onto a secure financial footing so that she can devote much more time to it. We've already planned to move our rehearsal day from Saturday to a weekday. So I can still work there - Sally will be my anchor!"

"So, along with the salary here, you'll be well set up financially," Timothy said, as he walked her through the numbers of her new post. As an academic institution, salaries were all on set scales, but there would also be the possibility of extra work for Tabitha if she wanted it. The figure mentioned made her gasp. On reflection, she realised it was a perfectly ordinary sort of number for the hours and the skills she would be bringing, but she had been without money for so long that it staggered her.

Angus was mean, habitually keeping her short of money. Since he'd stopped her involvement with The School for Scoundrels, the theatre company she used to enjoy so much, and required her to do admin and secretarial tasks for him (though she was never given access to any of his financial figures), she found she had to justify any expenses to him. She had become adept at inflating the prices of the groceries to Angus, cashing his cheque at the supermarket - he never entrusted her with cash - and being able to buy some more interesting foods and supplies with a bit of juggling. She seldom bought new clothes, and was a frequent flyer at the local charity shops. Even her long hair, which Jamie loved so much, was only long because a hairdresser was an expense she could not run to.

She was actually going to have her own money, and a very respectable amount too. And, of course, Sally was right - she too should be recompensed properly for her work. Tabitha now had a figure to gauge how much the school should be returning for its devoted organisers, so she could be sure Sally was getting the right pay. With two sources of income she'd manage very well.

She realised Timothy was asking her a question. She brought herself quickly back to the present and listened.

".. so, as you'll be spending a lot of time here, you may want to consider moving to the city and travelling back for your school rehearsals? Although your husband will have an opinion on that, I would guess," he smiled.

Tabitha smiled back and brushed over the mention of Angus by saying, "As long as I can find a place right for my dogs, I'd certainly be up for that!"

And as long as I can still walk in nature, she added to herself. She thought of the excitement of living in a city again, the buzz of meeting new people all the time, the busyness of the streets, the enormous energy of the students - when they were not affecting total indifference with a pre-Raphaelite languor as she had seen them do on her last visit.

She realised how hemmed in her life had become. She had continually given way to Angus's demands - anything for a quiet life, she supposed - finding herself isolated, poor, almost friendless. But with all this change and excitement, she had to maintain access to the landscape somehow. She realised how important it was to her - to be able to see the sky, the clouds, the beauty of nature. How could she ensure this while living in the city? She moved the thought to the back of her mind for the moment. Her life was on the cusp of changing entirely, and she found it incredibly exciting - it got her creativity moving, and new ideas were emerging as she and Timothy continued their planning session, which they eagerly discussed.

"Now, you had some questions about some of your own students joining the Academy?" said Timothy, when they'd got almost everything tied up.

"Yes, there are some who could do well in the business. And one who is gifted. I think so, anyway. The trouble there is that her parents - though perfectly well off - don't take drama seriously. She was saying only yesterday that her parents want her to go into some kind of office-based career where she can land a suitable husband. That's an awful thing for a sixteen-year-old to be thinking!" But as she said it, she remembered the sixteen-year-old Tabitha being issued with the exact same instructions by her own father. Previously, her father had always fostered her inventiveness, her being different, her quirky humour. What was it about these men that once they found themselves in a position of power, of management, that they tried to run people's lives for them?

"Well, we can look at this during our next meeting. But there are some bursaries that may be available. Moneys that were given to the School years ago with strict provisions on who should get them. Some of them have age or location constraints. We might be able to access some of those funds for your star pupil. And, of course, I'll be looking for more funding anyway. Named scholarships from individual businesses may be a popular way to go .... Would you fancy winning the Taylor's Trousers Award?" he mused with a smile, thinking of the large business at the entrance to Benjamin Square. Reassured, Tabitha relaxed a little. She knew Timothy would do what he said. She could wait to hear what he came up with for Jennie.

"Now," he said, clapping his hands and rising from his chair, "let's go down and explore where you'll be working! And I've got a few people I'd like you to meet - future colleagues. It's time they got to see my secret weapon," he winked, as he motioned Tabitha towards the door.

Tabitha felt so proud as she toured the rehearsal rooms and admired the theatre, which - being the largest space in the building - would be her own rehearsal area for the Junior Academy. She'd be rehearsing her charges in the NDS Theatre! It was almost too much to believe.

The School was busy, and there were activities in all of the rooms. Walking along the corridor, lined with photos from previous productions, framed theatre programmes and posters - their style and design clearly reflecting the era they were from, she could pick up on the mood of each rehearsal room as she passed, from the sounds emanating from them. She was excited by the surge of energy the small groups of students generated. Judging by the sudden bursts of laughter, they were loving their work. Timothy was obviously a popular Director, and seemed to have a very easy, relaxed relationship with the staff, and that enviable mixture of respect and joshing from the students. He introduced her with a flourish to each of the tutors as they invaded their rooms, and Tabitha warmed as she met all these fellow drama-fiends. Why had she been away from them for so long? It was as if cobwebs were being pulled from her face, she could smell the excitement of the theatre again. She felt as if she were coming home after such a long absence.

She was pleased to see, in one of these rooms, her old colleague Gerard, one of The Scoundrels. He turned to Timothy with a serious face, saying "Glad you listened to me and took up my suggestion," as he winked at Tabitha. Ah, so it was Gerard, she realised, who had mentioned her to Timothy. She smiled back at him, hearing Timothy say, "Now now, Gerard, you can't claim credit for all the best ideas!"

Gerard greeted her with a warm hug as a long-lost friend, reminding her of one or two of the antics they'd all got up to.

"Remember when Edward lost the keys to the tour bus and we were all standing around freezing at 2 in the morning while he tracked them down?"

"I do indeed!" replied Tabitha warmly, "and remember how we all wondered how he'd managed to not lose his glasses for once, but the keys to our bus instead."

Gerard's class students listened eagerly as he and Tabitha laughed together, hoping to catch a sniff of scandal from their tutor's past life, not to mention this new mystery woman he seemed to have history with.

"And how's that scenery guy .. what was his name? … um, Johnny?"

"Jamie!" Tabitha responded, seeing he was setting her up.

"Yes, that was it, Jamie. You knew him quite well, I think?" he added with a mischievous glint in his eye.

So they all knew, thought Tabitha, working hard not to blush, as she said, "Oh, I believe he's doing fine - still carpentering, I think." She recovered herself enough to change the subject by asking after Gerard's family, asking how old his children now were. It was easy to turn him to his very favourite topic, his family.

As they moved on to the next room, she mentally kicked herself for being so stupid. Of course they all knew! Nothing was a secret in the theatre - nowhere a greater hotbed of gossip and vicarious living. Who was more attuned to people's words and body language than actors? She wondered with a jolt whether it had ever found its way back via the writers and dramatists to reach Angus's ears. But then, she reflected, he was so supremely bound up in his own life and ideas, that he may not have given it credence if they had told him straight. He'd accused her once of having an affair – long before she actually was - because he completely failed to understand how a small touring theatre company could possibly be so absorbing. She wondered now if his accusation had given her the green light to connect with Jamie later. But he was barking completely up the wrong tree thinking she was having a relationship with Edward (Edward! of all people!) and she felt sure he never knew anything about Jamie at all.

As they completed their tour and introductions, and Timothy saw her off with their next date firmly in the diary, Tabitha compared her present feelings of fulfilment and excitement with the emptiness and purposelessness she so often felt at home. The only ones who valued her there were her dogs. Her dear dogs, who had been her rock in all this time. Something of her own to cling to. And they were the one area of her life where she totally stood up to Angus. When it came to the dogs, she was unswerving in her dedication. She was able to say "no" long and hard if she needed to. She was going to have to practice her "no" muscles! She wasn't going to be beaten down by another person any more. She was going to do what she wanted, and rejoice in it.

And after such a fulfilling day, on the train journey home she made another momentous decision. She would tell Angus tomorrow. Oh no, perhaps she wouldn't … Oh dear, already her resolve was buckling! She realised she felt a bit afraid of him. It was not that she thought he'd hurt her, but his temper seemed so unpredictable these days, and she always cowered before his outbursts. Perhaps she should broach it early in the day, before he'd got into the drink?

She was making all these plans for a new life, glossing over the fact that she wasn't allowing herself to think of the key part - that she was abandoning her difficult husband.

Somehow she had to face him.

# 16

The morning dragged on. Tabitha had walked the dogs, prepared tonight's dinner, cleaned, washed and cleaned again in her fidgetiness. She was beginning to feel butterflies. She felt faint, shaky. She had no idea when Angus would come home. She never had much clue what he was up to as he always kept her in the dark, or brushed off her questions with vague answers that told her nothing. Ending her marriage was a big issue for her. It put her integrity and her whole life in jeopardy. But when she thought of integrity she realised that there was only one decision she could make - and be able to live with herself.

Yesterday had been enthralling! Feeling accepted by Timothy and the staff, being quietly admired by the students - especially Gerard's, who by now would be busily telling the others all about her - she knew what her place was, her mission in life. The emptiness she often felt in her own home was replaced by a buzz of excitement and purpose, and drive! Yes, she loved her own little school and what it did for her students, but even that had started to be swallowed up by Angus's malaise of finding fault and looking on the gloomy side of life. If ever there was a person who saw the glass as half-empty, it was Angus. She had stagnated, and it had taken all this upheaval for her to realise where she was going.

She stood gazing out of the kitchen window, watching one of the hens - ever alert to possibilities - racing through the grass to snatch a tasty insect.

Had Sally come out with her suggestions without everything that had happened, she may have gone back into her shell and continued to stagnate.

What a loss that would have been!

A flash of energy came into her mind as she thought of the ever-industrious Sally. Sally's enthusiasm was great, and perhaps it had saved the school from being sucked under by the narrowness of Angus's vision - his vision for everyone else, that was! He was clear enough on the splendid vision of his own success.

She arranged and re-arranged things in the kitchen, she tidied the living room and plumped up the cushions. The dogs trotted behind her, wondering what was going on. She couldn't settle to any work. She had to get this out of the way, and hoped to be able to address Angus before the day was too long, before he hit the bottle again.

She had rehearsed what she was going to say over and over again. Yet she still wasn't sure how to go about it. She'd practiced different approaches in her mind. She thought of flattering him first - that always seemed to work, a bit. She thought of plunging in headlong. She thought of feeding him first then getting round to it - but there was a danger that he'd have had some drinks and just want to be on his own in his study. They never sat in the living room together any more. Tabitha would sit there of an evening with the dogs, knitting, reading, watching TV quietly. She wasn't allowed to listen to music. He would simply come into the room, pick up the remote without a word, and turn the television off. Music seemed to reach his soul (which Tabitha so wished she could) and had the power to disturb his work. He was unable to switch it off in his ears, so he had to switch it off at source.

She was turning this all round in her fevered mind when she heard the crunch of car tyres on gravel in the drive. Her stomach lurched and she felt prickles of sweat in her armpits. As she heard her husband arriving home her heart beat faster. While she urgently reminded herself of her purpose, she nevertheless felt disorientated … and she felt quite at sea.

"Ah, I'm glad you're here for once," he started as he came briskly through the door, tossing his file onto the table. It was only early afternoon, but he'd clearly had a few. Tabitha noticed that the dogs, who had been happily following her around the house all morning, Luigi with his ever-present teddy bear in his mouth, had slid onto their beds by the cooker and put their heads down. They were telling her - as if she needed to be told - that there was an Atmosphere.

"I want to know how you're doing with the arrangements for America. I don't seem to see much happening. You've got to buck up, Tabitha! You need to get moving on this."

All Tabitha's imagined openings disappeared as Angus took the initiative! But perhaps she could calmly steer him round?

"Well, I've been looking into housing over there - I can show you what I found if you're interested? The sort of thing you'd want - near the University, you know. I know they're going to provide something to start with." She felt flustered.

"Good!" he said, pulling out a chair and sitting at the table. "You'll find lots to do there too, I'm sure. You won't need to do much for me as I'll be able to use the college staff for admin. You'll need to have something to do." He pulled out a chair and sat down at the table, and smiled at her. "Perhaps you could join a theatre group? Get to know the other wives? We'll want to entertain. I want you to be happy, Tabitha." His grey eyes softened as he looked at her.

For a moment he seemed to have a shaft of understanding - that Tabitha had feelings and desires too. For a moment, just a moment, Tabitha saw the man she'd married - solicitous, generous, smiling, thinking of her. Why did this happen so seldom?

"But you don't seem to be entirely committed to this," he continued, leaning forward with his elbows on the table.

Tabitha felt herself weakening. Had he seen through her? Or was he just making a stab in the dark? But it was a stab which hurt her, dug at her heart. There were signs of the man she had known all those years ago, and she was gripped with guilt at her planned betrayal.

"I'm really not keen on going," she said. "Not right now," she hurried on. Yes! She'd said it! She had to keep going ... "Not while there's so much still to do with my school. Then there's the dogs ..."

"Oh, your *school!*" Angus laughed shortly at her. "How can you think that's important now?" Tabitha felt the blood rise into her head. She clenched her teeth. How dare he ridicule her school! But he was carrying on, "I only let you start it to pander to your obsession with acting. It's nothing compared to the opportunity I now have. *We* have," he quickly corrected himself. Tabitha reeled. He was completely oblivious to how important her school was! It was real to her - it changed the lives of so many of the children she worked with. Why did he think his work was so much more important? There was no way she would now mention her new project - the new Academy - to him. She couldn't bear to hear him ridicule that!

"And as for the dogs," Angus added, continuing to trample on her heart, "you can get new ones. Well maybe just one new one."

Tabitha was aghast. Her precious dogs! What could he be thinking?

"In any case, you're my wife." He said with finality. "It's your duty to support me."

"I'm not your wife." Tabitha was astonished to hear herself saying this out loud. "Not really. Not in the real meaning of the word," she added, very quietly.

This was the first time in years she had stood up to her husband - not since she had insisted on getting Esme, and at that time she had so surprised him with her determination that he had found it easier to capitulate than to argue. She couldn't believe the place she had arrived at. She felt powerful over what she had just said – she had actually said it! After all these years of silence. Yet she was fearful at the same time.

Angus looked at her, first blankly, then as the enormity sunk in, thunderously.

"You *are* my wife, like it or not. I've supported you and helped you all these years. I've encouraged you in your hobbies - yet you seem to inflate their importance beyond just being a parochial children's hour! Ha!" he said, hollowly. "I want you to start making the arrangements necessary. This house has to be sold, things have to be wound up here. And you have to start looking to the future." He smacked his palm onto the table in emphasis.

Tabitha flinched. Esme looked up, startled, while Luigi got up from his bed and silently crept out of the room in slow motion. Her moment of rebellion felt crushed. She didn't know this man. He wasn't the man she had married. He'd beaten her down, and when it came to it she was tongue-tied, humiliated, dumb-struck. She felt wretched. She had colluded in her own difficulties through her lack of confidence and inability to see her own purpose in life. She'd gone along with every twist and turn of their relationship. She had been compliant, complacent. She was utterly to blame.

She saw Angus pick up his file and start leafing through it. And yet she couldn't help but feel sorry for him. He had boxed himself into a corner, he had isolated himself from the one person who could have supported him and loved him. He was such a mixed-up person, with a past that cast long shadows over his life - and hers. She knew that his early family life had been difficult, with the loss of his mother, leaving him to be cared for by grandparents and minders. Maybe he formed his damaged ideas at that time? Maybe he'd always been afraid to let go, to commit to their marriage, for fear of being abandoned again? Maybe, if Tabitha could push aside the guilt she seemed to go to as her first resort she could see that it wasn't all her? She thought with a pang of the times, early on, when he'd encouraged her, taught her things, included her in his life. And was she being too harsh, disloyal, to this damaged person - who needed help? She looked away from him, a tear in her eye. She knew he was watching her.

She remembered their early times together. He was kind and attentive, amusing, entertaining, solicitous. He took her to concerts and introduced her to wonderful music – Bach, Messiaen, he showed her everything. They visited art galleries and he showed her hidden gems in the collections – the little Crivelli room in the National Gallery, the heart-rending and poetic Pre-Raphaelites, a wonderful portrait of a spaniel by Landseer, which she still so loved. He took her to strange dark parties with his literary friends, carefully watching over her and staving off any drunken advances. He was generous and caring. And he declared his love for her, with a sad puppy dog face she found irresistible: "I'm afraid I'm falling in love with you," he had said one evening as they walked the city streets. She really thought she had found what she was looking for! And she felt a huge responsibility for having engendered such feelings in him.

As it was her fault that he felt this way, she had had to follow through.

Her mother used to say, "You've made your bed so you must lie on it". She hadn't meant for this to happen, but it had. And she had felt duty-bound to stay with this man who was to become her husband.

Angus was muttering at the papers in his file.

"Here's stuff on immigration requirements. You'll need to look at this carefully," he snapped, thumping the papers onto the table, clearly still taut and annoyed. The very thought of moving permanently anywhere with him caused her chest to tighten, her breathing to feel suffocated. Life with him was just that - stifling.

Angus had claimed his religious beliefs as the reason there was no sex in their relationship - "That's wrong before marriage," he'd said, as he pulled away from her. This was something that puzzled Tabitha, who had enjoyed sex as fun with several previous boyfriends and did not see it as a troubling issue. It was when there appeared to be no sex *after* marriage as well that Tabitha had got confused. That was when she came to the conclusion that - as every normal male wants sex - it must be her fault that Angus didn't. It had simply never occurred to her to put together his early life, the early loss of his mother and his fear of abandonment, and the current situation, and see that he was not so normal a male after all. One thing that always shocked her was that he'd enjoy telling risqué jokes with his friends, with great belly-laughs of "I know what I'm talking about," to underline that he was a man of the world. But he wasn't. He joked about things he'd never experienced. He was a small boy lost in a sea of emotions that he couldn't control.

Right now that small boy was glaring menacingly at her. Was that why he sought to control Tabitha at every turn? She was easy - a pushover - as she had had her own ideas about marriage formed so early in life, of the subservient housewife-mother and the all-powerful out-in-the-world father. She had always dreamt of her wedding day, her beautiful dress, the lovely flowers - as an end in itself. She was compliant and biddable. She did what she was told. And that had so been the wrong course to take! With every little success, every time he leant on her desires to sublimate her to his, Angus's feelings of self-importance, of rightness, were bolstered. And she got pushed further and further - downwards. Was all this done to cover the broken heart of that small boy?

She looked towards him, now sitting with his arms folded, waiting for her response. This had all whirled so fast through her mind. Was she so wrong to be thinking of herself and her future now, when he so clearly needed her? Could she deliver the fatal blow and tell him she had made plans which did not include him - in the same way that he had made secret plans that did not include her?

Her silence led Angus to believe that he had won this round. He stood up and strode towards his study. "So let me know in a couple of days how far you've got with the plans," he said.

And as he headed to the door his foot kicked one of the dogs' toys which spun and hit the skirting board with a clatter. "Damn dogs," he muttered.

Tabitha sat down, miserable. Once more, she had buckled before him. Would she never be able to live her own life? Was it absurd, her idea of independence and fulfilment? She snapped her fingers and Esme jumped up as she headed for the back door, Luigi putting his head round the living room door to see if it was safe to come out. Tabitha had to get out. She felt she was choking in this house, she needed air.

And she needed warmth. Affection. Understanding. She felt a sudden yearning for Jamie and slipped her phone in her pocket so she'd be able to ring him while out and fix to see him again, soon. Was she vacillating over him as well?

# 17

They met on Peter's boat. Peter was one of Jamie's friends who knew all about Tabitha, but kept quiet about it. They'd used his boat before for assignations, Peter being happy to facilitate his friend, who spent time tinkering about on the boat with him. Jamie had quite a number of good friends. She was happy for him, though it made a stark contrast with her almost complete lack of them. Except for Clare, of course, coming back into her life. Tabitha wondered if that friendship could grow again. She really would love that.

Being on the sea leant a mystical quality to their lovemaking, feeling the boat rocking gently, hearing the water slap against the hull when another boat went past in the sleepy harbour, watching the shimmering patterns of sunlight reflected off the water onto the cabin ceiling as they lay beside each other, sated.

Tabitha had the dogs with her. They were part of her "cover" for spending the day away from home. The four of them had enjoyed a pleasant walk on their way to the boat. Jamie was good at throwing toys for the dogs and played happily with them. He was fit and trim and very, very physical. Tabitha loved watching the three of them play together. But as they got nearer to the main purpose of their meeting, Jamie's light manner changed.

"Dogs can stay on deck," he said peremptorily as he led her down the steps and put the shopping bag by the galley sink. "This is not a spectator sport," he smiled and put his arms round her.

"Oh no they can't," responded Tabitha hotly, pulling away. "They stay with me. They're people - they can't be left alone on deck."

"No. *We're* people. *They're* dogs."

"But they're people to me," she said, as his mouth covered hers and stopped her protests. She was torn between allowing the joy to flood through her, and realising that here was another man dictating how she should feel. The joy won. But so did she, by absorbing all of Jamie's attention while the dogs found a small corner of the cabin floor to curl up and sleep after the exertions of their games.

Tabitha managed to put everything else out of her mind - that swirling sea of worries and conflict that now seemed to occupy her every waking moment as well as disturbing her usually deep sleep - and immersed herself in the moment. She even banished the thoughts of their last meeting, when she'd felt so disappointed in Jamie. He was such an imaginative and delicate lover, and he knew her so well. They had a couple of hours of fun and laughter - a lightheartedness she hadn't been able to feel for some time. Jamie was in good form, telling stories, playing with her, relieved that she was back from the darker place she had been when they had last met. He was always able to summon a good mood at will, to grab the lightness of the moment and keep it alive. His game of pat-a-cake with her hand was punctuated with kisses - on her nose, her breast, her ears ("Turn your head, I have to kiss both of your ears. Must keep it fair.")

Tabitha gave herself up to the pleasure of the encounter. She relished Jamie's devotion - his adoration - and loved releasing herself to him. Life seemed so simple when they were together like this. How would it have been if they had taken the plunge and got together all those years ago? Her mind baulked at this image. It couldn't have happened. And it didn't happen. It wasn't just that Jamie was already committed, had responsibilities. However much she loved their physical relationship, and the lightness of their spiritual one, intellectually she always hesitated.

The differences between her and Jamie went much deeper.

She thought of the time when he had arrived at her home to do some work on hanging her new kitchen cupboards and she was listening to music. It was one of the Bach Cello Sonatas, exquisitely, heart-tearingly, beautiful.

"What on earth's that noise?" Jamie had said as he dumped his heavy toolkit on the floor with a crash.

"It's Bach," replied Tabitha, trying to keep the defensiveness out of her voice, "and I think it's some of the most ravishing music the world has ever heard. Do you not know it?" she asked him.

"Nope. Ignoramus, I am," he said, pulling her towards him for a kiss.

"You should know about this," said Tabitha, easing away from him. "I know it's not easy music to understand .."

"You can teach me!" said Jamie, smiling, holding her hand, stroking her fingers. "I'd love you to teach me about music. It's important to you, so I want to know about it."

"Ok," said Tabitha brightly, unwinding herself from his arms and heading for the music centre. "Let's find something more accessible ..." She flipped through her collection and chose a piece. The sublime melodies of Vaughan Williams filled the room from her speakers hung high on the walls of the kitchen. Something pastoral, easy to listen to - she thought it would make a good start.

After less than a minute, Jamie had turned to his toolbox and started to chuck tools around noisily. Just as the music was reaching a lilting crescendo into the sweetest melody yet, he started to talk about the tv programme he'd watched the night before.

Tabitha sighed. It was hopeless. He means well, she thought, but he doesn't have an ounce of artistic feeling. How could she live with a man who thought that Wagner composed "Here comes the bride" for fat women in helmets?

How could she spend the rest of her life with someone whose heart had never broken over a Bach Passion, a Palestrina Mass, a Bruckner String Quintet?

She felt she'd only be half a person with their physical connection and not the deep shared history she had with Angus. She didn't feel that it could last, if subjected to the scrutiny of everyday life. There were times when sex, even just affection, weren't the answer, thought Tabitha. She could see bills being unpaid and commitments being missed, with Jamie telling her not to worry, and trying to kiss away her concerns. She'd paid for the coffee and cream in the supermarket on the way to the boat. He'd said he had no cash and couldn't have the bill appear on his card for Annette to see. How true was that? She had turned the thought round in her mind for a moment then abandoned it so she could enjoy him now.

Staying with Angus had been in some part a defensive measure for her, to avoid having to face and discuss all this too deeply. She realised how she had been happy to mark time while using her married state as her get-out clause. At the same time the presence of Jamie as a pressure valve for her feelings had enabled her marriage to continue - perhaps longer than it would have otherwise. And now she had the opportunity to finish her marriage and - technically - be free to engage with whom she wished, she felt unable to confide her new change in circumstances to Jamie.

"Jamie," she said.

"Mm-hm," he answered drowsily.

"Jamie ..."

"Still here," he said with the corners of his mouth curving up. She so loved his mouth.

She went silent. "What is it?" he said, opening his eyes and turning towards her.

"Just ... this is a magical moment," she ended lamely, despite everything she'd said in the pub not so long ago.

She knew he'd start again on them disappearing to some impractical and imaginary location to be together all the time, and she didn't want him to do that. She knew in her heart that Jamie loved her, was in love with her, in love with the idea of them being together for ever, and that he felt that the things he said to her were real.

And now on the boat, as she stood at the tiny cabin sink and splashed cold water on her face to cool her rosy cheeks and neck, and Jamie beside her washed to remove her scent from his body, she wondered how many more times this could happen. She had a churning feeling inside her that change was inexorably coming. Once more she felt helpless.

They retrieved their scattered clothing and passed them to each other, Tabitha admiring Jamie's beautiful body as he dressed. And he said, "You're gorgeous," as she did up her bra. Yet another of his delightful compliments she found so hard to receive. But she also knew, even now - this blissful afternoon - that she was unlovable. It was her go-to thought. It all had to be her fault. So his compliments must be empty, though they seemed so pure and true when he said them. She felt a yearning for .. what? A different life, a life without the drama she was going through at the moment - an unattainable dream. She lay back on the bunk again and watched her lover as he fished the coffee things out of the carrier bag and started brewing a drink for them. This was a secret moment in Tabitha's life. This was not real. It was a glimpse of heaven which shut off again as soon as they were apart. She puzzled over the people who had this in their life all the time. People who had married their lover, or whose husband had become their lover. Was that everyone else? Was it only she who had missed out on this? Did everyone else have a life of perfect alignment and fulfilment?

It was hard to credit. There must be others like her. She turned onto her side, her hand under her cheek as she watched Jamie. Perhaps she should just think herself very lucky to have had it at all. It wasn't perfect, but it was something, and so much better than nothing.

And it was a very blissful something, especially after the torment of the day before.

Yet she kept her life in separate compartments. She had always told Jamie everything, but now she found herself unable to tell him about the momentous goings-on with Angus. Keeping him in the dark ran counter to what she had always done, but she feared opening the floodgates and being overwhelmed by yet another problem right now.

"It's ok if you don't want to tell me," he said, without turning round. She sank down as she felt a wave of finality settle over her. Was it to be the end with Jamie as well as with Angus? Would there be a life ahead where this turmoil would end? Perhaps, she realised, that would mean that neither man would feature. She let out a great sigh.

Jamie turned, one eyebrow raised quizzically as he poured cream into the coffee. Then he smiled warmly at her, giving her a wink. She loved his sensitivity and his happy-go-lucky acceptance. But she knew that today was a day to keep unsullied, precious, a delicious memory. She laughed and he reached out a hand and pulled her up so he could sit next to her on the bunk. Tabitha felt fears in her chest but suppressed them. She was going to enjoy this beautiful, innocent, moment, as Jamie had clearly decided to.

She leant up and kissed his neck and snuggled into his shoulder and sighed.

"I love you," said Jamie, drawing her closer, "I love you."

Tabitha smiled dreamily at him and snuggled further into his shoulder. She wanted to immerse herself in him, immolate herself. And yet it all felt as if it were running out of control, fast.

Esme got up and stretched, rested her chin on Tabitha's knee and wagged her tail slowly. "Luigi, here!" said Jamie, as the older dog got up more awkwardly, his feet struggling to get a grip on the smooth floor, and plodded stiffly over to him. Jamie used his finger to dot a little cream onto the old dog's nose, and they both laughed warmly at his comical efforts to lick it off.

Such moments were divine, precious. Could she really let this all go? Was there any way of keeping it?

# 18

"We'll have to draft a letter to the parents," said Sally, at their planning meeting a few days later. The interlude on the boat had kept Tabitha in a more elevated state of mind which had served her well while she focused on the plans that had to be made, and the numbers that had to be crunched. Angus's disapproval - even his positive discouragement - had always driven Tabitha to play small in her work, to shrink her passion down to what she could get away with. She felt that this was now a time of huge upheaval – a burgeoning of inspiration and ideas that she had so longed for.

"Indeed," replied Tabitha, as she finished the last sum on her chart of the new financial predictions for the school. She slapped her pen down on the sheet with a flourish, and leant back in her chair, stretching luxuriously. In addition to all the usual items, like hall and costume rental, printing the scripts, the flyers and programs, it included pay for Sally and also an official amount for Tabitha – a great novelty when she'd always just had the leavings, in a haphazard way. "We'll just have to explain to them that their dedication and support has helped grow the school in such a way that we now have to get it onto a better financial footing – so that it can carry on. Can give their child a much better experience, type of thing …" She turned to look at Sally, "We should mention the new tie-up with the NDS and what it could mean for their child - it's going to benefit their children hugely, access to speech coaches and so on. I hope they can see that - and accept it!"

"Well, there are bound to be some who moan and expect to get all this for half nothing. Kat's mother, for one! Remember when she complained about being asked to provide some sandwiches for the dress rehearsal? That she didn't expect to be used as an unpaid cook?" Both women laughed and shrugged their shoulders at the memory. "But I think most of them know the value of what they've been getting all this time. I do think they'll cough up. Just compare it with painting lessons, or gymnastics - that costs loads compared with us - even with the new figures. And anyway," she added, packing away her coloured markers and her huge sheet of neat planning diagrams - in such contrast to Tabitha's scribbled and overwritten sheets, and old envelopes with notes on - "once they hear that you've been headhunted for the National School, they should realise just how lucky they are." Sally smiled broadly, as Tabitha sighed and smiled back saying, "I still can't quite believe all this is happening …"

They had been plotting and planning for what seemed like hours. Much coffee had been drunk and several slices of cake and lumps of cheese had disappeared. They were feeling well satisfied with the outcome. With Sally on board, dealing with all the admin that Tabitha used to put off doing for as long as possible - admin really wasn't her *forte!* - her school was now secure. Tabitha would be able to do the planning with Sally, then just turn up for rehearsals and performances, and so it could all carry on while she worked at the National Drama School.

"Jason's father will be delighted with the new schedule," laughed Tabitha. "He always complained that he couldn't take Jason to football because his wife had forbidden it as Saturdays was our drama school day. And I think Thursday will suit very well. I don't know of any other group round here that has Thursdays after school."

"Well, we've just got to send out the letter and then duck the brickbats. They'll have to see - it's either that or nothing," said Sally, as she cut herself another sliver of cake. "I think it'll all work out fine. We may slim down a bit, lose some of the less committed, but I think most will be happy to join us in our new chapter." She munched for a moment then added, "And newcomers should consider it more valuable now we're setting a higher price on it. They would start with more commitment." Sally gazed at the warm summery greenness of the tree outside the kitchen window, licking her fingers thoughtfully.

"Anyway," she continued, "I am just so thrilled to be involved! Brendan will be delighted when he sees these figures. You know how he adores Maisie? And if Maisie wants the school to continue, then Maisie's wish is his command," she laughed. "But he'll be much happier about it once I'm earning - it shows that I'm valued. And I won't have to look for work elsewhere in order to feel I'm contributing," she added with a coy smile. What a difference, thought Tabitha. How wonderful to have that support at home, to feel encouraged in your ventures ...

"Oh, you certainly are valued!" exclaimed Tabitha. "I'm excited by all this too, Sally. You're a Godsend. I couldn't do this without you."

"Well, you can rely on me, Tabitha. I want you to know that. I won't let you down. And, you know what, I'm going to start training up some of the keener mothers of younger children in the school, so they can step in if necessary. I'll give them a small task and see how they do. I'll soon be able to separate the wheat from the chaff." She laughed, "Perhaps they'll take over entirely when I'm a grand impresario!"

"Right!" said Tabitha smiling happily upon her newly-elevated colleague, and picked up her pen again. "Now we have to work out next year's production schedule."

The two women smiled at each other and bent happily over their paperwork again. One of the plays they were considering involved a dog on stage. The dog would need to come on set and do one or two amusing things, including stealing a string of sausages and running off with it - something that would definitely appeal to the audience, especially the younger members. Sally had looked at Esme, contentedly chewing a bone on her bed under the kitchen counter and said, "Well, we won't have to look far for our dog-actress."

Tabitha's first reaction was her usual one - of inadequacy, self-deprecation. "Oh, I don't think Esme could do that. She doesn't really know any tricks." She stopped herself, realising she was Doing It Again. What would it take for her to realise she was an able person with her own special gifts?

"Really?" said Sally, one eyebrow raised in a mock-quizzical look. She was used to Tabitha down-playing her abilities and always tried to lift her. "Well,

I saw a programme on telly the other day," Sally went on, "I meant to tell you about it. They were teaching chickens to do tricks - you know, showjumping - only over tiny little jumps, up chicken-sized ladders, and through little tunnels and hoops. *Chickens!* - it was hilarious! The trainer swore that they did it all for a smidgin of grain. Actually they showed a bit of the training so people could see it wasn't cruel. I wouldn't have thought you could get a chicken to run through a tunnel unless you threw her through, or perhaps I never discovered their hidden depths of intelligence! I'm actually looking at our hens with new respect. So if *chickens* can be taught to do a whole agility circuit, then surely you can teach Esme to steal a sausage when you want her to?"

Tabitha smiled to herself. If she could tame a rabble of children, surely she could teach her dog not to be outdone by a chicken! "You know what?" she said, sitting up in her chair, "I'm going to take you up on this challenge! I'll see if I can find a dog trainer who can show me how. Not one of those old-fashioned ones that shout at the dogs like at a military bootcamp - no!" No way, thought Tabitha as she recalled a class she had once visited, when she first had Riffle, years ago. They all just marched in circles round the hall shouting "HEEL" and yanking the dogs by the neck. "They're horrible. That's why I've never taken any of my dogs to training classes. But there must be *some* nice ones. Maybe things have changed since then? Perhaps I'll ask those tv programme people." She added, "Maybe the chicken trainer man would know?"

"Great idea!" enthused Sally. "You can get on with that while I make out this spreadsheet with all the dates and requirements." Tabitha knew that Sally was in her element and never happier than when drawing up her spreadsheets and complicated plans. She was happy to leave her to it. Really, Sally with all her practicality and super strong work ethic was the perfect complement to Tabitha with her intensity and creativity and wandering mind. How could she ever have doubted her?

She thought about the possibility of teaching Esme how to play the part. It was tremendously exciting! She loved her dogs and loved spending time with them. This would be a wonderful opportunity to really achieve something with them. If chickens - she thought of her hens pecking about the garden and shook her head in wonderment - could be taught showjumping, kindly, then absolutely Esme could be taught to steal a sausage! She would start hunting down a trainer the next morning. This would be a great diversion for her, something creative to do away from the scene of conflict. She mused on what Sally had just told her.

"You know," she said out loud, "If they can teach chickens to jump through hoops - and they do it just by explaining it to them and offering them a bit of grain, then there must be more I can learn about how to get children to do things?"

"Oh, you have no difficulty getting children to do things!" laughed Sally. "You could be teaching the chicken-trainer a thing or two, to be sure!"

Tabitha smiled at her friend, happy that the misunderstanding they'd had had been so satisfactorily and productively resolved.

"You do me a power of good, Sally," she said. "Now, let's pack up for today. We've done masses, and you have a family to look after," she added, looking at the clock with surprise and beginning to stack the papers and stow them in her box file. She paused for a moment and thought how supremely happy she'd felt this afternoon - how much she'd achieved, how her plans were coming to fruition. This was true fulfilment, while the happy afternoon with Jamie had been ... what? a dalliance? an illusion? She was coming to great decisions and getting things done in her work life - her new and burgeoning work life - but the rest of her life was still a complete mess. Still she baulked at making any decisions and getting anything done at all. Time for some head-clearing fresh air for Tabitha.

"Seeing as you came by Shanks's Pony today I'll walk some of the way back with you - time to get this film star out in front of her public!" she laughed, picking up the leads and seeing Luigi scramble to his feet as Esme was already sitting in front of her waiting to be hitched up, her ears cocked, her head tilted quizzically to one side. Esme knew that something was up, and was making sure she didn't miss a thing. Little did she know, thought Tabitha, (she was a dog, after all, living in the moment) how much those changes would be affecting her! How could she know?

# 19

It wasn't many days later that Tabitha had a new project to look forward to. She'd really thrown herself into the idea of Esme being in the play! While it aligned with her new life, driving forward, trying new things, it was also a welcome distraction from thinking, worrying, churning everything round endlessly in her head. And the vision of herself actually being in the play alongside her students was a bit surreal - but exciting after such a long time away from performing herself. While she'd mainly be in the wings, she'd still be an active part of the performance - her timing would have to be perfect! She gave the dogs a shorter walk than usual that morning. She wanted them to be well-rested by the time Melanie arrived.

Melanie was the dog trainer she had discovered who she hoped would help with Esme. Tabitha had done a bit of research, then rang one of the parents who she remembered telling her at a recent practice that she had a rambunctious dog who was always getting into trouble, but was now reformed. And Jacintha had raved about Melanie, who had transformed her recalcitrant pup in no time at all - "and she never shouted at Dougie or laid a finger on him! Magic, that's all," she had added, still in awe as to how such change had been achieved in such a short time. "You know, I think it was what she taught *me* - to change how I saw Dougie - that did the trick," she added reflectively, as if the mystery was only just unfolding to her.

"Sounds just the job," Tabitha had said happily, so pleased to have found a possible person so easily.

"But why do you need a dog trainer? Your dogs are so good!"

"Oh, I want to teach Esme something new. She's so clever - I feel I'm not using her brain enough," Tabitha laughed. "Who knows, perhaps she could have a future on the stage!"

"Then you'll love Melanie! She does that weird thing .. what is it? ... Dancing with Dogs. I thought it sounded a bit creepy, but she showed me a video (made a change from Captain Pugwash, I can tell you!) and it's amazing! You can see just how she and her dog understand each other - not creepy at all. It made me cry, to watch it. Ooh, you'd be really good at it, seeing as you have the acting bit down already."

So Tabitha put the phone down then picked it right up again and dialled Melanie's number. Her recorded message answered:

"Hello, I'm out with some dogs. Please leave a message with Heidi and I'll get right back to you." This was followed by a mighty woof from a large dog that was presumably Heidi. Tabitha had laughed and left her message. She felt she liked Melanie already.

And so she did, when the trainer arrived a few days later, her large van bumping into the driveway and just fitting into the space. Melanie carefully adjusted the window openings, and spoke into the van, so Tabitha assumed she had some dogs on board. She welcomed her warmly and paused while Melanie admired the stunning view of the hills from the driveway. Gloom descended for a moment as the contrast between Melanie's arrival and Angus's homecomings stood clearly in Tabitha's mind. What on earth would he say if he came back early and "caught" her, wasting her time talking about dogs with a stranger?

"Would you like to let your dogs out in the garden?" she asked instead.

"No, they're fine, thanks," Melanie responded. They've just had a long walk and they'll be fast asleep in no time."

What a life! thought Tabitha - surrounded by dogs all day long. Her own calmest and most fulfilled moments tended to be the ones she spent with her dogs, especially when out in the beauty of the landscape. It was the time when she was renewed, restored. There was never any conflict or angst there, she thought ... so much easier than people, with their egos and hang-ups. Then, 'adults', she corrected herself, not 'people'. She loved working with her children too, who were still open to learning, to change. She wanted to get in there and open their minds before they became carbon copies of the adults in their lives. She wanted them to keep the joy and sense of curiosity they still had. When she got to them young enough, they stayed open to her for ever.

As Melanie came into the kitchen, Esme went straight over to greet her with enthusiasm. Luigi gave a few small barks then hung back and stayed on his bed, casting furtive suspicious glances towards this newcomer. Melanie totally ignored him - pretending he wasn't there.

"So this is Esme," said Tabitha proudly, while she attempted to get Esme off her visitor.

"That's ok, I don't mind dogs jumping up," said Melanie, "but I think I'll stop it now." Tabitha was worried for a moment at what Melanie would do - her heart hardened as she thought that if she had made a mistake and this trainer was at all harsh to her darling dog, she'd be booting her out of the door straight away!

But Melanie simply stopped responding to Esme's jumps and gazed out of the window for a moment. Esme, puzzled, dropped her feet to the floor, and Melanie bent down to her and fussed her while Esme stayed down at dog-level.

"Oh, that was simple!" said Tabitha, relieved and wowed. "I'd never thought of that. You didn't even say anything!"

"Quite often the less we say, the better," said Melanie. "After all, dogs don't have verbal language. Our babblings don't mean much to them."

"Of course," said Tabitha, "I don't make a big deal when a child is doing something I'd rather she didn't ..." she mused to herself. "Do you want to say hello to Luigi? Shall I bring him over?" She added, feeling slightly aggrieved on Luigi's behalf that he was being ignored, passed over.

"No no, let him come in his own good time," said Melanie. "He's not sure of me, so he can have as long as he likes to work me out. The faster you push a greeting with an anxious dog, the more anxious he'll get. His curiosity will overcome him eventually, and he'll relax."

"That figures," said Tabitha. "Just like Maisie and the other shy kids at my school. I leave them be till they're asking to join in." She realized she had been acting just now like those pushy parents she secretly mocked!

"I suppose you have all sorts in your school?"

"Oh yes!" replied Tabitha. "Some of them are there because their parents think it would be good for them to become more confident. Then there are some parents who just see me as a glorified childminder!" she laughed easily. "As long as the kids are out of their hair for a while, they're happy. But then there are others - these are the kids who have badgered their parents senseless - they're desperate to try acting, and they won't give up, whatever obstacles are put in their way."

"You have it all worked out already!" said Melanie, turning her grey eyes from Esme to Tabitha. "The dogs are just like your children, all different. There are dogs who love to strut their stuff - they're the ones who become champion performers - and there are others who'd melt away in horror! This is why my Rhys does so well in competition - he just loves it!" she laughed. "Heidi, though - I tried with her and found it was just too stressful for her. She worries about everything. Having a bombproof dog who really can get up on stage in front of a noisy audience, and do what he's meant to do without "playing to the gallery" - well, that's pretty unusual."

"Well, Esme has to enjoy it. If she doesn't enjoy it, and get excited when she sees me get out her props, then I won't ask her to do it."

"I like that. So many people expect their dogs to be robots - they want me to teach their dog just the same as some other dog they've seen." She had stopped fussing Esme, who nudged her hand, then sat gazing at her, hoping for more attention if she stayed still. "They don't seem to realise that it's not a one-size-fits-all. You have to find what the dog enjoys - and make sure she gets plenty of that."

With a lurch of her heart, Tabitha thought for a moment of the thing she enjoyed so much – Jamie – that was floating away from her.

Tabitha glanced over to Luigi to compose her face before continuing. "Do you know, there was a child whose parents were desperate for him to play a star role in one of our productions. The poor lad just wasn't cut out for it. He was ok in the chorus, or as part of the crowd. If he felt no one was looking at him he could do pretty well. But a starring part? Never! It took some diplomacy to get his parents to accept that he had chosen the role he would be taking in the play, and that it was important he had a say in what he did."

"Then you already know this stuff!" laughed Melanie. "Will I go now?" she smiled broadly, feinting a turn towards the door. But amidst the smiles from both women, she pulled out a chair and sat so she could reach Esme without having to bend over her.

Luigi silently got up from his bed and shuffled over to sniff Melanie safely from behind her chair. As he got a little braver and joined Esme in front of her, Melanie dropped her hand by her side so he could crane his neck forward and sniff it, then he headed off back to his bed again - satisfied - and relaxed. As did Tabitha, audibly.

"So tell me what you do in your school, Tabitha? They say 'Never work with children or animals.' Looks like you're doing one and want to start on the other!"

As Tabitha spoke she found herself getting more animated, fervent. She felt a kindred spirit in Melanie, and she found she so wanted her to understand what it was that made her put all this work into her school, what drove her to start it, and the enormous satisfaction she gained from watching her charges develop and blossom. She wondered if it was the same story for Melanie. Meeting a new person and finding someone who could understand – after so long in the wilderness where few seemed to understand – made her feel a little drunk, and very talkative.

"It's not the money," she said, "I hardly make anything from it."

"Tell me about it," murmured Melanie, with feeling and a wry smile.

"But I seem to have a way of getting strong performances from even the most unlikely children. It's something I'm good at, so I have to do it. Does that make any sense?" She frowned as she turned towards Melanie, realising that this wasn't something she'd articulated before.

"Oh yes, absolutely!" said Melanie, leaning forward keenly. "I suppose it's what drives me too. It's something I can do, something I understand. And if an owner can get an inkling of how much their dog can actually *do*, and treat them with the respect they give the rest of their family, then I've achieved something. Gradually others will notice and this will eventually become the norm. No hurting, no shouting, just understanding."

"I love that!" said Tabitha, enthusiastically. "How people can hurt children or animals is a complete mystery to me. I can't bear it."

"Same here," confided Melanie, shaking her head sadly, "Total mystery."

Through their easy chat they fell to discussing what Tabitha was needing from Esme. She gave Melanie a copy of the script they'd chosen, and pointed out a few of the things the dog would have to do.

"I have it all written out here. I hope you can understand the stage directions? I highlighted Esme's part."

"I think I'll get the picture," Melanie said, enchanted by the project and already busily making a note in the margin. "I can always ring you if I don't understand something. May I work through all this and come back to you with a plan?" she asked, leafing through the pages.

"Of course," said Tabitha. "But do you think Esme will be able to do it? She's a very outgoing dog and she's happy when she meets any of the children. I *think* she'd enjoy it?"

"Tell me - what's Esme's favourite thing in the world?"

"Food. Any food. All food ... definitely food," she added with a laugh.

"Well that's going to make our task easier!" smiled Melanie, "and how about toys?"

"Oh yes. She does love her ball on a rope." As she walked across the room to the dog shelf she added, "She absolutely loves chasing it, but she's not so quick to bring it back, although she always does eventually. She knows I can't throw it again till she's given it back to me. You're not daft, are you, Es!" She smiled at Esme whiile she handed the ball to Melanie.

Melanie took the toy and, holding it by the ball, started to flick the rope about on the floor. Esme instantly jumped from her bed and pounced on it.

"This is good," said the trainer approvingly. "Between the treats and the toy-drive we've definitely got stuff we can work with. And I can see that she's friendly but not hyper - good starting point. So I'll tell you what we'll do. I'll give you a few exercises to work on with Esme - well, she'll think they're smashing new games - and while you're doing that, I'll be working out the best way to work out these sequences of actions you want. We'll teach her bit by bit, starting with the last thing."

"The last thing?" Tabitha interjected.

"Yes. If you start at the end you can teach them the whole trick (it's all a kind of trick, this way of training) always ending up with the last bit - and the reward. So Esme will always know where she's headed. She'll feel confident because she knows what's happening next. Dogs love knowing what happens next. Do you see what I mean?"

"Yes! That's amazing! Do you know, I do something like that." An image flashed into her mind, of her and Angus talking earnestly in a coffee shop – such a long time ago. He was talking about how he mapped out his books, keeping his endpoint firmly in view as he wrote towards it. Such a conversation never happened these days. She mentally shook the image from her head, and continued, "We never start on page 1 of the script and work forward. I pick one of the exciting parts, which all the children are involved in - to give them an appetite for the rest. And when we reach the scene we started with it's very familiar to them - they feel comfortable doing it, understand their characters, know what they're on about. They can really throw themselves into it."

"Oh, I can see you're a natural!" Melanie laughed. "Let's just have a look at your timing in these games and see if you've got that licked just as well. You say Esme loves food. Does she like cheese? Sausage? Hot dog?"

"Yes, yes, and yes! She'll love those." Then she looked across at her collie lying patiently on his bed under the worktop. "Poor Luigi. He's going to be missing out."

"No, he doesn't need to miss out. I can chuck the odd treat over to him - just for staying quietly on his bed - and being beautiful, of course!"

"Oh I love that you can see he's beautiful," said Tabitha with delight. "Some people see him hiding behind me, or giving them a weird unfriendly look if they get too close. They don't like him at all." She realised with a start that it was mainly Angus who didn't like Luigi. He'd never, in all these years, taken the time to get to know the dog. To Angus he was just something that was in his house and had to be endured or avoided. Jamie liked Luigi well enough. He'd found out that he loved playing with twigs, so he had a way to enjoy the quiet dog. She felt the now-usual stab in her chest as she thought of the fun she had with Jamie and the dogs, then realised Melanie was talking.

"I have a soft spot for collies," said Melanie, putting down the script, "And my two collies couldn't be more different." As she rootled through her bag, looking for her box of treats, Melanie said, "There must be certain types of child you warm to? See the best in?"

"Actually, all the ones who join in and take part are perfect in my eyes. So long as they commit to working with me, I'll do whatever I can to make it work for them. Do you know, the other day one of the quietest children in the whole school just came up to me out of the blue and said 'I love this. I would die if I couldn't come any more.' That really surprised me. You just never know ..." She paused while she recalled the scene. She made a difference! She had to keep doing this!

"That's a great thing to have a student say to you! Though my students can't say that exactly," she smiled. She looked at Esme, now back on her bed, who was giving this interesting visitor rapt attention. "But I know they love it when they give me total focus," she laughed.

She twitched the ball for Esme again, then stopped dead as the dog came to join in. Esme froze too, her muscles all a-quiver, and the second Melanie moved it again she pounced on the ball. Melanie laughed and Esme tugged on the ball happily, tail wagging fast.

"What's really interesting - to me, at any rate - is that what works for dogs works for most other animals - killer whales, giraffes, pigeons, humans. And you seem to have sussed this out with your children, without knowing *any* of the theory behind it. That's why I say you're a natural. Do other drama coaches work the same way as you?"

"I'm afraid some of them are still stuck in the Dark Ages. There's another group a couple of hours away who were talking about doing a co-production with me. So I went down to one of their rehearsals to see what I thought. Oh, it was like an army training camp! It wouldn't have suited me at all - so no joint production there. But thank you for the compliment. I'm sure it isn't warranted!" Tabitha paused and blushed. There she was, Doing it Again. Why did she put herself down like this? But there wasn't time for introspection now - Melanie was pressing ahead with the lesson.

"Let's get started," said Melanie as she stood up, "and I'll prove you wrong." Tabitha smiled, reassured, and watched - fascinated.

Working very quickly with her tiny bits of cheese, Melanie had Esme's total focus in no time. Tabitha watched, entranced, as Esme worked harder and faster for her tiny morsel of food, giving Melanie the "spin" she wanted, and saw that every now and then Luigi would be tossed a morsel. This made her feel so much happier about the visit. Luigi was able to choose whether to join in or not, and he chose not. But he wasn't neglected. Just like Maisie, thought Tabitha. Encouraged by her mother Sally, Maisie had happily taken on the task of providing Tabitha's glass of water at rehearsals. She was able to join in before ever venturing out on the stage.

After she'd got a tight fast Spin going, Melanie played with Esme before handing her treats over to Tabitha, with "Your turn!" A few moments later, Melanie was coaching Tabitha how to get the same effect.

"You got it!" Melanie encouraged her pupil happily. "Remember to keep your hands still, you're distracting her ..."

Tabitha felt so like one of her new students! Trying to remember what to do in what order ... it was a lot harder than it looked! So a very short session was quite long enough. They took the dogs outside to the garden for a break and discussed the next steps they'd take.

Tabitha magicked a quick coffee for them both and they sat and admired the distant hills as they talked, a view which could always gladden Tabitha's heart, and which she was happy to show off. She wondered how much longer she'd be able to do this. She was proud of her home and its setting, and felt a momentary stab of regret as she knew she wouldn't have it for much longer. Where would she end up? Nowhere as lovely as this, she felt sure. But it was the price she'd have to pay.

"Oh, that must be Tom's place over there," said Melanie, peering into the middle distance.

"Yes! How do you know Tom?" asked Tabitha, thinking of the kindly farmer who let her walk his fields.

"He had a dog - a pet, not a working dog - who was thinking of chasing stock. So I taught her an instant Down. Did the trick!"

"Ah, Nell's black labrador?" asked Tabitha. "I saw her out riding with her the other day. You must have set Tom's mind at rest."

Esme was happily sniffing and mooching about the garden, while Luigi flumped down at Melanie's feet.

"Oh, he likes you now," said Tabitha. "You're a glutton, Luigi, so you are!"

Tabitha felt supremely happy. She loved interacting with her dogs, and the way Melanie had shown her to get such quick responses from Esme was exciting! She couldn't wait to get started on her homework with her. Though she had to keep in mind that Melanie told her to work for only one minute at a time and not overload Esme. Perhaps she'd have to use the kitchen timer to make sure she didn't get carried away and wear the poor dog out! An idea to try at the next rehearsal, she thought. She could actually get some of the children concentrating longer if they had only to keep going till the timer buzzed. And Melanie's instruction to her of keeping a training diary was something else she could introduce into the school - she could see lots of possibilities here. This session had been full of surprises for Tabitha!

The sky was clear and the sun shone comfortably on them. And her mind felt clear too - clear in her direction. She had completely forgotten all her worries as she shared coffee with her new friend and thought of the fun she would have teaching Esme her part. Tabitha had to admit she'd felt anxious before Melanie came. She would hate anyone to be nasty to her precious dogs. And Melanie had come up trumps, and apart from ruffling Esme's ears gently when they finished the session, hadn't even touched her.

"I do what I can to change people's attitudes towards animals - and dogs in particular - just one dog at a time. It's what I can do," she added as she squinted at the horizon. "Maybe it's my legacy." Melanie smiled and stayed looking away. "I get on better with dogs than with people, so I use what I know works with dogs. And it seems to work with people too!" she smiled again, and turned back to Tabitha.

"Oh - a legacy - that's just how I feel!" enthused Tabitha. "My little school is nothing, really, but I hope I can somehow have an impact and help children to feel better about themselves." She thought about her own feelings of inadequacy as a child, and then of the impact she actually was having, and how her new position at the NDS was evidence of this. She had to catch up with herself! She no longer was that inadequate child! But how true was that, really? She paused for a moment as she thought of her total inadequacy in the face of Angus only a few days before. She had to realise she had value.

And she thought of the irony of her helping children to feel better about themselves while she felt so wretched about her own life. How would it have been if Tabitha had had a Tabitha to help her in her early life? Would she have got herself into the mess she now was in? She felt able to weigh in with advice to Jennie - it was time she gave some to herself! But she was so thrilled to be talking to her new friend - someone who seemed to understand exactly how she felt, and what she was trying to achieve, its importance.

At the same time she wondered if she had the same one-track mind as Melanie, who was still gazing at the far hills. Then she turned to Tabitha, twiddling the coffee mug in her hands, and said, "Of course some people prefer to blame everything on the dog - the dog's stupid, the dog's stubborn, if you give him an inch he'll take a mile - you know the sort of thing. But it's often because they can't face their own failings that they have to lash out and blame others." She placed her empty mug on the grass. "I can go to a house to deal with a problem dog. And when I get there, I find that it's not the dog that has the problems."

This hit Tabitha right in the midriff. She suppressed a gasp. She had to process that statement later on, what it had immediately meant to her. She had been blaming herself all along for the insufficiency of her marriage. She had felt selfish, putting her own needs first. And she saw now what was perhaps obvious to everyone else. *It wasn't her.*

"I gather you do Dancing with Dogs?" Tabitha asked brightly, quickly changing the subject so she could carry on the visit without breaking into tears.

"Oh yes! I love it!" Melanie replied, relaxing back into her chair at the thought of it. "You'd be good at that - you should try it!" she added, turning to look straight at Tabitha. "Most people have difficulty trying to look as graceful and agile as their dog. You'd have no problem with that! When we get going with Esme's training program you can come along to a show and see what we do - would you like that?"

Tabitha felt she could burst with the warm feelings surging up within her - feelings she had all but forgotten in her worries - apart from her stolen moments with Jamie, those blissful, happy moments which she knew were coming to an end. Now she was being given a licence to spend time "playing" with her dogs! Delight was not lost to her, not forbidden. She could still find joy and fulfilment in other things. And as she reflected, she realised that neither of her menfolk would be the least bit interested in that joy. Jamie would be glad she was happy, sure. Angus would not be glad. Anything that took the focus off him grated with him. What was going to be important to her in the future? What was she going to choose for her life path, now she was going to have the freedom to really decide for herself?

She saw that this new world of working with her dog was something she might get good at, and she'd meet other new people with the same interest. She remembered how kind her father always was to animals - he would go to such lengths to help a moth out of the house so that it didn't batter itself against the lampshade, and he'd get out of the car to check a bird lying in the road, to see if it could survive if he moved it into the hedge. She had inherited that from him - and while she had always felt that she had disappointed him because she didn't have the conventional family life, hadn't produced grandchildren for him before he died, like William had done - this was something he'd surely have approved.

"I'd absolutely love that," she found herself saying happily, as yet another exciting adventure in her new life began to open up before her, "You've got a deal!"

# 20

Walking round the 50-acre the next day was invigorating. Though it was mild, there was a brisk wind which was sharp in the shade of the tall trees, so she kept to the sunnier parts of the big field. It was probably as well that she keep Luigi away from the ditches too. He'd struggled to get out of one the other day, and she'd had to scramble down into the black muck to pull him out. Dear Luigi was showing his age these days. He was getting stiffer and less agile.

She was using her walk - as usual - to enjoy the undiluted pleasure of being out with her dogs, and to think things over. She felt so much better than she had a few short weeks ago after Angus dropped his bombshell and disturbed the predictable but enclosed world that her life had become. Then, she had felt shocked, desperate. It had been like ripping a plaster off an infected wound and forcing yourself to look at it.

She'd done so much looking at wounds over the past while, and was feeling very ready to look forwards, to a better life, and healing. The new opportunities that had all presented themselves since that bad day amazed Tabitha. It was as if clearing out a cupboard of old unwanted things had made space for lots of new exciting things to flow in. To think that she had been stopping the good things happening herself - just by staying firmly in the old, wrong, place! Once she was forced to look at where she was, what she was doing, indeed where she was going, everything had changed.

Timothy's offer, Sally's enthusiasm, Maureen's wise words, Melanie's exciting insights, even the surprise reconnection with Clare, and Jamie's failure to see what was important to her, were all factoring into what was going to happen. Not to mention what had kicked it all off - Angus's bombshell. After years of nothing happening, she sensed a huge upheaval looming!

Her thoughts were interrupted. "What's wrong, Esme?" she asked of her young dog, who was scrabbling at her mouth with her front paws. Her claws were scratching her face as she desperately tried to dislodge something from her mouth. Tabitha clamped Esme between her legs as she bent over her and gently opened her jaws. She had a broken stick wedged across the roof of her mouth, digging into the gums on both sides. Tabitha flipped it out without difficulty, Esme smiled at her and went rampaging off again.

How easy it was sometimes, to alleviate someone's pain, she reflected. Esme may never have been able to get that wedged stick out without help. And without help it could have caused pain, infection, sickness - even death! Tabitha had been self-reliant too long. She needed to look around her and accept the offers that seemed to be there all the time, but that she'd never noticed, in her island fastness. She thought she had to do it all alone. She had thought nobody cared. But she had not allowed them to care. What was hard for Esme had been easy for Tabitha. And what was hard for Tabitha could seem so easy to others.

And what Melanie had been saying about insufficiency and blame-placing when she visited a house with a "problem dog" came back to her, now she'd had time to think it over.

Could it be that Angus was so angry with her all the time and treated her so badly because she was living witness to his own failings and inadequacies?

Could it be that he showed no physical affection because of what was going on in his own convoluted mind, and it was nothing to do with her, not her fault? She stopped abruptly for a moment, drew breath, and walked on.

Maybe she wasn't that unattractive to him, but she brought up feelings within him that he couldn't cope with for some reason? So he suppressed them.

Could this explain why he withdrew more and more from her on an emotional level, treating her more as a member of staff than family?

A shaft of light penetrated the gloom. Not that she felt she'd be able to live with him even with this new knowledge and understanding - but that she had been so wrong about herself for so long!

She wasn't ugly, unattractive or stupid! Surely Jamie had shown her that? And that brought up a huge realisation about why she had taken up with Jamie in the first place. It was not her fault her husband had spurned her all these years. It was not because she was inadequate that she was not a mother. It was entirely Angus that was not functioning properly as a man - not that she was failing as a woman.

As Melanie had said, she wasn't a problem dog: she had a problem owner!

She felt suddenly invigorated! Confidence flooded her and gave power to her thoughts, the strongest of which was "I can do this!"

And if Jamie found her beautiful because she was (she blushed to even allow herself that thought) - and hadn't Jacintha and Melanie both talked about her grace in movement? - then she had no need to have this pathetic gratitude. Jamie - nice as he was, and forever powerfully attractive to her - was just a guy who was enjoying a relationship with her. She'd been making it so much more complex for so long. She was part of Jamie's great fantasy of changing his life and living in a world with her where there were no bills, no dirty nappies, no schoolbooks to buy, no creaking hinges to fix, no getting tired of the partner who knew all his failings. And while she had often lain in his arms thinking similar fantastical thoughts with him, when the slightest possibility of it actually happening occurred she had kept the information entirely to herself. She knew that reality was what could shatter their relationship. And she wasn't ready to lose him quite yet.

Everything had changed so much in such a short time. And so much of it was change within Tabitha herself. She'd been treading water for way too long. It was time for her to cast off the heavy weight of gloom that she'd been carrying, and to move forward into what could be a wonderful time of light and excitement.

She was not so naive as to think that there would never be more problems. There were bound to be teething troubles with the new enterprises - both of them - but the difference was that there was nobody to blame but herself. Far from diminishing her, as she began to shed the people who were preying on her, she felt empowered! Yes, even Jamie was a predator in this sense. He took what he needed and offered so little in return, in reality. For such a long time her life had been closing in, getting gradually smaller as Angus shut down her associations with this friend or that group. Some of them refused to be shut down though! She thought of steadfast Maureen, and now Clare who'd popped up out of the blue. Because of her strong - yet misplaced - sense of duty, she'd gone along with it all. She now saw how very wrong she had been. She had deceived herself in thinking her responsibilities were more important than her soul.

So she sat on the grass and gazed at the hills she so loved to look at. She pulled her hood up against the fresh wind, and put her arm round Luigi who had come to lean against her in this welcome break in the walk. Down at dog-level Tabitha could smell the crushed grass beneath their feet, see the scurrying insects, feel the warmth of the earth where the wind didn't reach. Esme found a twig and placed it very gently on Tabitha's knee waiting for her to respond. They all watched it tip over and fall on the ground, whereupon Esme grabbed it up and tried again. This attempt at balancing the twig on Tabitha's knee went on for some time till Esme tired of it and went to cruise the hedgerow. Tabitha smiled indulgently at the two real loves of her life, gently ruffling Luigi's neck.

At last she was beginning to emerge as a person with her own agenda. And - she stopped short as she realised - one of the top things on that agenda would be finding somewhere for her and her dogs to live. Her stomach lurched as this thought hit her. This was real. This was tangible. This showed that her new ideas meant business. She was going to have to start moving things along. She'd have to tell Angus her decision. It really couldn't be avoided much longer. It wasn't fair on him to string him along, just because she couldn't face the reality herself. Yes, she'd tried to tell him a few days before, and he hadn't accepted it. She'd felt herself buckling under the force of his words, just as she always did.

She knew she'd made the decisions - about both men. Wasn't she going full steam ahead with the plans for her future? It was unkind not to be straight with them, both of them.

What could she do to get the strength to approach Angus? She thought of the time when she had wanted Esme. She had known the time was right for a new puppy. Riffle had died a good few years before, and Sparks not long after him. And by that time she had got Luigi. But Luigi had always been an anxious, shy, dog, and she felt that a companion would help to boost his confidence and help him worry less. So she'd picked out Esme. She was so sure she was going to have her that she almost forgot to mention it to Angus. And when she did, in passing - to make less of a big deal of it - his response had been "not more bloody dogs". She had ignored his moaning and complaining. She was going to have Esme and that was all there was to it. She was sure the new pup would be a tonic for Luigi (and how right she had been!) and besides, she loved this little puppy's happy-go-lucky character. She wanted her in her life. And she had got her.

She jumped up from the ground and Luigi got slowly to his feet.

That was what she needed now. To know that what she was doing was right, that it was her truth, the way she had to go, and nothing would stop her. She should give her own future the same importance she had given Luigi and Esme. After all, she'd be no help to them if she couldn't help herself first.

So as she turned towards the gate, both dogs turning with her - Esme bounding about still, Luigi at a plod - she felt a surge of power within her. She would do this thing. She'd do some more phoning and sorting out Angus's departure, and she'd tell him. Straight.

# 21

Tabitha heard Angus's car wheels crunch on the gravel drive. She put down the phone and stretched her arms over her head.

"On the phone again?" he said, as he came through the door. Even though local calls were free on their phone tariff, he always acted as though they cost a pound a minute. He hated Tabitha talking on the phone. While he used thrift as a reason, Tabitha now realised that he didn't want her to interact with anyone else. It was one of those many demands of his that chipped away at her freedom. Each thing seemed fairly insignificant in itself, easy enough to go along with at the time to keep the peace, but as they heaped upon each other, she had found herself constricted and trapped.

He picked up a notebook out of the papers on the table. It was Esme's training notebook, covered with coloured stickers and a photo of the dog. Tabitha was taken with the idea of introducing this plan into Shooting Stars and had been experimenting.

"'Esme's book'?" he sneered, tossing it away again. "Really Tabitha, don't you have any real work to do?"

She gathered her notes together into a thick pile and banged the sheets into shape, putting Esme's book safely on her side of the table. "I've been working on your American adventure," she said, hoping to keep the conversation light.

"Oh?" he said, taking off his coat and tossing it over a chair. Tabitha looked at it for a moment, then got up and picked it up and hung it on the coat hooks in the hallway.

"Yes. I've invited a couple of house agents to come round and give a valuation for the house," she said as she came back into the room and went to fill the kettle, "and I've been working out your itinerary. It's a good thing the university is organising the accommodation. That would be very hard to arrange from this distance."

"What's with the 'your itinerary'?" said Angus, biting into an apple noisily. "It's 'our itinerary', surely?"

Tabitha turned and leant against the sink, her heart in her mouth, her breath short and gaspy. "I really think it would be best if you went alone," she began. "It's honestly not something I want at all."

"*You* want?" roared Angus. "This isn't about you! This is my big break, what I've been working for for years. Recognition. Acclaim. Why do you want to make it about you?"

"I … It's just not something I want to do," stammered Tabitha. "I have work to do here. People need me …"

"*I* need you!" he shouted, slamming the apple down on the table in a splatter of juice and pips. "I'm not having my big opportunity wrecked by you. It's always about you and your little projects. Well this time, it's about me, and you are expected to accompany me."

It's all going wrong again, Tabitha thought, as she turned back to the kettle, gripping it tightly while she recovered herself. She wondered how much her husband had had to drink today. The drink always made him angry and overbearing. With a lurch in her stomach, she saw that when he was like this she was frightened of him. And it made her feel sick to acknowledge that. What a state for a marriage to get into!

"I've supported you all these years," he was continuing behind her, "and it's your turn to support me."

Tabitha gasped inwardly. How could he say that?

"Nobody needs you here. You're superfluous. Your place is at my side, organising things, entertaining visitors. And that's where you'll be."

Tabitha's insides were in turmoil. She just needed to get away from this onslaught. How much more could she take? Angus seemed to be able to get to her, every time. He played on her feelings of guilt - and God knows she had plenty enough of those!

She wanted to tell him that he had not kept his side of the bargain. She wanted to say that marriage should include love, and a family. She wanted to scream about how much she had given up for him, how much he'd changed. She knew she should talk to him, say it straight - what she was really thinking and feeling. But she was afraid of how he'd react. She just didn't feel able to.

The atmosphere was electric, the dogs lying flattened on their beds while Angus stood stock still, waiting for her answer.

"Alright," she said meekly, turning back to him but avoiding his face. "I'll look into it. Take those sheets of paper for now and have a look at the plan I mapped out for the journey."

He stared at her for a moment, snatched up the sheaf of papers, turned on his heel, and headed to his study, slamming the door. The pressure lifted from the kitchen, the dogs lifting their heads and beginning to stir.

Tabitha felt wretched. She'd done it again - caved in. She was crying with frustration and ran out of the door with the dogs. This could not go on. She had to go through this split, painful as it was. She could not live with this bully that her husband had become. And yet, when she thought of what they had had once, she felt the guilt wash over her again. She had tried - oh, how she had tried! - to make this marriage work. She had taken blow after blow. And she had now found herself backed into a corner: how had that happened? Time after time, Angus just had to say the word and she knuckled under and did what she was told.

Where did this fit with the independent person she had always thought herself to be? Where did it fit with the advice she so freely and passionately dished out to her students? How could she face herself, never mind the rest of the world, if she couldn't stand up for what she felt was right?

"People can only hurt you if you let them." Who had said this to her? Isn't it the sort of thing Maureen would say? She tried to make her agitated brain remember, and failed. But she recognised she was as guilty as Angus in this mis-match. She had let it happen. She had felt everything was her fault and that therefore she had to acquiesce. And every time it happened her self-esteem took another blow.

As she clambered over the gate and started walking the 50-acre, Tabitha felt that her life was all askew. She knew what she believed in. She *thought* she knew what she believed in. And yet when push came to shove, her belief was not strong enough to stand up to any opposition. Her schooling, her family, had brought her up to believe in subservience - to a father, a husband, a teacher, an ideal, a greater good. And look where this had landed her! Her mother had always seemed happy enough in this set-up, and her father had been kind and appreciative. The system clearly worked for him! Perhaps her mother didn't feel driven to express herself in another way. Perhaps being a housewife and mother was enough for her?

Thinking of settling for motherhood brought another pang to Tabitha's heart. When she had married, she truly thought it was for ever, and it would lead to a family. A house bursting with love and laughter, activity, dreams ... not a barren house echoing to shouts and fights.

She felt betrayed. She had kept to her side of the bargain, yet Angus had not. And now he didn't even seem to be the same person. Did she have to stay married to someone who was not the person she married? Really? Was her life so worthless that she should be sacrificed on the altar of integrity and faith?

She really ought to say this to him. Face him with how she felt. But she was afraid to. She certainly wasn't going to return home and go to his room to start a fight there. Her thoughts - which seemed so far from his - stayed bottled up inside her.

Her endless circling of questions in her mind, echoing the endless circling of the field, was interrupted by a text on her phone.

Jamie.

"Need to c u. Red Indian at 11 tomo. Got something to ask"

She didn't feel at the moment she was any use to anyone, but the diversion would be good, and she wondered what he "needed" to see her about. Was Jamie going through some momentous upheaval as well? Was he going to suggest they live together at last? Her thoughts ran away with her. She was beginning to break the ties with her husband. What was she thinking of - jumping straight to another person? But she'd have to wait till tomorrow to find out what he wanted. She could fit the meet in with the weekly shop. At least she had something to look forward to tomorrow, though it seemed a long night she'd have to endure before she got there.

In her haste to leave she had forgotten her coat so that when she eventually came back home she was cold and wet. As well as miserable and resentful. She knew she had to make a better plan about Angus. Perhaps just telling him straight was the answer? But supposing he threw her out? She needed to sort out that accommodation, fast! Then she could tell him and bolt. She resolved to avoid Angus as much as possible and think rosy thoughts about the National Drama School instead. And she was determined - "I will not lose this opportunity!" she affirmed to herself.

# 22

Tabitha wondered why Jamie had chosen the Red Indian cafe to meet. It was heavy with meaning for her. It was where they had gone after they had bumped into each other after their long break, and slid down the slippery slope again.

The cafe was in the middle of a large business park, very busy at lunchtime, but mainly frequented by van-drivers stopping for a break the rest of the day. It was actually called The Pit Stop, but it was known by everyone on the estate as the Red Indian Cafe because the owner was a Native American Indian enthusiast. The walls were decorated with splendid feathered head-dresses, spears, tomahawks, horse gear, bows and arrows, all collected on trips to America. (America again: could Jamie have possibly found out about Angus? Or was her brain going feverish, ascribing motives where there were none? She banished the ridiculous thought.) There were many fascinating framed photos of important Chiefs standing outside their tepees, or wigwams, or whatever they were called, she was none too sure - she had been too preoccupied to pay attention on her previous visit. They had exciting names - Running Horse, Soaring Eagle, Spotted Elk, and the like. There was even a library of books - some of them rare - about these noble people and their sometimes awful history, that customers could browse while they took their coffee break. This strange and unusual place had added an air of mystery and suspended reality when they had gone there to discuss urgently what they were going to do, when they'd met again.

So Tabitha wasn't sure whether there was a hidden meaning to this appointment. She was early, and studied the exhibits on the walls while she waited. She saw him walking across the car park - and he had a lovely girl with him. It was Karen! Tabitha realised - she hadn't seen her for a good few years but she was instantly recognisable, and so grown up now.

Karen was "that baby" whose conception had so upset Tabitha all those years before and caused her to break up with Jamie the first time round. Since then she'd met her on a few occasions. Karen was a quirky child, nothing like her mother Annette, and only like Jamie's wilder side. But she had always been a fan of Tabitha. At a chance meeting a few years after their split, the young child had turned to Jamie and said: "I love Tabitha. She'd make a good mother." Such words - out of the mouths of babes and little ones - had bowled Tabitha over, and given her a lot of thought about whether she and Jamie could ever make a go of it.

Now this rather exotic creature was entering the cafe with her father. She was slim, very tall, her dark hair streaming over her shoulders, and with rich-toned skin. She moved her lithe body with such grace. Was this really the baby she had resented? And, curiously, she was so much more like Tabitha in appearance than like either of her parents. Another changeling, perhaps?

And as they greeted and settled at a table, Tabitha was to find that she was like her in other ways too.

Jamie launched straight away. "I wanted you to meet up with Karen again. She's working in one of the businesses here - 'work experience', you know - so this cafe is handy."

Ah. So it was just convenience. No tripping down Memory Lane for Jamie, Tabitha thought, with a twinge of disappointment. And no connection with America or lectureships either – Jamie probably still had no idea.

"She's got a crazy idea, and I thought you'd be the person to talk some sense into her."

"I want to be a dancer," blurted out Karen.

"Ah," said Tabitha, "that explains the grace and fluidity of your movement." Unlike what her own response would have been to such a compliment, Karen's reaction was a soft smile. She wondered why Jamie never mentioned this to her before? "I remember your Dad telling me you went to dance classes, but I didn't know it was with such passion."

She had a feeling that this meeting wasn't going to be so straightforward. She wondered what her position was meant to be - clearly very different for Karen and for Jamie! She didn't want to offend or disappoint either of them, get between father and daughter.

"I've been going to lessons for ages, and now that's all I want to do. But Mum and Dad say I have to get some exams under my belt before I can think of what I'm going to do after school."

"Absolutely right," grunted Jamie, sounding remarkably like someone twice his age. Miss Wiseman would have approved, thought Tabitha wryly.

"I can understand why they should say that," said Tabitha, treading carefully. "You know they want the very best for you?"

"Yes. I know. Kind of. In a way ..." Karen tailed off. "But they don't really understand!"

"It can be so frustrating when you've got something burning in your heart, and yet the world seems to demand something else of you," Tabitha went on, thinking that here was Tabitha talking to Tabitha again. She wondered what line she should take so as not to alienate one of the family before her. Karen was sitting forward and attentive in her seat, while Tabitha saw out of the corner of her eye Jamie shifting uncomfortably. "Tell me about how you see your life - what kind of dance? Where? Tell me what you know."

So they fell to discussing Karen's dreams. The girl would look furtively at her father before reeling off all the answers to Tabitha's questions. She had clearly done some serious research. Tabitha dug a little deeper: "Where could you study? How much would it cost?"

It seemed that Karen had it all worked out. She knew what government assistance was available, how much she'd have to work to cover her costs, what school was best. Tabitha was impressed with her thoroughness, and felt herself warming even more to this "ugly duckling", so unlike her parents.

"This is all jolly fine," interjected Jamie at last, "but it's not realistic. Dancing is not going to pay the bills in your future life. You should be thinking of a career where - not only will you make a bit of money - but maybe meet the right sort of person to spend your life with."

Tabitha's jaw dropped. This could have been her own father speaking. This was Jamie - her lover! - not an old man. Clearly Jamie had asked her along to speak sense to his daughter. But she found herself very much applauding the girl and, just as she had with Jennie, wanting to encourage her to follow her star regardless of her family. But she couldn't do that. She couldn't betray Jamie's trust, even if he had dropped her right in it!

So she tried to convey her feelings to Karen without actually saying anything that would go against her father's wishes.

"Why don't you stay on at school long enough to get your basic exams? You can be concentrating on your dance lessons at the same time."

"We're not made of money," Jamie said, now sounding petulant. Tabitha started to feel irritated with him. Was her mystical, magical hero getting feet of clay? Now she saw him in the trenches, dealing with everyday life and family problems, he actually was becoming someone she didn't much like. Wasn't this what she'd always feared? And was this the real reason she hadn't told him about Angus?

Karen was wowed by Tabitha's grasp of the situation, and the coded messages she was sending her. She gave her admiring glances, grateful to have an ally at last.

"There's one thing I could suggest," Tabitha added, leaning forward with an elbow on the table, "if the practical details could be worked out," she said, nodding towards Jamie. "I'm hoping to put a dance sequence into our next production at Shooting Stars. We have a few dancers amongst the younger children, but you could lead them, Karen. What do you think?"

Karen clearly thought highly of this idea, as she gasped and held her hands to her face.

As soon as the suggestion was out of her mouth, Tabitha had wondered if she'd gone too far. She was planning on breaking it off with Jamie – this was becoming more obvious with each day that passed – and this suggestion would involve her in his family in a new way. She was already detaching from him and seeing him as she viewed the parents in her school. But once again she saw herself in Karen, as she had seen herself in Jennie. She couldn't fail to help her. This was perhaps what her whole life had been leading up to, this is why she'd had the experiences she'd had – knowing she could now make a difference in the lives of young people who needed encouragement at a defining moment.

"It would give you a goal to work towards, to show that you can do some advanced stuff - actually choreographing the sequences, teaching the younger ones. It would stand you in good stead when you get to applying to those schools you mentioned - *after* you've got your exams!"

"I'd absolutely love that, Tabitha!" Karen enthused. "Could I, Daddy? Could I go and do that? I'd really work at it."

Jamie smiled lovingly at his daughter, and nodded his approval. "As long as we don't hear any more about you leaving school early, eh?"

"Deal!" said Karen excitedly. "I have to fly now - I'm due back at work. Bye Dad," she added, throwing an arm round her father's shoulders and kissing the top of his head, and "Bye Tabitha, thanks *so* much!" with a cheery wave and a beaming smile.

Tabitha watched the flurry of energy that was Karen disappear from the Red Indian cafe, and in the ensuing stillness, turned to Jamie.

"You must be so proud of her?" she asked him.

"Yes, of course. The funny thing is, she's always reminded me of you. She was born shortly after we split up - the first time," he smiled lopsidedly at her, "and I always thought of you as I watched her growing up. Thought of the children we should have had together."

Tabitha's heart missed a beat. Then she quelled the feelings. Those were from another time. They were not relevant any more. Her course now was set. No regrets.

"And now she's turned into an arty person like me!" And she has the same challenges, like me, she thought to herself. Jamie was still living in his fantasy world: Tabitha now knew with certainty that they would never be together. Just his reactions to his daughter's dreams had cemented that fact in her mind. She hoped she had helped Karen in some way. She hoped she had helped Jennie too. Why was she so intent on helping these young girls, but not helping herself?

She was still young herself - she had plenty of life left to live! It was time to start putting herself first and working out a life that would be the best for her. If only she could have Maureen's simplicity and clarity.

As they walked to the car park, she said brightly, in an attempt to lighten the mood, "You know I want to do some tricks with Esme? Well I met this amazing dog trainer – Esme can already spin in a circle!"

"That's good," said Jamie, without even an attempt to feign interest. Tabitha was deflated and relapsed into silence.

She mused on these thoughts as they left the cafe and its splendid feathered head-dresses and set off to somewhere more private. It couldn't end here. Watching Jamie and his reactions to his daughter's plans had made him look so old, fuddy-duddy - not her glamorous and delightful lover. Tabitha felt as if the scales were falling from her eyes. She had resigned herself for so long to how things were, and she was only now realising they didn't have to be that way. It was *her* life. She had the opportunity - with everything that seemed to be happening right now - to strike out on a new path. And why *was* everything happening right now, she wondered? The catalyst had been Angus's bombshell, the last straw in their relationship perhaps. And it had made her start seeing everything else she accepted as normal as … not so normal!

She didn't have to continue on this same path. Her marriage vows? Well, why should she worry about them as she'd never really had a marriage. She had a pang of regret for a moment. All those years wasted, with both Angus *and* Jamie.

If only she had found a life-partner who combined the best of both these men! The intellectual plus side of Angus, without the sour and domineering person he'd become; the self-confidence, acceptance, love, excitement, of Jamie, without the shallowness and predictability. But that was not what had happened. Her parents had once, long ago, dismissed a friend who was wanting to leave his marriage: "He's made his bed. He must lie on it." It seemed so hard-hearted to Tabitha at the time, though she had thought that marriage was sacred - and she had thought that perhaps they had been right. Only now, when she saw the reality of life, did she realise the pain of being forced to stay in a marriage that was not just wrong, but actively attacking her.

She had been following Jamie's pick-up truck all this while. He'd found somewhere new for them to spend time together, and it seemed to be at the end of this bumpy lane they were headed along. As she got out of her car, she breathed in the fresh scent of pine. There were fields glittering in the sunlight to one side of the lane, and the other side was a dense pine forest. As they set off through the brambles, Tabitha knew that now was her moment to talk to Jamie.

# 23

Tabitha gazed up at the canopy of branches above her. She sighed as her breathing slowed, then said, "Ouch - damn twig."

Jamie drew her to him as he reached over her and under the blanket to pull out the offending stick. He smiled as he held up his trophy - that tilting up of his mouth that Tabitha so loved - before tossing it into the brambles and bracken surrounding them. He pulled the covers up to her chin. Tabitha leant back and nuzzled into his neck.

The woods where they lay were remote. They'd only seen one person, an old man wearing a cap and old tweed jacket, with a small brown spaniel darting about enjoying the cover. They'd huddled under the dark cloth and stayed still and silent till he passed about fifty yards away, not even knowing they were there.

"Are you going to tell me now why you're wound up as tight as a watchspring?" Jamie said quietly, as he threaded his fingers into hers.

Tabitha found it harder than she had anticipated, telling Jamie about Angus's announcement. Telling him she was leaving Angus would open up the path to her and Jamie being together, and she knew - now she had given it such exhaustive thought and watching him playing the heavy father with Karen - that this was not what she wanted. And of course Annette was tough, and would never let it happen. But neither did she want to start a fight with Jamie! He had been her only ally for so long. Even though just lately she'd found out how important Maureen and Sally also were to her, giving her support that she'd been reluctant to accept - damn her pride! She wasn't sure where to begin, how to phrase it. But she threw caution to the winds and jumped in with both feet.

"Angus wants to go to America. He's been offered some high-flown lectureship at a university. He's told me I have to arrange everything for him as he's too busy - or too important, I'm not sure which - to do it himself. He's talking of selling the house, that we go away and stay away."

There. She'd said it. And there seemed to be silence coming from Jamie. He hadn't leapt in with an "Oh no!" or an "Over my dead body." There was nothing. Tabitha knew that she'd passed a point of no return. She didn't want to hurt Jamie. What could his unaccustomed silence mean? Did this potential parting suit him well? Was he tired of her?

"He wants me to give up everything and go with him," she added, for emphasis, prompting him to respond. She felt she was showing herself up as a victim, a pawn, helpless. Would her knight in shining armour ride in and say "NO! that cannot happen! Those things are too important to you." And did she *want* to be rescued, after all her thinking in the 50-acre about pursuing her truth, being unstoppable? Did the child within her just yearn to be cared for? To feel that love and devotion again? What did she expect poor Jamie to do?

"And what do *you* want to do?" he asked instead, so quietly, as if he were afraid what her answer may bring.

"It's the last thing I want!" said Tabitha. "I have so much here." She stopped herself, thinking he may assume she was including him. He wasn't to know that she had, in her mind at least, discarded both men.

"Where would you go? What about your school?" he asked tentatively. "What about your dogs?" And slowly, "What about us?"

She looked at the problem with fresh eyes. She was a little surprised by Jamie's response. She'd expected him to dive in with excitement and start planning their life together. But did he suddenly feel trapped? That he'd have to come good on his fantasy and expressed desires after all these years of impossibility? Tabitha hadn't foreseen this! But hadn't he just brought Karen to see her? Hadn't he just brought some of his reality and laid it before her, making her a valued part of his life? Had he moved her from the "lover" box into the "family friend" box - a natural ending to their long relationship?

And what about us? What, indeed. This was the one thing she had spent most time over. What about Jamie and her? For so many years they'd been so important to each other, such a vital part of each other's lives. Even in the fifteen years they had been apart, the ache was always there. He had always been present for her, if only in her heart. It had been an impossible relationship then, the first time, and it had been an impossible relationship now. But suddenly - it was becoming possible, and yet neither of them seemed to want it! Tabitha knew that she'd already made up her mind about Jamie. It had crept into her being in all the turmoil and upset of the last few weeks. All that tramping round the 50-acre had told her. Fight it as she may, she and Jamie were done. But she hadn't bargained on his quiet acquiescence. This was a bit of a shock for her.

What had caused the many tears she'd shed in the last couple of weeks was the slow and painful realisation that it was not to be. They both lived this endless dream - clinging to each other like children in the storm - that they were kept apart by circumstance. And yet, now they had a chance! Perhaps Jamie had simply been stunned into silence. Or had they been deluding themselves all this time? Their love was real. There was no doubt about that. But could it not stand up to reality? She knew the answer, in truth. But now that it was out in the light of day, she felt pain, the pain of loss. And a bitter disappointment – that Jamie was not grasping this opportunity, the opportunity that perversely she didn't want him to grasp!

"I have ideas - a move forward with my career," she said. "It's an opportunity for me to make huge change in my life." She waited for a response, which didn't come. "Sweeping changes ..." she added, for emphasis.

She pulled her hand away from his to wipe her eyes. She hadn't realised she'd been crying, the tears trickling down her temples and wetting her hair.

"Here," he said, holding her tighter and kissing her wet cheek. "I want you to be happy. That's all I want."

There. Again. He was not talking about their chance to be together. She'd only just told him, to be fair, but she knew he'd had an inkling something was up already. She'd expected him to launch into wild and fantastic plans about the place they'd have on the edge of a lake, with mountains behind them - just them. And her dogs. But instead, there was a crackling silence. No plans, no excitement.

Was he grabbing the opportunity to dodge out of the relationship? And, she knew with a jolt of her heart, that that was what she really now wanted. That *he* should leave *her*, rather than her be the one inflicting pain.

"My whole life as I know it is ending," she said in a choking voice, with no intention of sounding dramatic. She needed to convey to him that it was over. But she couldn't say it outright. Not after all this time!

'Not a day has gone by without me thinking of you,' Jamie had said when they had met again after that long break. For someone who thought that nobody thought about her ever, it had been a staggering - and deeply moving - revelation. Jamie had given her - not just the physical adoration which Angus was incapable of - but the strength to bear all the adversity of her marriage. She realised now that she'd almost hoped his reaction to her news would make her firmer in her resolve to end it. She had imagined herself soothing him. Instead it seemed to be the other way round. She'd known for so long that their relationship was more about fantasy than reality. But she hadn't expected Jamie to be so reticent when confronted with the actual possibility. She kicked herself for her stupidity in wanting him to beg her to live with him. Was this too much of a leap for him after so many years trapped in one sort of relationship? Too hard to transform it into something else?

And what was she expecting of poor Jamie? That he should leap with excitement and start planning to leave Annette and the children and start a new life with her? But - she knew with certainty now - that was not what she wanted! And clearly not what he wanted either, when truth be told. So what *was* she expecting of him?

Out of her confusion a realisation was dawning in her. All these years she had sublimated her own desires to fit in with others. First Angus and his delicate self-esteem, which couldn't be challenged or upset or he'd be unable to write. How much she'd given up for him! How he had gradually closed her down, "forced" her into a deceitful affair, made her feel small and helpless. It was always she who had to change, to manoeuvre, to accommodate, to take the blame. She felt anger rising in her. She wasn't going to do it any more!

And as for Jamie - yes, of course she had colluded in the affair. It suited her as well as him. But was she just fitting in to fulfil his love fantasy with no real commitment from him, so that she got the short straw in her relationship with him as well as with Angus?

The two men in her life represented what Tabitha had always considered the two halves of a perfect partnership. On the one hand there was Angus, super-intelligent, older than her, established in his career path, who could converse with anyone about all the same subjects that fascinated Tabitha (except, of course, for animals!), but struggled to operate any tool or machine or cope with the practicalities of life at all. Then she had Jamie, with whom she had enjoyed the rapture of love, and the funniness of friendship, his comic ways, his practical approach - and she had overlooked his relative paucity of education, his failure to notice this omission, his lack of understanding of anything spiritual or artistic. He didn't dislike it - he just didn't understand it. It had never impinged on his life till now, when his strange daughter - that daughter who seemed to be Tabitha's in spirit - wanted to pursue it as a career. Efforts to teach him - to make him more like Angus - had failed. And efforts to make Angus more like Jamie had failed equally spectacularly.

All these years, one of them had made up the shortfall in the other. Now Angus had become impossible to live with, and Jamie suddenly seemed so lightweight. She hated herself for thinking of him that way. But when it came down to it, could she be happy with him?

She felt a pain sear across her chest, and reached her hand out for his again.

"Hey! What's with all the tears?" he asked, stroking her face and kissing it dry.

"I feel as if I'm at a turning-point," she said, slowly. "Everything is changing for me."

"All I want is for you to be happy," said Jamie again. "If that means you going to America, so be it."

"I'm not going there. I'm not going anywhere. But everything's changing. This is it, Jamie," she sobbed.

The pain seared through her again. She knew that this was the end of her and Jamie. It had been so long, yet it had taken so little to fracture them, and her heart. The tears flowed more freely and for a while she allowed herself to sob, while Jamie held her close, seemingly unable to offer her an answer.

She felt so alone. She could almost be here in this pine forest on her own. Jamie was there for her physically, but at the same time he seemed so far away. Had he been thinking about ending it for some time? He seemed to be taking it so quietly, so calmly. She had expected something more: excitement, disappointment, even anger. And he was giving her nothing of these.

And what if he had given her the answer she had expected? Supposing he had rejoiced that their love could now be fulfilled? It was so unfair of her to expect him to think that, when she didn't think it herself.

Perhaps she was stronger than she'd always allowed herself to be. Perhaps this was the moment she could come into her own - stop fitting in with everyone else. Stop depending on others to bring her fulfillment. Everything she'd always believed - about herself and her place in the world, about marriage and companionship - it was all disintegrating before her eyes. She had always been a fiercely loyal person. She had always taken the blame for Angus's sexual shortcomings - was it really her fault? She had always stayed "in the wings" with Jamie, not upsetting his family life, thinking it utterly wrong to take him away from his children. Now, it seemed, she was just a family friend, someone to help with advice. The only people she had left to be loyal to now were her dogs. And her school, her teaching - her ability to inspire and enthuse others. That had been affirmed repeatedly over the last few weeks. She was forced to believe that just maybe she did have gifts. And how could she overlook Sally and Maureen, who went on and on about this relentlessly!

She took a deep breath and stopped crying.

"I'll always love you, no matter what happens," Jamie murmured to her. It was his love that had sustained her all these years, had given her belief, a measure of acceptance. Could she manage life without that love supporting her? Did she really have the strength to go on through her life alone? She knew with certainty that she would never again have someone who loved her as Jamie did. This was it.

There was a space between them. Not a physical space - he was still holding her close - but a gap had appeared, a chasm that could not be crossed.

"I have to go," said Tabitha, as she reached for her clothes. She couldn't bear the pain any more. They said that a child was born through its mother's massive pain. Her new life was being born. And the old Tabitha was crippled with the pain of it. They broke camp in silence. And gently and sadly held hands as they trekked back through the undergrowth to the cars. And the real world. A new world. A world where Tabitha had to rely on herself, not others. Where she would make the decisions, where *she* would protect what was precious to her.

"So I guess we won't be making another date?" said Jamie quietly. He knew.

"I think not," said Tabitha, looking straight into his eyes. She gave his hand a final squeeze, then let go.

And as they loaded the blankets back into the car, her mind was already moving ahead, beginning with organising Angus's trip without her. And her own home without Angus. Just her and her precious dogs, in her new life. It was easier to plan than to feel all this pain.

# 24

Two days after the momentous day of the Red Indian Cafe, her chest aching still with the anguish, Tabitha was sitting in Maureen's garden, rather clumsily trying to make a daisy chain for Sean. Sean was Maureen's "Lammas lamb", born so long after the other three. He was "driving" his toy digger across the daisy-strewn lawn, with appropriate "brm brm" noises. Tabitha needed the feel of a normal home. Maureen seldom came to her house now, as it had become just that - a house, not a home. The unhappiness lurked in the dark corners of the rooms and was seeping into the fabric.

Tabitha felt her friend's tender gaze on her. Esme was snuffling about in the long grass which formed part of Maureen's chaotic vegetable garden, and Luigi lay at her feet watching Sean. Tabitha felt drained. Hollow. Knowing that Jamie was over had left her feeling rudderless. After so many years, and two tries, that relationship had failed. The only two men she'd ever got deeply involved with, and both times she'd failed. She'd given way to Angus again - her courage had deserted her when it came to it - and she felt so trapped. She had taken the lead in ending it with Jamie, but she was left empty.

Maureen could obviously see that something big was happening. But she did not pry. Tabitha found this genuine love and understanding comforting. And she so needed comfort at this time! Maureen accepted her for herself, she didn't judge and she didn't pontificate.

Instead she focussed Tabitha on the mundane.

"You haven't forgotten about next Thursday, have you?" she asked, as she topped up their coffee from the cafetière perched on the rickety table - one of

Kevin's early efforts.

"Of course not!" Tabitha almost lied. She *had* forgotten, for the moment. But she was happy to be reminded, to have something completely outside her troubles to think about, where she could focus on her friend, making her anniversary the best day ever for her.

"We have everything lined up - it's going to be a great party! The children will all be here for it."

"I'm looking forward to it. Really. It'll be lovely!" said Tabitha. "Twenty-five years of happy marriage is something to be cherished and celebrated." She should know. She'd barely had a couple of years of happy marriage. And that only because she'd been deluded, thought that it was her fault, thought that they would work it out. She'd spent years waiting, waiting for Angus to change (which was never going to happen) ... only to be so bitterly disappointed.

"And we don't want anyone driving home worse for wear. So Gary's wangled a whole floor of rooms for our guests. He and Larry go way back - Larry's the hotel manager - so he got a great deal on the rooms."

"Wow! that's amazing. So do we settle up with Larry direct if we want a room?"

"That's it. I'm afraid that after pushing the boat out for the party we can't run to the rooms as well ..."

"No no, of course not! But I'd love to take you up on that offer - can you put me down for a room? I'll ring Larry this afternoon to book it." Tabitha sipped her coffee and leant back on the garden bench. "That will make things much easier - I hate drinking and driving, so I'd expected to be on lemonade all evening."

She closed her eyes for a moment, and everything rushed back into her poor, battered, head.

She felt a bit like an invalid, disabled by the flood of emotions she had experienced over the last few days. When she'd arrived at Maureen's door she couldn't miss the look of shock on her friend's face as she looked at her drawn and pale face. She needed to snap out of it and get going with those decisions. She needed to get strong enough to resist Angus and tell him straight what she would be doing. But she was still dragged down by her feelings of guilt and indebtedness, heavily encouraged by Angus's contempt. These feelings were already bad enough before Angus had underlined how much he'd done for her, as if she were the "deserving poor".

Maureen's unquestioning support made her feel vindicated in her beliefs. She didn't feel so lonely.

Tabitha tried so hard to get her emotions under control. She'd read somewhere that anxiety does not exist in the present. It is only a memory from the past or a fear of the future. But the wretched feelings permeated her whole body. She felt unable to dismiss them. She'd tried staring them in the face. She'd tried saying to them, "Get behind me, bad thoughts! I am not a failure. I'm a fully functioning human being. And I have a right to happiness, just as everyone else does." But with her heart still aching over Jamie, she felt she'd need a bit of healing time before she could really cope.

And time was something she didn't have! Weeks had gone by since Angus had sprung his news on her. And there weren't many weeks left till he would be starting his new job while she started at the NDS. This thought added a dash of panic to her already-heavy heart.

Seeing her friend needed diversion, Maureen was chatting about her children. The two older boys had both left home - Brian was at Business School and Kevin had just started an apprenticeship. Kevin had always been good with his hands and the fruits of his labours were all over the house - a rather wonky cabinet in the hall that he'd put together when he was eleven, the wobbly table supporting their coffee, the hen house he'd constructed out of packing cases and other salvaged material, with vinyl left over from the kitchen flooring to make the roof waterproof. He'd even made the bench Tabitha was sitting on, mercifully constructed more recently and with more skill, making it safe enough to use.

"So I'll have some extra space here," she continued. "If you ever need somewhere to lay your head …". She looked at Luigi and added, "and of course I know well that where you go, these two ragamuffins go too."

Tabitha looked fondly at her friend and fought to hold back her tears. She couldn't talk to her about her breaking heart, but she knew that Maureen knew.

"Thank you, Maureen. I hope it doesn't come to that, but thank you. It's wonderful to know you care – that you're there!"

"I feel as if I'm watching a beautiful butterfly being crushed," Maureen added. "It's all wrong. You're such a lovely person, you have such gifts - so much to give. I want to see you taking your rightful place in the world."

The tears wouldn't stay held back. They started to roll down Tabitha's cheeks. She looked across at young Sean, now scooping up sand in his sandpit with more digger sound effects, and her mind transported her back to the day when she was in her sandpit and she learned that she was not good enough as she was. That she had to be changed to be acceptable to her family and the world. Had it all stemmed from there? Perhaps that day had stayed in her memory because it was a shock to her.

She remembered one of her earlier students at Shooting Stars who was suffering badly from bullying at school. She'd talked to the parents, who had decided to send their son to the School to help build his confidence.

"You can only be bullied if you allow yourself to be," said the boy's forthright mother. This was what she'd been trying to remember! It had stuck in Tabitha's head ever since. And it was Maureen who'd said something similar. It must be local knowledge hereabouts! She was seeing ever more clearly where she had fallen short in this marriage. She had allowed herself to be bullied. Never wanting a confrontation, she always pulled back, gave way, crumpled.

She was back to blaming herself again! And she knew that really wouldn't do. She'd get dragged down into a morass of self-pity. Just like that time she was walking into Tom's corner field when there had been a lot of rain and the tractors had been in and out of the gateway working on the ditches, her boots had sunk into the deep wet mud and were sucked in. She had had to get a much younger Luigi to help pull her out while she kept hold of the last inch of boot that was still exposed. She wasn't going to be that boot! Sucked down into the mud with no escape.

But day after day, year after year, at home, at school, with Angus, she'd been made to feel inadequate, falling short, not enough. The continued relentlessly dripping disapproval had deeply affected her soul. But it was she who had allowed it! From now on she was going to do what she was good at without heed for others' opinions. She wasn't going to "fit in" any more. She had to strike out and fend for herself. If people wanted to disapprove of her, that was their issue, not hers. Why had she never seen this before? It was like a flash of light!

She only needed one or two true friends to stand at her back, and Maureen was one. She didn't try to control Tabitha or tell her what she should think. She was a soft, comfy, cushion to support her. And even if she hadn't had Maureen, she had her own integrity. She knew that where she had drifted to in her life was the wrong place. She'd gone so far down a cul-de-sac that she had to make a dramatic change to get where she should be. She'd already made a start by losing Jamie (and this thought threatened to start the tears flowing again).

"I'm going to fight to save that butterfly," Tabitha said now in a hoarse voice, turning her tear-streaked face from Sean's sandpit to her friend. "It's hard. It's so hard ..." she sobbed again.

"If it's right, then you can do it," replied Maureen quietly. "Keep faith with yourself - what you truly believe - and it will work out right for you."

Keep faith. She had to know what was right and act on it. She always felt so conflicted around Angus. He was so distant yet so brutal. She merited better than this! She closed her eyes and leant back on Kevin's hard and uncomfortable bench. She needed this solace, the sun on her closed eyes drying her cheeks - her friend with her normal home. Yes, she could come back into the world! She could contribute! She did have a place!

She had loved and lost Jamie. Now to turn to the one she no longer loved. She had to find a way to overcome her misplaced feelings about Angus - and stand up to him. It was inevitable. She just had to do it. Once she had plucked up the courage to say what she truly thought - and what she knew had to happen - she'd be able to move forward.

# 25

The next day was the day Tabitha had promised to meet up with Clare. She really didn't feel in the mood to trip down Memory Lane with her old schoolfriend. Clare was bound to be happy and flourishing in her chosen life and would make Tabitha feel even more uncomfortable just at a time when she needed to build up a little confidence. She was still in great pain from finishing with Jamie, and there was still some self-criticism lurking - that she'd got rid of the relationship she loved while she was still stuck with the one she hated. Yes, hated. She had to admit that that was how she now felt about Angus.

So she was a little distracted when Clare arrived at the coffee shop, looking like a million dollars and bursting with confidence and enthusiasm.

"Hi, Tabitha!" she said with a broad grin, leaning forward to embrace her fondly. "You look *just* as I remember you." She still had her attractive Irish lilt and seemed exactly as Tabitha remembered her.

Tabitha smiled a little shyly at this outgoing and capable woman. "Well, *you* don't!" she responded, suddenly caught up in the moment, and glad about their meeting. "Last time I saw you we were still at school! You were in a bit of a state about getting pregnant, having to leave school under a cloud without your exams, and it wrecking all your plans. Weren't you planning to do English Lit at University? What happened? You kinda disappeared ..."

"Oh," replied Clare, after they'd sorted their coffee orders and settled themselves, "'The past is another country - they do things differently there'," her easy quote showed that her interest in literature hadn't waned. "I had no idea what to do. I was wracked with guilt over my stupidity at falling pregnant. Everyone was saying "I told you so." All my plans for university were gone - poof - in a puff of smoke. Jonathan was ok about it I have to say, and we got married and went to his country pile in County Meath to be near his family."

"What about being near *your* family?" asked Tabitha.

"Oh, they wanted nothing to do with me. I was a big let-down for them. Old West of Ireland thinking, you know. Da's still in Kerry, while Mum has stayed on in London. Well, it was ok for a while. There were two children before long, and Jonathan had a decent income so we did ok. It's a nice life out there for the "West Brits", I must say - swanning about in a smart car, spending afternoons with the children and friends riding, entertaining, gossiping. Staff to do all the work. But I wasn't satisfied. It didn't feel right, being waited on, not doing anything worthwhile. When the children were off at boarding school there was just acres of beautiful estate and empty time. That's when I did an Open University course in English and got really wrapped up in it. By the time I finished it I'd started writing some articles for magazines, the children were grown and off on their own paths, and Jonathan and I just drifted apart. It wasn't bad. We just weren't satisfied with each other any more, that's all. We still get on fine, in fact, and of course we both support the kids in their lives. But I needed more!"

Tabitha was gripped by this narrative. Clare was not at all what she had expected. She had just assumed … big mistake! At school Clare had been all about romance and passion, and when she became pregnant and went off with her man, Tabitha had taken that as the end of the story. "I just thought you'd found what you wanted in life - albeit a little faster than you had intended."

"We were so young then. What did we know about life? We were babes in the wood. And what did we know about other people? Our heads were stuffed full of romantic notions from literature - all very well, but not necessarily relating to suburban Twentieth Century teenage girls. Remember Veronica who was so pious and we always thought she'd be a nun? Well, I heard that she has six children now!"

"No!" laughed Tabitha, at the thought of plain Veronica who had always disapproved of the other girls' fantasies.

"And as for Yvonne," Clare went on, "the sexpot who was always courting trouble? She never married. She's something quite high-up in the City."

"Wow. I've fallen right out of touch with everyone from back then."

Tabitha reflected on the fact that she'd allowed Angus to separate her from everyone she used to know. At the time, she had just thought she'd grown out of her old schoolfriends and into a new, grown-up, circle. But really, it was part of Angus's apparent plan to isolate her. Her heart lurched again - what was he doing it for? "That's why I was so surprised when you wrote. And now? You've left Jonathan, you've left Ireland…?"

"Yep. I'm carving my own career now. The articles I wrote got around, and I've been headhunted by one of the big magazine syndicates. So I thought I'd come back to where I began. This is a lovely part of the country, and I don't have to put up with that endless rain any more!"

"That's impressive! Well done you!" She was glad now that Clare had got in touch. She had that shared history with her, those angst-ridden teenage years, and was warming to her by the minute. Clare had already set out on her path to independence. It didn't feel so frightening to Tabitha when someone she knew had already done what she had to do. "English Literature was always your subject. So you're back to what you always wanted to do?"

"That's it. I'm so excited about it! And, of course, it's an education for the kids, travelling across the water from one parent to another. Hopefully they'll feel freer about what they want to do as a result. Tell me, though," she continued as she picked up her coffee, "what about you? I always remember you wanted to act - but I think your plans got changed too, didn't they?"

"Too right," said Tabitha. She wondered just how much of her story she could tell Clare. She still felt so very sore, broken, over Jamie - perhaps she'd miss that bit out? But no, she decided it would be good to share with someone. Someone who didn't know anything about her present-day life, someone she felt sure wouldn't judge. So she told Clare everything. She felt the load lightening as she spoke. It was the first time she had ever spoken about all of this to another person. She did well to tell her story dispassionately, without breaking down. She kept it as matter-of-fact as she could.

And at the end Clare sighed and said, "You too. But you've suffered. Poor Tabitha. Mine was an easier choice - it was born out of pure selfishness," she smiled. "But it sounds as if you've been tortured all this time. So what do you plan to do? You're not staying in this no-man's-land?"

Tabitha recounted the rest of her story - about the development of Shooting Stars, about the plaudits of the Director of the NDS and the new post, about the terrific support she'd got from her true friends - who asked nothing but gave everything - about her feelings of fulfilment at last, her yearnings to make it all work. She even added in her new-found fun with her dogs and Melanie, becoming very animated in the telling, which just seemed to be rounding out her life.

"It really puts it in proportion, just talking about it. I've been holding on to all of it for so long. Just saying it out loud ... Now I can see the insignificance of some things, and the enormity of others. And ... what I have to do."

Clare was giving her rapt attention, frowning and apparently thinking hard. It was as if she had a particularly juicy bone she wanted to sink her teeth into.

"Ok, this is what you're going to do," she said finally. "You're going to leave your no-hoper of a husband. He doesn't deserve you. You've already chucked lover-boy who you were marking time with. You're going to make a huge success of both your business ventures. And you're going to fill what little spare time you have playing with your dogs." She leant forward, staring straight into Tabitha's eyes. "This isn't news to you. You already know it all. You've already worked it out. But I think you could possibly do with a little push. You know what you have to do but you still seem to be caught up in what you feel you *ought* to do."

Tabitha breathed out. She felt so refreshed at having unburdened herself. It was the first time she had put her life into words like this, and she was staggered to see how crazy it appeared when you looked at it from the outside. She had felt anxious to begin with as her head spun with all the drama of the recent days and weeks. But now she had found yet another friend, someone who could really understand exactly what she was going through, someone in whom she could confide utterly. And Clare had picked up the reins of their friendship as if no time had elapsed since they were last together, in those torrid emotional times when they were both emerging adults.

"Heaven knows why you married this guy in the first place," exclaimed Clare. "Why did you?"

"I ..." Tabitha sighed heavily. "I thought I was such a failure. I couldn't do the drama I so wanted to do as my parents wouldn't finance me. I thought I'd have to settle for marriage and children - which is what had always been expected of me, and which I really wanted too - and I thought Angus was someone who could give me that life while keeping a bit of the Bohemian world I craved. I was so wrong. I was so naive. I was so compliant. I just did what everyone told me to do. I can't believe how weak I was ... I despise myself now for that."

"No despising. We can't go back to where we were. We made decisions which seemed to be right at the time. That's the best we can ever hope to do. It doesn't matter why. But we owe it to ourselves to make the right decisions for us now. Imagine if you were to stay where you are now till the end of your days! You'd so regret it!"

Tabitha's heart sank at the thought of her newly-found freedom slipping out of her grasp while she slid back into her dead-end marriage, and she shivered. Not going back. Can't go back. Not staying like this, she shook her head slowly.

"It seems to me that you're worried that you're responsible for him," said Clare, settling back in her chair.

"I feel that I'm abandoning him!"

"It's more like he's abandoning *you*, Tabitha. But anyway, just look at it a different way." Clare looked at her now-empty coffee cup then gazed out of the window for a moment. "Imagine that you can release him to the life that he deserves. Maybe you both made a mistake. You don't have to live with it forever. And also imagine that by releasing him you release yourself to the life that *you* deserve. Had you thought of that?" she added, with animation.

"No. No, I really never looked at it that way."

"I'm damned sure you didn't. But It's true, Tabitha. Just because there's something that you decided years ago, it doesn't mean you have to hang on to it for ever. You were, what – a teenager? Would you take life advice from one of your students now? We only have one life - just the one! And you've got to make the best of it. You don't get another go!" Clare bounced in her chair, waving her hands expansively. "So what's the point of staying stuck in something that isn't working? And what's the point of keeping Angus stuck in something that's not working for him? It's not helping either of you. Open your eyes, Tabitha! Look at the world around you. It's there, waiting for you."

She leant forward again: "Everyone is wanting a piece of you. Everyone is wanting what they can get from you – in good and in bad ways. Your old man is keeping tabs on you all the time – keeping Tabs!" she laughed at her pun. "Everyone's trying to 'Keep Tabs'. And it's you who needs to 'Keep Tabs'." She sat back in her chair again, pleased with her play on words, then urged Tabitha: "You've already done the hard part, getting shot of Lover-boy. Now do the easy bit. Hubby next!"

Tabitha thought about Veronica and about Yvonne, and she thought about Clare as she looked at her sitting opposite. She realised that people's lives can be very different and don't have to be dictated by what happened in their youth. She saw that she needed to set her own life in motion at last in the direction *she* wanted to go. It wasn't too late to change course!

"But you're *not* going to stay where you are," said Clare, as if reading her mind. "You've already started moving - it's so exciting!"

Tabitha wondered for a moment why Clare was so keen to get her moving? She asked her.

"I've seen the light! I've broken free! So I want you to, too!" Just as newlyweds want everyone to get married, Clare had the zeal of the new convert. She wanted everyone to experience the heady rush she was feeling, at setting out on her own path at last.

"You see," Clare went on, "we all think we can control everything. I don't know why, but we do. And when things happen that we can't control, and people do things without our approval, we panic and think we're useless. That was rather how I felt, that trying and failing to control my family - a sure recipe for frustration! - meant that I was a waste of space. It was only when I realised that the only thing we can actually control is what's inside our heads

- not events, not acts of God, not what other people do - that I relaxed and found some freedom. It wasn't my job to control my family! They had to learn to manage themselves!" She picked up her bag and slung it over her shoulder. "It's not what happens in the world that matters - it's how we react to it. And that's always our choice."

Tabitha gasped. She thought of the amazing advances she was having with teaching Esme new things - the dog learned so quickly because she had the chance to choose. It was just the same for her! She had a choice - had always had a choice. She had simply been making the wrong choice, over and over again. It was now a question of making the right choice and sticking to it.

So the meeting that Tabitha had not looked forward to had turned out to be cathartic after all. Clare's fresh face was enough to spur her on, to lift some of the heavy weight from her heart. It was as if she now had permission to follow her own star, to be "selfish" as Clare had said *she* had been. The overwhelming guilt she had been experiencing was sliding away a little. She felt she had a right to happiness and she was going to take it! Would it be easier to talk to Angus without this unwanted and unwarranted heap of guilt on her? He certainly knew how to rub it in. In another flash of light she saw how manipulating he had always been. Maybe to protect himself and his own vulnerability, but that was how it came over for Tabitha. And she had played right into it. What a disaster of a partnership! No wonder it had at last crumbled, being built on such awful foundations.

The old friends shared a warm hug and exchanged phone numbers as they parted, with promises to keep closely in touch and spur each other on. Clare even offered to help her find somewhere to live. She was pushing things forward fast. And the urgency was necessary! Time was flying by to September.

Tabitha felt stronger in her resolve than she had for ages. She had a fellow conspirator! She had a completely new way to look at things. And she was going to continue to push forward in her new direction. She was having a planning meeting with Sally the next day, and she hoped she'd find that things were actually happening, and that it wasn't all talk. Things *had* to happen! Watch out world, Tabitha is on the move!

# 26

Tabitha was really impressed with Sally, and she made sure to tell her so.

"Sally, you're a marvel!" she enthused. "You've achieved so much in such a short time. You're a Shooting Star yourself!" They both laughed.

They were sitting together at Sally's kitchen table, planning the forward march of Shooting Stars. As usual, Tabitha had brought a bag of cakes to help them keep their energy up through the afternoon, to give the meeting that chocolatey sweetness that smoothed it along.

The school's finances were all untangled and arranged in neat columns in a spreadsheet entitled "Shooting Stars Financial Projections". It was way beyond what Tabitha had ever managed with the backs of envelopes. Sally's face shone as she unveiled more of her miraculous planning documents to Tabitha. Everything had a place, and everything was considered. And Sally had been canvassing the parents with the letters she and Tabitha had drafted at the last planning meeting - early responses were very positive. They almost all valued the school enough to pay proper fees. Those who saw it as a free childminding service would be on their way. And those who genuinely found it a hardship would be privately catered for with reduced fees, payment plans, and so on.

"We've had great take-up on your idea of them paying for a whole term in advance and getting some sessions free," said Sally. "That gives us plenty in the kitty to get things moving where we need to pay for things, and subsidise those who need a bit of help."

"It's so important that we don't deny any child who really wants to be there," Tabitha said. "Needs to be there, in fact," she added, thoughtfully, gazing at the sky beyond the window.

Sally nodded sagely, "We can sort that out quietly for them - no problem," and made a note on her pad. "I think Sharon may be one ... Now Linda's on her own with the three kids."

Sally was also working on local sponsorship which would be able to provide scholarships for deserving pupils. Keeping it open to everyone was something that both women utterly agreed upon.

Sally was always careful not to meddle in any way with the creative side of the School - how many rehearsals, who was to get which role, and what they were actually working on for the next production. But she excelled at translating Tabitha's sometimes wayward ideas into form and shape. ("Perfection," thought Tabitha to herself.) And now Sally was really excited at the prospect of Karen joining them and had already had a planning discussion with her.

"Karen's going to craft a routine which will suit the younger children who've got no dance experience," Sally was saying. "And she'll be able to do something with the older girls who can dance already. Apparently she's already been doing this at her dance classes. She's been the best in her class for ages, and her teacher's been encouraging her to develop her choreographic abilities."

Another find, thought Tabitha. Do I deserve this?

"I'm just amazed at how everyone is stepping forward to help, now we've decided on a new course. And things are just happening - look at Karen popping up out of nowhere!" And she reflected on the fact that her and Jamie's trust in each other had transcended their parting, so that Karen could still take up this chance. There was goodness there.

Jamie had held true to his promise and driven Karen up to Sally's place. It saddened Tabitha that she had felt the need to keep away, but she had to stick to her guns. It would be so easy to fall for Jamie's charms again - he was, after all, the love of her life. But she knew she had to remain strong. It was as if a force were ripping through her life. Starting with Angus's bombshell - the shockwaves had spread through her whole being, tearing down the fragile structures that she had built up over the years. It was a time of transition, of transformation. That butterfly had to fly free!

"Between the little children's dance routine and Esme's sausage-stealing antics, this performance is going to be a wow!" she said, happily, reaching for another brownie.

Tabitha kicked herself once more for taking so long to let others inside her precious School. She didn't have to do it all herself! Sally was a find, and she had been knocking on the door for a while before Tabitha saw sense and got off her defensive high horse. To think she'd actually been afraid to allow Sally to help her! And worried that Sally and Brendan were trying to move in on her business!

Brendan had proved beyond doubt how helpful and positive he was about the School. He was delighted that Sally had a project she could sink her teeth into and use her business talents while still being a stay-at-home Mum.

"Well Tabitha," he'd laughed, "you've kept this one from having to go on the streets to avoid going out to work!" He'd smiled lovingly at his wife, while clapping his hand onto his daughter's shoulder. "This is a perfect solution for me - you're keeping Sally amused while she's still able to wash my socks and get dinner on the table!" This last had been accompanied by guffaws - they all knew how much he valued his wife and doted on his family, and how he was ready to chip in and make the dinner when Sally was at full stretch.

Tabitha realised he had only been trying to protect his wife when she had ascribed underhand motives to him. He was now whipping up support from the fathers and the older girls' boyfriends to volunteer for the heavy work and for building the props and scenery, while Sally had a whole rota of helpers hunting down clothes and shoes in charity shops then organising sewing bees for the alterations. These were all heavily disguised as coffee mornings, while Brendan's group always had a supply of cans to help them in their efforts.

The new times and dates had been sorted and booked at the hall, and Tabitha was surprised to see how many people preferred the weekday sessions, leaving their weekends free for family. True to Sally's prediction, Jason's father had jumped at the plan. "Now if you want me to come out on a day other than Saturday to help with scenery, then I'm your man!" he'd told

Brendan happily. Football first in his family, but he was happy to join the lads during the week for a beer while wielding a paintbrush or screwdriver.

It was a bit of a shock to her to realise that she had got so stuck in a groove, finding the School harder and more stressful as it grew, and spending so much time on organisation and firefighting that she now saw how little time she allowed for creativity and forward planning - the grand arc of progress that she had envisaged when she began the School. A bit like her marriage, which had all the duties and responsibilities of a marriage without any of the perks or joyful moments that made it all worthwhile. Both had been slipping downhill together.

Thank heavens she'd seen the light in time! Sally was able to take a small salary and commit her indubitable energies to the School, excelling at all the things which were not Tabitha's *forte*. "I'll deal with that, Tabitha," or "That's right up my alley!" was music to her ears!

So she was thrilled to see Shooting Stars on an even keel, course plotted for the future. Thanks to some canny free advertising Sally had found, it looked as though it would actually grow, and auditions were being scheduled for the following week. So she now had two burgeoning projects to manage - exciting!

For the first time in a long time, Tabitha was feeling valued. She licked the sugar off her fingers and thought of how she'd always undervalued herself. Her hesitancy and lack of self-confidence undermined her opinion of herself. And Angus's constant carping and dismissing her ideas as unimportant hobbies had worn through a lot of her resolve.

But she could do stuff! The renaissance of her School was proof of this. She had only to get to grips with her feelings about Angus, get strong ... and tell him she was leaving him. Why was she so stuck on this? Why did she become disabled whenever she tried to tell him? She thought of her resolve when she told him about Esme. It was just a fact. Esme was coming. Now Tabitha was going. Just a fact. "Get that into your head, girl," she said to herself. "It's all done bar the shouting!" But how much shouting would she have to endure? She shivered at the thought.

She realised she was sliding back into her negative, self-deprecating thinking again. Of course she deserved it! She had dedicated her life to others, one way or another, and it seemed that it was now pay-Tabitha-back time.

The two women worked together for another couple of hours, till all the brownies were gone save the one they had saved for Maisie, who arrived home on the school bus - Justin was spending the afternoon at a schoolfriend's house. Just as well, as he was like a small and noisy tornado, in total contrast to his shy older sister. Maisie was happy to sit at the table doing her homework and eating her cake, feeling very grown up.

Tabitha had a momentary pang as she sat next to the child at the table. This was what she had expected her life to be, having children to devote her energies to, like Sally and Maureen and almost the entire rest of the world. She knew she would never have children of her own now. Her experiences with the men in her life meant that she was not going to be looking for a replacement partner. She was bruised and battered and exhausted with love and maintaining relationships in ridiculous circumstances. Her gifts - and she was getting stronger every day in her belief that she did have special gifts - lay elsewhere. And she was excited to release her old hang-ups and pre-occupations and get stuck in to them. She was being offered a great life. Not what she'd once hoped for, but a great life all the same. She was ready to move into it.

Leaving Sally's home, with lovely warm kisses and hugs from both mother and sticky-fingered daughter, she set off home. She was going to see Timothy tomorrow at the NDS and was all set to immerse herself in planning the meeting this evening. She knew she was putting off the hour when she would confront Angus and come clean. But she also knew that the next day at the National School would give her strength.

# 27

Another day, another planning meeting - this time with Timothy. And Tabitha was really enjoying it!

Planning meetings had taken on a different hue thanks to the fact that she was now able to focus on the creative side of her work, while all the practical details were worked out by someone else - by Sally for Shooting Stars, and by the efficient office staff for the NDS. Having ideas and vision was easy for her; working out the nitty-gritty of how to put the ideas into action was wearing and unrewarding. She remembered what Melanie had told her about how motivating your dog to do things for you was easy once you knew what he found rewarding. Tabitha had found what was rewarding to her about documents and planners: handing them over to someone else to deal with! This freed up so much of her energy for the important things that only she could do. She preened herself, her new allowed-to-be-creative self.

She and Timothy were sorting out the advertising for the new intake of students, and fixing the schedule for the auditions. Timothy appreciated her fresh approach. Without the need to justify decisions, as they did with older students by having a large panel of interviewers, there would need to be only a small panel, giving much more freedom for the sort of idiosyncracy that was the essence of how Tabitha worked.

"I love looking for genuine talent, combined with a genuine interest," she explained to him. "I keep auditions very informal. If the child is shy, for instance, I'll have them sit next to me on a sofa rather than facing me."

"And what do you do with the unfortunate children who've been pampered and preened all their lives, and think they're the next big thing?" asked Timothy, smiling gently as he looked intently at her.

"Well … you have to see past their posturing and their me-me-me and find out what's real about them. It takes time, sometimes, but it's worth it to see if there's actually talent and desire there. You have to disregard the face they're giving you because they think it'll impress you."

Timothy leant back in his chair as he heard her answer - the right answer - and made his secret smile, the smile that made him look like the cat who'd got the cream.

"Of course," she went on, "with the NDS I'll have to be more choosy about who gets accepted. I get it - it's a nursery for talent to feed into the main School! So I'll be looking for any signs of this talent in a possibly shy or downtrodden child." She smiled at Timothy as he nodded and went on, "I've seen enough children go from shy and tongue-tied to brave and outgoing as they've come up through the School, to know that there are almost no no-hopers. Those I've always let down gently, suggesting that perhaps individual music lessons or a sport may be more suitable for them."

"We can do that," said Timothy. "Often the parents feel that they're auditioning themselves, as their aspirations for their children are more about them than the child himself! We even find this with our older intake of students. You've obviously learnt how to deal with this sensitively, Tabitha! I'll let you carry on …"

There would be others on the audition panel, and Tabitha expressed her concern to Timothy.

"I know that I haven't got experience with the older students," she said carefully, "but I'm not sure how much experience the other tutors have with young children?" She didn't want to say it, but she was worried it may be a source of conflict. Some of the tutors were a little more old-fashioned in their views; as well as not having the experience of turning ducklings into swans.

"Don't worry, Tabitha," Timothy had said, nodding sagely. "I'm going to trust my gut - and your expertise - over this, and I'll make it clear that mine will be the final decision."

Tabitha relaxed back into her chair. She trusted him, and she certainly didn't want to start out on the wrong foot with her future colleagues. She hadn't sensed any jealousy or animosity when she had been introduced to them before, but the possibility was always there, that this blow-in could be some kind of threat to them.

She was meeting some more of the staff today, over Timothy's weekly sandwich lunch in his office. This regular event was designed to cement relationships with his fiery artistic teachers and provide an informal outlet for any gripes or complaints before they boiled up into anything significant.

Tabitha was looking forward to this hugely! And it started as soon as they finished their planning meeting. As she cleared away her papers, the office staff swooshed in with plates of sandwiches and fresh tea and coffee, adding them to the already laden table at the side of the large room, and refreshing the room with their energy and bright smiles.

It didn't take long for the room to fill up with the "starving artists" who were the teaching staff. And, as ever, when theatre people got together, there were stories and in-jokes to enjoy, and lots of gossip.

"Ooh, she *didn't!*" exclaimed one of the camper-looking tutors, wearing a yellow bow-tie and dark green velvet jacket, and the whole of his little group burst out laughing.

"Come on, Rory, we've all heard this one before," teased Gerard, when the junior voice coach started a story. "And don't let Drusilla hear you tell it either!" added Janey who was carrying coffee and milk jugs and topping up people's mugs. With so many trained voices in the room it made for a pleasant sound, with a sonorous background hum to the occasion. It was an enjoyable hour, and it seemed to be a meeting that the staff relished.

After a while, Timothy tapped his teaspoon against his cup and got everyone's attention. Or nearly everyone's. In the arts there's a fine tradition of freeloading - accepting patronage in kind from those who could afford it and who enjoyed colouring their house-parties with actors, writers, painters, and musicians. So, true to form, some were absorbed at the food table, performing a balancing act of sandwiches, sausages, and cakes on their plates.

But those who chose to listen heard Timothy announce with pride that the new much-rumoured Junior Academy had a new Director and was starting in the Autumn term. "And so I give you Tabitha Thomasson!" he finished, with a flourish and a bow. Tabitha smiled sweetly at all her new colleagues, blushing the while. Partly because she couldn't get used to being Tabitha Thomasson again after so many years.

It had been Clare's idea, to go back to her maiden name. They'd met up again shortly after their reunion - they'd both enjoyed it so much. Their friendship was warm and had endured the long break. And this was so heartening to Tabitha, who thought she had no friends left. She'd dropped round to Clare's one evening when she knew Angus would be out at some writerly function.

Going out in the evening! This was something she hadn't done in an age. So she felt conspiratorial - almost naughty!

What would Angus say when she got home? Well, she hoped she'd get back before him and avoid any trouble, but she had nothing to hide - except, of course, Clare's name. She was not going to lose a single nother friend!

"Cut the ties! Be yourself!" Clare had said as they'd enjoyed a glass of wine that balmy evening in the garden of her flat. "Tabitha Morpeth thoundth ath if you've got a lithp!" she'd laughed. "Tabitha Thomasson has a nice ring to it. And that's how I always think of you anyway. What do you think?"

Tabitha had had to agree. Using her own, her very own, name seemed the right thing to do. If she wasn't going to be Angus Morpeth's wife any more, then she shouldn't make off with his name. So she'd given Timothy her new name and got it down on the paperwork in the office. She really felt as if she were a different person when she came into the NDS now and swept up those stairs. And once she'd been formally announced, lots of people were wanting to meet her, welcome her, congratulate her. There was only friendliness in those eyes that looked keenly at her as they spoke.

"Welcome *my dear*," proclaimed Drusilla, the senior voice coach, apparently speaking for many. "We all *love* it here. You'll soon get used to our *idiosyncratic* ways!"

Through all the greetings and congratulations, Tabitha was pleased to see Gerard again. He really seemed happy here at the NDS.

"I'm so glad I got this post, Tabitha," he confided. "It's no joke being a jobbing actor - more often than not a *resting* actor - when you've got a family to feed." He munched ruminatively on the last of his egg and cress sandwich. "Helen's much more settled now we have the security of this job." He put down his plate, brushed the crumbs from his hands, and went on, "And I love the hours too! Not too early in the morning as a rule, and only really late when we have performances to put on. Are you looking forward to it, Tabitha?"

"Oh yes," she enthused, "I can't wait for it all to get going. I really feel as if I belong already. Everyone's been so welcoming!"

"Haha!" rejoined Gerard, "they're only too glad that this Junior Academy is going to happen and feed half-fledged students into the main school, and they don't have to have anything to do with dealing with small children with grazed knees, runny noses, and overbearing parents! They're delighted with you."

"And I'm only too glad to play my part," she laughed. "About the hours, Gerard ..."

Timothy had explained to her that she'd be on an annual contract to begin with, but assuming everyone was happy, she'd be able to become a permanent member of staff thereafter. This was an amazing thought for her, who had paddled her own canoe for so long. So she chatted with Gerard about the working conditions, the perks, his hours, and so on.

"The best thing is being able to pick up private coaching," he said. "Most of us do some, and we can use the college facilities. It's brilliant! You just book it with the office. And that's one reason for the low turnover in staff here. What we don't get in salary we get in kind. Where are you living these days, Tabitha?" he went on. "We do get *some* late evenings, you know, and - much worse! - some early mornings on occasion. It's handy to be nearby."

"We-e-ell," said Tabitha hesitantly. "I'm still in the same place - out in the sticks. But you're right. Living nearer would be a good move."

"Then I have good news for you, Tabitha," interjected Drusilla, who had just joined them again, floating in a billowing dark blue and green kaftan-type garment, her plate overflowing with sausage rolls, as she dusted some of the telltale pastry flakes from her slightly wobbly chin and equally wobbly bosom. "You know Genevieve has just retired, Gerard? Well, I hear she's moving to the South of France - a dream she's had for ever, bless her."

"Lucky her!" responded Gerard quickly, "she deserves a change after so many years. She seems to have been here since the beginning of time," he said, silently nodding at Janey as she refilled the mug he held out to her. "But why is this good news for Tabitha?"

"Genevieve has lived for donkey's years in the annexe in the grounds of Lady Despont's big house - this is the woman who funded a lot of the scholarships here, a great drama fan, my dear," she said to Tabitha, placing her hand confidentially on Tabitha's sleeve, and leaving some more pastry flakes there. "The big house and grounds are a kind of oasis in the middle of town, and the annexe is a kind of *grand* Summerhouse. Well, I'm sure Lady Despont would be keen to keep the connection with the NDS. It might be just what you need, Tabitha."

Tabitha was open-mouthed. Could more things fall into her lap? Is this really what happened when you started to make changes in your life?

"Oh," Drusilla was misinterpreting Tabitha's silence as lack of interest. "Perhaps you've got a partner, a family, and the little house wouldn't do?"

"Oh no," said Tabitha, "it sounds absolutely perfect for me! I just couldn't believe my luck. But does ... does Lady Despont like animals?" she added anxiously.

"Like animals?!" Gerard and Drusilla both chorused, looking at each other and clutching their stomachs as they laughed loudly. "She insists on turning up to previews with a lapdog in her bag." added Gerard. "In a *handbag?*" quoted Drusilla, spluttering pastry flakes, as Gerard muttered, "Mad as a basket of frogs .."

"Quite dippy," added Drusilla crumbily, her mouth now full of sausage roll again.

"That's just what I needed to hear," exclaimed Tabitha, glowing with excitement. "I've got two dogs, you see, who I adore." So Drusilla and she swapped numbers, so that she could be introduced formally to the person who she hoped would become her new landlady. And this gave Drusilla the perfect opportunity to talk at length about her cats, who *she* adored.

As the lunch ended, Timothy bade her goodbye. "I almost forgot to say," he said, smiling at her fondly, "your Jennie has just been offered a scholarship, starting in September."

"That's wonderful news," gasped Tabitha. "I didn't like to ask - I know you're so busy."

"If I say I'll do something, I do it," smiled Timothy. "That's why I don't often say yes to people!" he added with the slightest wink.

"Jennie will be thrilled, absolutely thrilled." Tabitha felt a flood of emotions threatening to overcome her. She had got this great opportunity. Timothy thought he was the lucky one - to have landed her to direct the Junior Academy - while she knew that this came straight from Heaven, or wherever good things came from. There was a possibility of a wonderful place for her to live where her dogs would be not just tolerated, but welcomed, and to cap it all, she'd been able to help Jennie escape her confines and get set to blossom.

Her heart felt fuller and lighter than it had done for ages. Yes, she'd lost her beloved Jamie, but it had never been unalloyed happiness. Intermittent joy, yes. But there was always the lurking feeling that people were being deceived and that grated with her. She hadn't realised just how much it grated till she finished with Jamie and felt a load lifted from her. Just as that young Tabitha had felt the load lift when she let her old dog Simon go. That she was no longer lurking in darkness and could come out into the light. And she was beginning to feel a liberation she hadn't expected. Perhaps better to be free of love and free of regrets? But she was so glad she'd experienced Jamie's love, even if it had caused her pain down the years. That love was something she would never forget, an experience that could never be taken away from her.

Would she feel more heaviness lifting once she got brave enough to talk to Angus? She felt sure she would. She had been carrying a heavier and heavier weight on her shoulders for so long. She felt freed here at the Drama School, amongst people who understood her. She was uncomplicating her emotional life while doubling up on her creative life. Everything seemed to be falling into place. There was just one huge hurdle to leap - telling Angus. And that was what occupied her mind on her journey home. She just had Maureen's party to go to—and she certainly couldn't show up all dishevelled as she would be if she came after speaking to Angus. But she would definitely, absolutely definitely, tell him when she got back on the Friday.

# 28

It was Friday afternoon when Tabitha arrived home after her night away. Despite herself, she'd hugely enjoyed Maureen and Gary's party, which finally petered out after lunch. While not being much of a party-person herself, Maureen *was*. So Tabitha had thrown herself into the occasion and done her best to make sure everyone was included and well-fed. The boys were assiduous at keeping all the guests' glasses topped up, and there was even a bit of a sing-song as the evening wore on. Daphne was enthralled by being at a grown-up party, and allowed to stay up for all of it. She looked lovely in her light blue lacy dress with her blonde curls tumbling down her back.

There were lots of old acquaintances to catch up with and she'd put everything out of her mind and "let her hair down". When asked the inevitable question about what she was doing these days, she just answered as if it were a couple of months earlier.

"Yes, still running the children's drama group ... Yes, Angus is fine, thanks! Busy on his new book."

This grated even more than she expected, but she couldn't breathe a word about Angus until she'd told him herself. That was only right. Once that's done, she thought, tomorrow, I will be a new person! Only a few more hours ...

So she refused to talk about what was as usual uppermost in her mind and concentrated on enjoying herself and making sure that Maureen did too.

The whole family was there, even young Sean who stayed up till he fell asleep next to Daphne on a comfy sofa. He was as bright as a button at lunch the next day, unlike many of the adults who were still feeling a bit delicate. It had been very late when the cake had been cut, the speeches made amongst much hilarity, and they had all headed for their rooms and the welcoming comfort of their beds.

It had been a pleasure to enjoy a night in the comfortable and homely hotel room, and to have a delicious lunch prepared by someone else. So she felt good as she returned home. She knew that her promise to tell Angus had to be fulfilled. She couldn't let herself down again. Perhaps a little later ...

As she came into the kitchen Angus was making himself a cup of tea. "How was the party?" he asked.

"Great!" she said, as she dropped her suitcase and ruffled Esme's head as they greeted each other ecstatically. "There were loads of people I hadn't seen for ages, and ... *Where's Luigi?*" she interrupted herself abruptly, suddenly becoming aware of his absence, that there was only one flurry of tail, and not the usual two.

"Er .. he had a fall on the stairs last night," said Angus, turning his back to her as he tended the teapot.

"But I told you not to let him on the stairs! That's why there's a stair gate!" She felt her voice becoming brittle, shrill.

"Well, he fell anyway."

"Where is he?" Tabitha said, looking frantically all round the kitchen, and at Luigi's empty bed. "*Where is Luigi?*" She was beginning to panic.

"I thought he'd be alright in a while, but I couldn't stand the screaming so I buzzed him down to the vet."

Tabitha was aghast. Luigi screaming? Oh my God, she thought, my poor Luigi. She scooped up her car keys again. "I'll go now."

"No, don't." said Angus, turning, but still avoiding her gaze. "The vet said it would need an operation - expensive - and as the dog was so old ..." He shrugged his shoulders, a helpless look on his face.

"*What have you done?*" whispered an ashen-faced Tabitha.

"He thought it would be best to destroy him. So I left him there. Sorry," he added, as an afterthought, as he turned back to the tea things.

Tabitha stood paralysed. Her beloved Luigi! Injured and in pain through her husband's carelessness, then transported to a strange place and left to die alone. She couldn't bear the thought. If she had been home she would have nursed her beloved old dog day and night if need be. She wouldn't have baulked at the expense. She would have paid anything to have him back with her right now, his dear old head cushioned in her lap, his scruffy fur under her caressing fingers.

She should never have left him! She cursed her selfishness, and the folly of leaving something so precious in the care of someone so uncaring. What was she thinking? But how hard was it for a grown man to look after an old, obliging dog in his own home? She'd left him strict instructions on what to do with the dogs, what their routine was. He didn't have to walk them - just feed them and settle them at bedtime. He'd lived with them all their lives, but what they did and liked seemed to have completely eluded him. He must have been drinking. He must have staggered upstairs and left the stair gate undone.

"You were drunk!" she said bitterly, accusingly. "You were drunk and forgot to mind my dog. You care nothing for anyone but yourself." Tabitha drew Esme to her and clung to her. She felt her heart - broken yet again - hardening against her husband.

"I had a drink, yes. Nothing wrong with that," he added as he edged towards the door.

"There is *everything* wrong with it." Tabitha knew her voice was coming out loud and harsh and tight. "I left the dogs in your care for just one night. You couldn't even stay sober for one night. Oh, Luigi!" she started to sob.

"Oh God, not the waterworks," said Angus, and smartly left the room.

After a while Tabitha recovered herself and got the phone. She rang the vet and asked for an account of what had happened.

It was a different vet from her usual one, a new partner in the practice - someone she'd never met - and it was a very different story from what Angus had told. "The dog had badly torn ligaments and some broken ribs," he said. "I don't know how he'd got all that from a simple fall ... I suggested I keep him in and treat him. He needed painkillers and rest. I said it would take time for him to recover. But your husband said that he had strict instructions from you that as the dog was so old he was to have no suffering, and that I was to put him down."

Tabitha gasped with a muffled cry.

"Sorry?" said the vet.

"I want to fetch him, bury him here at home," said Tabitha tightly, keeping back the tears in her aching throat.

"Er, I'm sorry, but it's too late," replied the vet, choosing his words carefully. "I was also instructed to dispose of the body. So ... no burial, I'm afraid," he finished a little lamely.

Tabitha just managed an almost silent thank you before replacing the receiver. She started to cry again.

He lied! Angus lied to the vet. And he'd lied to her. How could he do that to her? Had he no idea what her dogs meant to her? She rubbed her hands over her face, stood up as straight as she could, gave a tearful crooked smile to a much quieter than usual Esme, and headed to the 50-acre.

She walked. She cursed. She cried. She sobbed. She ranted. She cuddled Esme. She sat on Luigi's log with Esme beside her and felt the old tree's crumbling texture under her, as she gazed at the distant hills framed by the blowsy-leaved summer trees. She walked and walked. And she lay on the damp, soft grass exhausted from weeping.

Her life looked bleak. She could see no further than her immediate tragedy. It was hours later when she went home. She couldn't eat. Her throat was hard and dry and sore from crying. She went to bed early and tried to sleep. She thought she'd be tired after so little sleep the night before, but she woke repeatedly in the night to find herself crying for her lost dog and the disgraceful way he had died. She was racked with guilt that she had not been there for him, and that he had died unnecessarily, through a deception - a lie.

"Oh, for Heaven's sake, can't you stop crying?" said Angus tetchily in the small hours. "I'm trying to sleep."

Whenever she drifted into sleep she'd wake again straight away, crying out, "Luigi! Luigi!" She cried and cried till she was all cried out. It was as if this man in her bed were a total stranger. Someone who neither knew her nor cared about anything she held dear. He had no understanding of the depth of her distress. For a moment Tabitha wondered whether he was just trying to block out what he'd done by blaming her for what he thought was her excessive response. ("It's just a bloody dog," he had said.)

When she rose from her awful night, she had a new determination. Whichever way she turned it, he had betrayed her. He had done a dreadful thing. He had killed her precious friend. Everything that had happened before was as nothing compared with this. This far and no further. For all the thinking she had been doing - the reasoning, the rationalising - when it came down to it it was her visceral reaction to what Angus had done that decided her. No more thinking necessary. This was it.

She found herself shaking off any feelings she had ever had for her husband - though in truth there were not many feelings left by now, except guilt. She couldn't bear to think of how Luigi had received all his injuries - the awful seed the vet had put into her mind. It was better for her sanity to accept Angus's explanation. She went over other events in her life with him, stories she had accepted as true, but now saw were not. How often had he lied to her in the past? With her readiness to see the best in people, she was so easy to deceive! As she viewed her life in a new light, her self-esteem began to soar, along with her determination.

She got up, packed her case again, loaded Esme's food, toys, and bedding into a bag and headed out. She would take Maureen up on her kind offer. She'd camp out there while she got things sorted. Angus must now realise he'd gone too far, that she couldn't stay with him. Or maybe, in his supreme self-centredness, he didn't? Tabitha couldn't bear to speak with him another minute. She grabbed a sheaf of paper and stuffed it into Esme's bag. She'd write him a letter. Maybe it was cowardly, but if she did that she couldn't be badgered out of it again. She had to make it final.

It was over.

# 29

As soon as Maureen came to the front door and saw her, standing forlorn on the step with a suitcase, a bulging bag, and a dog, she opened the door wide and greeted her with a silent hug. Tabitha was so grateful that she had no need to explain anything to her friend.

"I know you," she added. "I know you're doing the right thing." And she took the suitcase and carried it in for Tabitha, who released it willingly, now overcome with exhaustion.

"Slight problem, though. The children are all still here for the weekend. The boys are headed back to their own places on Sunday night. Hmm … "

"I'm so sorry, I never thought!" said Tabitha, reaching for her case as if to go.

"Not so fast, Buster!" laughed Maureen. "We'll double them up - they'll be fine with it. You're not going back." She leant towards her and studied her sad face. "And it looks like the first thing you need is a square meal and a rest. So settle down here in the kitchen with me while I start on dinner. Hello Esme!" she added, looking around for Luigi, as they went to the kitchen.

"Hey everyone," Maureen addressed the children who were all in the kitchen already. "Tabitha's staying for a couple of days, so could you two bunk up together?" she asked Brian and Kevin.

"Sure," said Brian. "Kevin's room is a tip, so I'd better move in there and you can have my nice tidy room." He gave a little bow.

Kevin opened his mouth as if to complain, but a glance from his mother told him that now was not the time. Maureen addressed herself to her daughter: "Daphne, this is sort of private. Can you keep it a secret from your friends? Better not to let people think things, and gossip. You'd be helping Tabitha."

"I'd do anything to help Tabitha," said Daphne brightly, smiling coyly at her heroine. "I won't tell a soul - cross my heart! Can we play with Esme?" she added - "but where's Luigi?"

Seeing her friend's stricken face, Maureen said, "I'm sure Esme would love a game in the garden, wouldn't she, Tabitha?" At Tabitha's nod, she said, "Off you go - take Sean with you and make sure he doesn't annoy the dog."

"Boys, fix a couple of gin and tonics, would you? And then sort out the bedrooms for me." Then she added quickly, "Kevin, could you run up and look after Tabitha's hens?"

"They're great boys - young men," said Tabitha, as they jumped up to get the glasses and slice a lemon. "They were such good hosts last night ..." she felt her hard dry throat making her voice sound drab and distant.

"Gary's always maintained that the children should know how to look after guests, and tending to drinks is an important part of that. And you look as though you need fortifying before you spill the beans." She put her hand on Tabitha's arm gently, "It's time you did, Tabitha."

And so they settled in the comfy chairs in the kitchen, Maureen to prepare apples for the pudding and Tabitha shelling peas. Kevin reappeared with two glasses on a tray, and Tabitha took a refreshing sip as she got started unfolding the whole ghastly story.

She focussed on the events of the night, and her desolate response - that she knew she could take no more. Maureen quietly topped up Tabitha's drink while she nodded and tutted by turns, encouraging her friend to unburden herself as much as she wished. So it wasn't long before she had picked up the whole story about Angus. Tabitha told her things she had previously only guessed at. She knew full well that Tabitha would have loved children - now it was all explained, starkly related here in her cosy family kitchen. And while Tabitha knew Maureen knew about Jamie, she left him out of it - apart from saying that she had no one now. She managed to tell her story dispassionately, without tears. She felt empty of tears. She'd cried the last of them for Luigi.

Tabitha explained the position with the National Drama School - accompanied by "wows" from Maureen - and the possibility of a new dog-friendly home. "It has to be right for the dogs," she said, correcting herself sadly, "I mean, *dog*."

"It looks as though everything is changing for you Tabitha," said Maureen. "It's a lot to cope with. You can stay here as long as you like."

"You're so kind, Maureen. But I aim to move on as fast as possible. I'll follow up the lead for the Summerhouse, take my things and let Angus deal with selling the house. He can do something involving real life, for a change."

It was the first time that bitterness had crept into her voice, and she instantly regretted it. "I never thought I'd be in this position. I never thought I'd be one of those people who bunked out of a marriage when the going got tough. I've always thought marriage was sacred - that you make your promises and you stick to them." She blushed as she thought of the promises she'd broken with Jamie. But that didn't count. She'd justified Jamie to herself over and over. Angus hadn't stuck to his side of the bargain so there was no need for her to. "I don't know what I'd do without you, Maureen," she smiled at her, somewhat bashfully.

"Listen," said Maureen, who was now rolling out pastry at the worktop, "you've given so much to so many people over the last few years - including me and my family. It's your turn to do a bit of receiving now." She deftly cut a circle of pastry round the pie plate. "But when are you going to tell himself?"

"Uh." Tabitha sighed as her stomach lurched. "I'm such a coward. I've tried to tell him a couple of times and caved in. He kind of overpowers me and I end up a gibbering wreck and don't tell him. But now it's irrevocable - after what he did to Luigi." She screwed up her eyes and pressed the heels of her hands into them, wiped away some more stray tears and took a drink from her glass before saying, "I'm going to write him a letter. I'll put it all there in black and white, and make it final. He's not going to talk me round again."

"May I give you a tip?" asked Maureen, as she made little thumb marks all the way round the splendid pie she had made. "Take a copy of the letter. You never know when you may need it."

"Good idea," said Tabitha. "I've brought paper with me. I'll write it tonight. Now, let's get this supper organised," she said, standing up and taking her glass to the draining board. "I'll just check on Daphne and Sean and Esme - though from the laughter I can hear things are going just fine out there. This is a special family time for you, so I don't want them all feeling they have to keep out of the way."

It was later that night when Tabitha took a pen in hand and wrote her letter.

*Dear Angus,*

*It is with a heavy heart that I write this. I've tried to tell you already, but I feel that writing this will make it clearer.*

*I can't go on with this life of ours. I can't stay with you. And I can't go to America with you. It's out of the question. I had already made up my mind that unless you changed dramatically I would be unable to stay. But I realise now that that is impossible. Your callous treatment of Luigi was absolutely the last straw.*

*I feel that I have become more and more alienated in our marriage. I feel that all the allowances have to be made by me. I feel that you expect more of me than I can give. I'm sorry that it hasn't worked for us - I tried so hard.*

*You have great gifts, and I have enjoyed watching you grow as an author and speaker. I'm holding you back in your development and you'll be much better off without me. You needn't worry about me, as I have plans in place for sufficient income for me and Esme to live on.*

*I'll come and collect my things over the next few weeks, and clean and tidy up the house so you can arrange for its rental or sale. If you want to pass on anything for my share of the marital home, I'll be able to put it to good use.*

*Please don't ask me to change my mind. I am decided. We don't need to involve lawyers as I have no wish to marry again. And you shouldn't.*

*With sadness,*

*Tabitha*

She sat back and read through the letter several times before making her copy. And she reflected that the only times she'd stood up to Angus were over the dogs. It seemed she had to have a strong driving force to take her own feelings of not being good enough out of the equation, and be able to focus on something that really mattered to her. Once she had a mission, she was unstoppable. And having that mission would help her resist what she felt sure would be the inevitable tide of letters, calls, and texts from her angry husband.

This letter was what she took to the house when Angus was out the next day. As she went into the kitchen, Esme ran to Luigi's bed to see if he was there: a final sadness. She collected a few more of her things and left the letter on Angus's desk.

And as she closed the door behind her she felt as if she were emerging from a sticky cocoon into the freshness of the day. She looked firmly forward as she set off from her home for the last time to walk in the 50-acre, knowing that she had so much to finalise to organise a new life for her tiny little family.

# 30

A couple of days later, sent off after a splendid breakfast prepared by Maureen and Daphne, Tabitha found herself in the huge drawing room of Lady Despont's big house drinking Earl Grey tea out of little floral-patterned bone china cups whose faded rims still bore remnants of gold. The room had been designed - and last decorated, she thought - some time a century or two earlier. It was like a room in the stately homes she'd visited when her parents had considered such house tours as a suitable, educational day out for their children - although Tabitha's mother liked by turns to imagine what it must be like to have a fleet of servants while bemoaning the starched splendour of the main rooms of the houses. It seemed that this house had not changed an iota in the last hundred or so years. While they could look out - through the massive bay windows - to a distant landscape, the room itself was dark and silent, and a bit musty.

Tabitha was glad that Drusilla had made the introduction as promised, and painted her as the ideal tenant!

"My dear," Lady Despont had drawled in her old-fashioned aristocratic voice as she had met Tabitha at the majestic front door, "Drusilla tells me you are an absolute *paragon* of clean-living virtue, and that you'd be *perfect* for the Summerhouse."

"I think I'm going to be very busy at the Drama School," Tabitha had responded, blushing slightly at the nice things Drusilla had said, "and I'm not much of a party-person, so you need have no worries there," she added with a rueful smile, reflecting on the fact that she had next to no friends to party with anyway.

"Well, let's go and have a look at my little Summerhouse first of all," said Lady Despont, heading down the hill in a sprightly manner which belied her years. "Oh, is that your dog?" she said delightedly, turning towards Tabitha's car.

"Yes!" said Tabitha, always proud to show off her darling dog. "That's Esme." She reached inside the window and opened it a bit more, so that Lady Despont could coo and fuss her wagging dog.

"What a delightful little person," she'd said as she led the way down the front drive, her bony fingers plucking at the sleeves of her cashmere cardigan, "Dogs are so *dependable*. I'll bring you in the front way," she added, as they curved round and down from the main house. "It's really a very charming house."

As the drive rounded a copse it changed from tarmac to gravel, making crunching noises under their feet. Tabitha could feel her phone vibrating angrily in her pocket. More of those texts from Angus, she had no doubt.

Without troubling to open the latest messages, Tabitha flipped off her phone entirely, and looking up, she stopped abruptly and gasped. Before her was a long, low building, the whole of one side all full-height windows and French doors - the glass shining bright in the late summer sun - with attractive carved woodwork painted lovingly in white - and a tall chimney with ornamental brickwork patterns winding up into the sky. The silver birches shielding the house from behind waved in the light breeze, their leaves sparkling in the sunshine.

"Is this it?" she blurted out, gazing at the Summerhouse.

She was instantly enchanted with the little house - it looked the perfect harbour for Esme and her, an escape from the storms! They stepped in through the main door, also glass. Inside it was largely open-plan, with comfy old sofas facing those french doors, and a small kitchen tucked away at one end. There was a woodburning stove with a mound of logs beside it, which explained the chimney she'd noticed from the outside. Lady Despont indicated the two doors at the other end of the house, and Tabitha peeped in to see a bathroom behind one door, and a bedroom behind the other, the bed covered in what seemed to be an ancient patchwork quilt. The whole house was light, bright, pretty, and uncluttered.

"I love it," she said, with what she felt sure was a daft enraptured expression on her face, "I absolutely *love* it!"

She turned away and started looking round the main room more carefully. She could see where she could put her bookcases, and the little table and chairs provided were just right for any supper-parties she may have. (Yes! she thought, I can have friends round! I can actually have friends! And she laughed out loud.) She chose the perfect spot for Esme's bed, near where her own feet would be when sitting on the sofa with a book … With a questioning look at her hostess, she reached towards the big French doors. Lady Despont nodded, "Of course, my dear - explore!" and Tabitha opened them both wide, feeling the warm summer sun on her face, marvelling at the view from the paved terrace outside.

The grounds were all laid to lawn, with clumps of flowering shrubs here and there, and taller trees guarding the perimeter. The land - covering at least three acres, she guessed, and already boasting a smattering of early Autumn leaves - sloped up to the big house, which was facing away towards the distant hills, enjoying the magnificent view which had doubtless been the reason the Despont ancestors had chosen the site. You'd hardly know you were in a busy town! It was quiet, apart from the birdsong, and glorious!

"You'll have the use of the grounds, of course, Tabitha. And I want you to make *full* use of them," she leant towards her, smiling conspiratorially. "It costs a *fortune* to keep them nice, you know, and I shall love looking out of the window and seeing you and your dog enjoying them."

Tabitha was wowed by the magnificence of the grounds - which she would actually be able to use as her own - she could scarcely believe her luck! She could come home late from the NDS, or from Shooting Stars, and still take Esme for a walk without having to travel out again.

Tabitha found that old feeling of insufficiency creeping up on her, feeling that she didn't deserve such fortune. She beat it back down again, telling herself firmly that she had every right to a lovely home. She turned to Lady Despont with shining eyes, barely keeping back the tears.

"I just love it! I hope I can manage all the outgoings …" she added, nervously.

"I'm not a shark landlord," laughed her potential new landlady, "and if Genevieve could manage it on her NDS salary, I trust you can too. Come, my dear, let's go into the house and I can show you all the doings."

So that's when they repaired to the house for tea, with Lady Despont insisting on going via Tabitha's car again so she could have a proper joyful meeting with Esme, who so quickly won her over. "Mitzi will think I'm such a *tart* when she smells me!" she said, smiling at Tabitha over the flurry of ears and tail.

They'd agreed the rent and outgoings, including free logs from the estate and that - amazingly - the cleaning and the many windows would be done by Lady Despont's housekeeper. Genevieve had raced off to France as soon as the school term had finished, so Tabitha could move in straight away. Glowing with joy at her new home, Tabitha enjoyed meeting Lady Despont's little dog Mitzi - the one who travelled in her handbag to plays.

Mitzi had come trotting in from the kitchen when Maddie, the housekeeper, had brought in the tea things. The little dog sniffed her mistress suspiciously, gave the stranger a wary eye, decided she was harmless and hopped up on to her lap to get a closer look.

"*Really,* Mitzi!" exclaimed Lady Despont, leaning forward. "She usually takes a while to warm up to visitors you know."

"I think I must be deemed dog-friendly," smiled Tabitha, stroking the little dog, whose fluffy tail was now wagging easily.

"Mitzi is a bit fiery," added Lady Despont, "and *not* a lover of other dogs, I'm afraid." Tabitha was able to reassure her that Esme was the mildest-mannered of spaniels and was very easygoing with dogs. "I couldn't imagine her ever getting into a fight. She'd just move away, and find something to sniff."

"Oh, I'm sure that's right," said Lady Despont, having just met the happy little dog herself. Tabitha wondered to herself if she'd be able to use some of the skills Melanie would be teaching her to get Mitzi to learn some tricks? She would enjoy that! Such a cute little dog would be very appealing, twirling and bowing. And she knew Lady Despont would be quite delighted. What a lovely thought!

"I'm just so thrilled that you've arrived at the exact right moment," said

Tabitha's new landlady. "I was so sorry when Genevieve told me she'd be leaving - though I've known for years that she *longed* to go and live in France. But now you're here and I won't feel *quite* so lonely. This is a big house to rattle around in with just Mitzi and Maddie for company. I'm sure Mitzi will get used to Esme after a while and at least tolerate her. Maybe they'll even be friends?" she mused, happily.

"That would be wonderful, Lady Despont."

"Darling Tabitha, you simply *must* call me Georgia," said the lady in question, with a little moue.

"Ok, Georgia it is," smiled Tabitha back.

Tabitha still marvelled at her luck. Since this whole sorry affair had started such a short few weeks ago, things had just fallen into place for her. First Timothy, then Sally, now a home. Though she'd been through the mill herself in that short time: Luigi had had to die before she plucked up the courage to do what she needed to do. She stared at the empty cup in her hands for a moment. So much had changed. A life she had thought immutable - that would go on for ever in the same way - had been shattered. And as the shards fell around her they exposed a new, warm, vibrant, and fulfilling life - one that she had yearned for. In her mind she pictured the Summerhouse down the hill, basking in the summer sun. This was a symbol for her life now.

She had been looking in the wrong places for fulfilment in her life. She had thought it lay with other people. She thought that she had to fit in with others in order to be successful. She had always felt that she didn't quite measure up, that she wasn't worth anything on her own, always falling short. She now saw that she had to follow her own star, do what was important to her, to have a satisfying life. In a way she could have learnt that from Angus. After all, the most important thing in his life had always been himself and his career. Though she wondered for a moment just how satisfying that life could be if he'd made such a mess of what should have been his most important relationship. And her trying to serve him and his writing, fitting her own interests and gifts into the margins of *his* life, had led her down a fork in the road which had taken her way off course and ended in loss and despair. At last she realised her mistake!

What was it Clare had said? That we have to make our own decisions, and that others have to make theirs. The only thing we can control is our own response to something, she'd said - and Tabitha had made such a mess of that ...

She was ready to blossom - to do what she now saw she had been born to do. To bring the joys of acting and drama to those who would most benefit - youngsters trying to get to grips with this turbulent and sometimes-baffling life. She knew she could give them a lifeline in those confusing teenage years. She would do her best to see that the children in her care were not dismissed, their gifts and yearnings downplayed as hers had been. She would foster their strengths and encourage them to be brave enough to put themselves out there - to follow their own star, wherever that may lead.

She wanted to ensure that they didn't become pawns in someone else's game, as she had been all her life. Shame on her to give in so easily to everyone else's demands and requirements! Always taught to be polite, to accommodate others, to put herself last, to be humble to the point of grovelling. She would teach these youngsters, through what she was naturally good at, to be their own person, to look inside themselves for inspiration, to know that their own thoughts and feelings were valid, important, their own, their truth.

Maybe she would end up like Lady Despont - alone with her dog, slightly scatty. But if she could help others along the path, she would feel vindicated. She would feel that she had contributed something to the world she inhabited, no longer just a passenger being swept along by others' wishes, desires, and intentions.

Her new life was going to be so busy! She would be surrounded by people who understood her, understood what she was wanting to achieve. She'd still be able to work with her own students at Shooting Stars - keeping close to her roots was so important to her! - hopefully funnelling some of the children into the Junior Academy as appropriate. And Sally would be dealing so well and enthusiastically with all the tasks which Tabitha found irksome. That alone was a reason to rejoice!

"You know, my dear," Georgia spoke into the silence with a faraway look, "I had a dear friend once - long gone now, I'm afraid," she added quickly.

"He had suffered terribly during the last war. He was a Jew, you see. Persecuted, punished … you know the sort of thing. I can't bear to think of it. But do you know what they couldn't do? They couldn't break his spirit." She took a sip of tea from her flowery cup. "His favourite words - his 'catchphrase' I think you'd call it? - were 'Life is wonderful'. He truly thought that. After all he'd been through, he would say 'Life is wonderful'. He lost several members of his family, he had to abandon his studies, escape Vienna and start a new life in a foreign land, in exile. And yet whenever anyone complained about things going wrong, Hans would say 'Life is *wonderful!*' It didn't matter what happened, he'd seen worse, and yet he always said 'Life is wonderful!' In our comfortable lives, we don't really have too much to complain about, do we? Where there's life, there's hope." She sighed. "There's always a way." And she glanced at Tabitha to see if her message had reached home.

And it had. Tabitha wondered how she knew. Perhaps it was written all over her face: loss, despair, tragedy, rebirth … Yes, Life was wonderful. She had just managed to miss so much of it.

Tabitha blinked and smiled at her with gratitude. She had truly found a comfortable life – this was no time for weeping.

"I hope you'll be very happy here, my dear," Georgia added. "I think you need a safe haven - I hope this will be it for you and your lovely Esme."

Perhaps Georgia wasn't as scatty as she appeared, thought Tabitha as she smiled at her new friend, who had proved to be perspicacious and sensitive as well as rich and dotty.

She no longer had to ask the world's permission to do what she wanted with her life. She had autonomy at last.

# 31

Amongst all the busyness and excitement of leaving her old home, moving into her new one, starting with the new children at the Junior Academy, and beginning the new play with "her own" children at Shooting Stars, Tabitha made time for her lessons with Melanie. Sally had come up trumps again for the move, and volunteered Brendan and his van. And one of Maureen's boys had been home and helped with the heavy lifting. Tabitha hadn't wanted anyone else to know - she still wanted to keep Angus's dignity intact. She was still taking the blame, inside.

In fact, she wouldn't have missed a lesson with Melanie for the world - it was a high point of her week. While the whole plan was to enable Esme to take part in the production, the sessions had taken on a life of their own. Her insights into her dog's mind were sharpened, and she wished she had known more before, so she could have helped Luigi with his fears. But then, if she'd known more before, it wouldn't have been "before". You can't go back into the past. She knew well now, that you had to start from where you were. The past would never disappear, be wiped out. There was a lot there to learn from, and to enable her to understand more about herself. But there was no need to carry it round with her for ever, like a deadweight on her back.

The complaints and messages from Angus were thinning out a little, becoming less frequent, and less vitriolic. There had been so many. He sent texts because she'd stopped taking his calls when she found that they were just a litany of whingeing and moaning and listing her faults. These calls were often late at night, after he'd been drinking all evening. He was upset at having to deal with the house sale, and though she had visited the house many times when he was out, so that she should remove any trace of herself from it and get it clean and tidy and ready for sale, he still found plenty to complain about. For a while he'd been in denial. He decided Tabitha was just having a strop because of "that damned dog" and that she'd soon come to her senses and knuckle under. So as the weeks went past and there was no sign of her crawling home, he started to rail against her, against fate, and against anybody else who got in his way.

To begin with she was upset and wavered a little in her resolve, wondering if she was being selfish as he said. Her shoulders would droop, her heart sink, she seemed to see fingers wagging at her, teachers from the distant past telling her off for thinking only of herself. She still felt guilty at his pain, as she knew that was the cause of his fury. But gradually she had grown stronger, thought of poor Luigi, felt her resolve on that awful day, and knew that Angus's dominion over her was history. She was her own person at last. She could do this. She paused for a moment as the thought of how easily Jamie had accepted the end of their sweet relationship contrasted so much with Angus's resistance and lashing out at the end of their bitter one.

She felt sorry for him, flailing about in his distress, blaming her, the world, everyone but himself. But appearing to harden her heart to his entreaties had paid off. She knew that she was not the "selfish, hardhearted bitch" he had called her. At first she had been hurt, wanted to cry out that he didn't understand her. But she knew - and could remain strong in the knowledge - that she had acted honourably and done the right thing. That this was no longer the life for her. Angus was by now in America, building his new life. And she felt sure he was actually better off without her. He'd find someone else to cook and clean and wash his socks. He didn't actually need a wife, a companion. Just a "Maddie" would do. The gradually growing distance between them removed the shackles from her heart and allowed her to breathe easily. The fear of him trying to snatch her back - and her giving in yet again - was over, and she hoped he would gradually heal. They both had healing to do.

As to her other set of matching baggage - her life with Jamie - she was at peace with that too. It had been a desperate attempt to find love in her life, the love she felt she needed, the acceptance she craved. Now she knew - to start with painfully, and then with a cheerful realisation - that she didn't need adoration or admiration to live her life. She didn't need the approval of others to do what she wanted to do. She had come to know that her satisfaction was all within her own hands. It was for her to make her life her own, create her own life, make time for what she wanted, without heeding the judgments of others.

She loved her new work at the NDS, she loved every moment at Shooting Stars, but nowhere did she feel lighter in spirit than in these sessions with Melanie and their dogs.

She'd been doing fairly well with what she was teaching Esme, but needed help to tidy things up and avoid confusing her poor dog by not understanding the principles of teaching, herself. It was all giving her such insights into teaching the children! When Esme was confused she just stopped doing anything - or started trying to do everything at once to see if something worked. Tabitha had sometimes seen the same response in her students - and realised how she could be so much clearer and yet at the same time give them the opportunity to work things out for themselves. That was where the strength of this style of teaching lay!

As Melanie and her crew arrived at Tabitha's new place the van barked a bit, but was soon silent when the unseen passengers realised that this was not their time for a walk. Melanie clambered out with her things, stood and looked at the little Summerhouse and said "Wow, Tabitha - you've certainly landed on your four paws here!"

As Tabitha ushered her into the house, she paused to look back at the splendid grounds. "And you get to walk in all this?" she asked, eyes agog.

"Absolutely," replied Tabitha. "And we love it, don't we, Es?" she added as Esme wiggled about their legs, excited to see her favourite friend.

Fortified by hot coffees, the fresh aroma filling the little house, its doors closed against the autumn chill, they got down to work. Tabitha got out her notebook - the one decorated with the big photo of Esme and the words "Esme's book" - and checked exactly where they'd got to in the last session, and how many practice sessions she'd had since then.

"We're on scene 7, the sausages," Tabitha said, as she located the page, getting herself up and ready to get started.

In the play they were working on, the dog had to steal some sausages and race off with them. Esme was now able to pick up her string of sausages, having started with a couple of knotted socks to make it easier to pick up cleanly and turn fast, so today they practiced Tabitha standing off "in the wings" calling her and getting her to spin round quickly to run off with her prize. She needed to grab and turn and run away in one movement, while the children in the scene made as if to chase her. Getting this going well - much sooner than expected - they went on to learn spins and turns.

"Let's see how these are going," said Melanie, sitting down on the sofa again. "Not so fast!" she added as Tabitha gave a snappier hand signal and Esme started to spin out of place, "you can build up speed once it's accurate."

"This is handy for me to keep in mind with the dances the children are doing. Mercifully Karen seems to teach them very well so I don't have to get involved - though there's always *one* who can't tell her left from her right," she smiled.

"Have you tried tying a ribbon to one of their wrists?" Melanie asked, adding, "a trainer friend of mine struggled with this, so she tied pink and blue ribbons to her dog's front paws. Instead of Spin or Turn, she'd say Pink or Blue!"

"Now that's not a bad idea," said Tabitha, smiling at the thought of her "corps de ballet" adorned with pink and blue ribbons. She slowed down and got Esme doing it right again. She was happy to follow Melanie's guidance, as wasn't this just the way she aimed to teach too? It wasn't a question of making the student do what she wanted - rather allowing the student to do their best, giving them the space to "work it out" as Melanie would say. Endless encouragement didn't lead to a soft learner - it led to one who tried ever harder to get it right. She'd developed this system of getting results from the children down the years, but never put it into words as Melanie did now.

"Take the pressure off," she'd say, when Esme hesitated or looked worried.

"Give her time to work it out," she added, to slow down Tabitha's impatience.

And "Why do you think she's doing that?" always got Tabitha thinking, finding the answer Melanie knew she knew. There it was again - Tabitha knew the answers, she just had to look inside and find them.

Melanie was a natural teacher and had only the dog's welfare at heart as she taught. It was all about the learner. At one stage in the session Tabitha looked past Melanie and caught sight of the photo on her desk, of Luigi and Esme in the sunshine on Luigi's log. It served as a reminder that she had a reason to drive forward. She would never let herself or her dogs down again.

They were getting to the end of their session when they heard a car pulling up on the crunchy gravel outside. Of course Esme responded to this "rural burglar alarm" first, her nose pressed to the glass of the French doors, her tail waving low, alerting Tabitha to the impending invasion. More joy for Esme: it was Clare, another on her list of top favourite people. Clare was due for a visit to work on the article she was writing about Tabitha's new venture at the NDS, and she was a bit early.

"Oh, it's Clare!" said Tabitha, "I'd love you to meet her. She's a feature-writer - maybe she'd like to write a piece about you and your dancing dogs?"

"I'd love to meet her," said Melanie, "and we're done now anyway. Esme will be exhausted," she laughed. But Melanie wasn't exhausted, and was happy to have another coffee and meet Tabitha's old friend.

After the noisy introductions - Clare always breezed about the place and loved getting Esme excited - Tabitha was persuaded to show off one of Esme's tricks. Esme was happy to oblige, and performed several of her new skills, with much tail-wagging and bright eyes.

Knowing that "stage fright" could interfere with the performance, Tabitha was careful to avoid what she assumed would be Melanie's critical gaze. But she needn't have worried: Melanie was smiling proudly at her pupil's efforts.

"That's amazing!" gasped Clare. "I knew you could do wonders with your kids, but you can do all this with just a dog?"

"She's not 'just a dog'," protested Tabitha with theatrically downturned mouth. "She's Esme, and she's precious." And she laughed and glowed with pride over her little dog, ruffling her neck, as she went over to turn on the kettle again and get out three clean mugs.

She looked over and saw that Clare was chattering animatedly, and from the way she was listening to Melanie's responses with rapt interest, Tabitha had a feeling that her plan had worked, and Clare saw the makings of another article there. She waited to return until she saw - with delight - the two of them swapping contact details, then carried over the tray with the mugs and fresh cafetière she'd just made.

"Now let me look at you," said Clare, turning to face Tabitha. "What's with the trendy hairstyle?" She grinned, knowing full well that it had been she who had prodded Tabitha to make the change.

One of the first things Tabitha had done after moving into Georgia's was to have her hair cut. Having a regular income from the NDS - and Shooting Stars actually producing revenue at last - enabled her to join the rest of civilisation by spending a little money on herself! After years of tight budgeting and zero spend on "fripperies" she was able to make her modest earnings stretch well. So she now had a neat dark cap of hair which made her look not only smarter but also, apparently, younger. Or so the students said.

"I like it," added Melanie, who had a trim head of red curls. "Much easier to manage when you're bent over checking a dog's paws, or walking in a stiff breeze."

Tabitha smiled at them both. "I love it." She said with a warm smile of acknowledgement to Clare. But she reflected that while she knew that the reason she'd always worn her hair long was because she couldn't afford regular visits to a hairdresser - Angus always being so tight with money - she admitted to herself that that was not the only reason. Jamie had always loved her long hair. Annette had a short trim style that befitted a busy mother of five always bent over the oven or the ironing-board. But Tabitha had had long silky dark hair which Jamie would twirl round his fingers, stroking it over her shoulders ... She touched her short hair now with her hand, to bring her back to the present, and gave her guests another warm smile.

She sat, stretched her legs out and leaned back luxuriously in the battered old sofa. She watched her two friends as they chattered animatedly. Melanie had become a real friend and was so much more relaxed and less distant than when they had first met. Esme had indeed taken herself off to her bed and was fast asleep already.

Tabitha had a new life - and she was loving it.

She felt so fulfilled. She had a home. She had two new good friends who valued her - and of course, the support of Maureen back home, back at her old home, and her new protector, Georgia. She had the warmth and support of her colleagues and mentor at the NDS, and the enduring love of her rural families at Shooting Stars. Her family was just Esme now. But the bond between them was fierce. Having Esme to look after was the one strong thread running through these past months of turmoil. Esme had helped her keep her feet on the ground, while it quaked and heaved beneath her and threatened to swallow her.

# 32

"Aren't you glad you've moved to the metropolis and you're not dealing with country bumpkins any more?" one of the younger staff members said at a tea break - albeit tongue in cheek - a few weeks into the Autumn Term.

And Tabitha was pleased to be able to reply with all honesty, "Actually, I love it all the more. The contrast is brilliant. But you know, they're all just children, wherever they come from. We all have the same concerns and worries as we grow up. And of course, gifts are scattered fairly equally throughout the population!"

"I might argue with that when I look at my group!" joked the young man.

Tabitha's love for Shooting Stars was undiminished. She'd been worried that she'd be so consumed by the NDS project that she'd lose interest in her "nursery school" - which she now saw was her own nursery, for her own development, as much as a nursery for talent and self-expression.

But that fear had turned out to be far from the truth. She still loved it just as much as before, and always looked forward to her trips to rehearsals and the camaraderie of the Shooting Stars family. On every visit she felt she was being welcomed home. The simplicity of the children in general - along with the complexity of every individual one! - kept her humble. It kept her in touch with her roots - her "why". The NDS was simply another stage on this path of helping young people develop - develop their talents, and develop their personalities. Giving them the time and space to express themselves in a way that society tended to stamp out of them. To help them avoid the wrong turnings that she had taken.

She reflected on this as she was tidying the Summerhouse one Sunday morning.

Melanie's 'My Book' idea had gone down a treat with her "country bumpkins"! She'd enjoyed getting the children busy making their own books, with pictures of them - in costume where possible - and reminding them to write into their books after each rehearsal. A couple of the mothers had brought old magazines and scissors and glue and set them up on a table at the back of the hall so those who were not rehearsing could enjoy working on their books. The older girls had decorated theirs with images of them posing like their favourite models and film stars. The younger girls had let loose with the coloured markers, including lots of drawings of unicorns and ponies and kittens. The boys? They had macho images of their heroes, guns, soldiers, men jumping out of aeroplanes and the like. But they were all proud of their creations, and kept them up to date. They loved sharing them with each other. Maisie had proudly showed Tabitha her book, adorned with a picture of her with her rabbit. So the books were altogether a success, and now just might spread into the Junior Academy too ... It was a great way to infiltrate their drama experiences into the rest of their week, at home.

They brought their books to rehearsals and left them in an untidy heap on Tabitha's table while they worked. At the end of one session, Philip - not so long ago the new boy with the difficult mother, but now firmly one of the group - had picked up Maisie's book and said, "Couldn't you find a photo of you instead of a hippo?" and laughed uproariously.

"Let me see," said Tabitha, taking the book gently from Philip. She looked at the photo of plump Maisie, her eyes screwed up against the sun. "I see a lovely young girl who is kindness itself. Don't you remember how Maisie helped you when you first came, Philip? Run along with you now. You'll appreciate her one day."

Philip took the book back and handed it to Maisie, saying, "I remember," under lowered lashes, before spinning round, spreading his arms out wide and zooming off making aeroplane noises. Maisie smiled up at Tabitha, hugging her book to her, then set off to find her mother Sally, and help her with the tidying up.

In every moment, Tabitha reflected, we have a choice. We can be kind, or we can be unkind. We can help build someone's confidence or we can shatter it.

She still marvelled at the fact that she'd needed a cataclysmic event - or indeed, a series of such events - to catapult her into her new life, her true calling. She woke daily in the little Summerhouse full of optimism and fire for the day. As she walked with Esme in the fresh, chill air in the beautiful grounds she knew how lucky she was that everything had fallen into place. It was as if her fervent desire for a better life had caused all the obstacles to simply vanish, leaving her new path open to her.

It was Maureen who had pointed out to her that it was her openness to change that had allowed all these things to happen.

"I'm a firm believer that good things happen to those who deserve them," she'd said on Tabitha's last visit. They had sat huddled in coats in Maureen's much-loved, rambly, garden, hugging their coffee mugs close and enjoying the fresh sunshine that October day.

"But they have to do something themselves to make it all happen. There's no such thing as luck. As well you know, Tabitha! You've done so much good, you surely deserve the good things now."

Esme was sniffing the weed-filled border. "What's a weed?" Maureen would always say, "They're all beautiful, in their way." And Tabitha had responded quietly, "Yes, that's how I think of the children, too." Esme started, and took off at speed to the far end of the garden where she'd spotted a rabbit. Thwarted by the tiny gap in the fence the rabbit had shot through, Esme feigned nonchalance and carried on sniffing. Maureen and Tabitha enjoyed the moment and laughed together.

She felt very secure amongst her friends. Those who really appreciated her had come good. She had felt so alone in those dark days with Angus, and now her life seemed to be filled with colour and laughter and opportunity.

Tabitha returned to thoughts of Shooting Stars, particularly the latest rehearsal, with Sharon's mother Linda now helping Sally with all the new recruits, as a thank you for her reduced fees. It was so busy, and Karen had come up trumps! She was really blossoming in her new role as dance leader.

She was so confident in her dance abilities - as well she should be - that she had nothing to hold her back. She was proving so popular with the children that Tabitha and Sally had shoe-horned some more routines into the production. And she did wonders with tidying up entrances and exits, especially with the younger kids: she was so good with the young ones - helped, no doubt, by being one of such a large family herself.

"Tabitha, I'm just so happy with what you've done for me," Karen would tell her, repeatedly. "Mum and Dad are actually beginning to come round!"

"You've done it all yourself, Karen!" Tabitha had said. "You'll be able to hold your head high when they see just what you've achieved. And you'll be choosing a dance school soon … This is bound to help your application!" She knew that Jamie and Annette would be coming to one of the performances, and she was calm about it. To help them see how proud they should be of their daughter - that what she did was worthwhile - was a final gift she was able to give to Jamie's family as a kind of thanks and farewell. It had worked out for the best, in the end. Seated now on her sofa, Tabitha took a deep sigh, releasing it slowly as she hauled her mind back to the present.

She was able to greet Jamie when he drove Karen up to the hall without pangs and heart-churning. He seemed relieved to see this, and his smile always combined a little sadness with open relief. This proved to her that she'd moved forward with her life, and that he had with his. She had no regrets over Jamie - he had absolutely been the love of her life - but she felt that she'd "been there, done that," and could look forward, without yearning for what was past. Her desire for him had gone, and left in its place warmth, affection and gratitude.

And her new friends had really come into their own. It was Clare who had cheered Tabitha on from the sidelines, whose splendid article about the new Academy was now published, and done wonders for the sign-up rate at Shooting Stars with her glowing profile of Tabitha, with some lovely photos of her and Esme outside the Summerhouse. Several copies of the magazine were to be found around Georgia's house, some of them open at "Tabitha's" page, so that Georgia could show off her protégée proudly to her friends. And Clare was a frequent visitor to the Summerhouse, which she saw as a haven away from the busyness of the city it hid in and the speed of her own life in it.

"Don't you realise what you have to offer?" Clare had asked her a few days before on one of her visits, her smart shoes kicked off so she could sit on the sofa with her feet tucked under her. "You've spent all your life believing what you've been told, by people who got off on keeping you down."

"But why would my mother want to keep me down? She did, you know." Tabitha had replied, in puzzlement.

"You said yourself that she was attractive, took care with her appearance, was good socially - entertaining for your father. Of course she didn't want you competing with her for looks and presence! Having a shy and frumpy daughter was her way to shine. Can you not see that now?"

It was a body-blow for Tabitha. She'd always been puzzled by her mother's attitude to her, treating her as the ugly duckling, unsuccessful at finding a decent mate. But she hadn't realised that it had been in her mother's interest to have her think this! She knew that her mother had never meant to hurt her - it was simply the way she'd been brought up, to rely on her looks and marriageability. And that included a tendency to choose plain friends who made her look better, as well as not trying to force her reluctant daughter to shed her natural diffidence. She'd accepted so much of what she'd been told, for so long, without question. Without ever looking for an ulterior motive.

The more she learnt about the children in her care, the more she saw that the same event could be viewed in as many different ways as there were people to view it. Other people's opinions were just that - other people's opinions. They were no more the truth than people's perceptions of weeds as bad, as opposed to Maureen's open appreciation of them.

"You have special gifts," Clare had carried on, unwinding her feet and handing Tabitha a tissue as she leant forward earnestly. "You have something to offer the world. You *should* offer it! It would be wrong to have these gifts and not allow others to benefit."

Clare leant back in her seat again, the movement causing Esme to lift her head from her paws, wondering if there was going to be some action. "You owe it to them."

This had so helped Tabitha feel her own power in her work. She had thrown herself even more into both her groups - at the NDS and at Shooting Stars. The students were responding with equal vigour, and now her colleagues - her equals - were recognising this by the way they spoke to her. She truly felt she had arrived in a new chapter in her life - a chapter where *she* mattered.

There was only one thing that niggled, that blighted her happiness. She felt she'd ducked out of facing up to Angus. There had never been a final resolution, an ending, as there had been with Jamie. This one remaining source of dissatisfaction would make her cheeks burn with shame - when she allowed it to.

# 33

It was Tuesday, so that meant it was Timothy's sandwich lunch day. After a few weeks at the Drama School, Tabitha enjoyed the lunch as much as the old-stagers - her new colleagues - clearly did. She observed again with amusement, that once artists discover that people are prepared to feed and water them in return for their company, there's no keeping them away! Just the sniff of a free lunch was enough to ensure that this was always a well-attended event. In finding ways to unite his staff, Timothy knew what he was doing!

So the room was full of chatter as the various tutors solved the world's problems, discussed recalcitrant students, told stories - racy or tedious, as suited their character - and generally felt at home and valued. Timothy's office, usually still and smelling of leather and polished wood, now was full of noise, colour, and the smell of fresh food and coffee, as well as the myriad scents the tutors had chosen to adorn themselves with. Tabitha had slipped into the NDS family easily and comfortably. She felt as if she'd come home, had been there for years. She worked very hard, and while she got the new group of children shaping up into a team - always excited and happy to arrive at their classes - she was also getting used to the new routine at Shooting Stars, with Sally so keen to ensure that it all worked smoothly, now building a new team of helpers herself, of which Linda was the keenest.

Carrying her mug and her plate, she joined one of the groups at an opportune moment, as Drusilla was talking about Jennie as one of the more promising students. "She's had to hold her own in the teeth of her parents' disapproval. Just what we need - *dedication!*" she said, with emphasis.

"Jennie's a hard worker," agreed Tabitha, "and she seems to get on well with the other youngsters in her year."

"She's quiet, but yes - she has opinions when she needs them!" agreed Drusilla.

Jennie was blossoming too. And Tabitha realised that one of her gifts was undoubtedly being able to recognise raw talent. While she had been under her husband's thumb she had not been able to help these young people in the same way. Encourage them, surely. But she had no "in" to an organisation that could really move them forward in their lives. Since she had emerged as that butterfly who Maureen had feared would be battered to death as she beat her wings against the cage that held her, she had discovered her power.

By freeing herself she was able to free others. And save them from following the desires and whims of other people. They would know where they should go, and point themselves firmly on that track!

"What's all this?" Gerard came up, brandishing a copy of the glossy magazine, opening it at Clare's article and holding it up for all to see. "Do we have a star in our midst?" he asked, smiling at his old friend.

Drusilla snatched the magazine and demanded of Gerard, "Since when do you read *lifestyle* magazines?" as she scanned the piece, nodding approvingly.

"I don't!" said Gerard, looking a mite uncomfortable. "But I had to go to the dentist and there it was. I thought it would do better service here than in the dentist's waiting room ..."

"So you *snitched* it!" said Drusilla, laughing loudly. Then, "Tabitha, my dear, this house looks gorgeous! And what a sweet little dog you have."

Tabitha smiled happily, feeling something between shyness and pleasure, agreeing with them enthusiastically.

"Yes, it's perfect. I love it there. Thank you so much for setting it up for me, Drusilla!"

"Well, I knew Genevieve lived there, but I never *imagined* it was so charming," she replied.

She knew both Gerard and Drusilla were impressed with the article, and once Drusilla had the magazine, everyone in the school would soon know about it. It would probably fetch up pinned to a noticeboard.

"What happens to your dog while you're here stuffing your face with Timothy's largesse?" asked Gerard, moving beside her as Drusilla, heading back to the sausage roll plate, accosted the Director with the magazine that she was waving in front of him.

Tabitha gulped down her mouthful of prawn mayonnaise sandwich, waving her hand by her mouth as she tried hurriedly to swallow it. "Georgia will let her out for a run in the grounds," she said.

"Oh, it's 'Georgia' now, is it?" smiled Gerard.

"Oh yes, we're firm friends," laughed Tabitha. "Actually it's brilliant. Her Mitzi is quite anxious about other dogs, a bit frosty usually, but Esme is so easy-going that there's no problem. They get on fine and even start chasing games with each other sometimes. It makes Georgia very happy to think Mitzi has a friend. Remember the dog trainer I'm working with?"

"Sure. Some madwoman who talks to animals, isn't she?" Gerard looked deliberately vague.

"I told you! *Melanie*. She's fantastic with dogs. She understands them. And she gets them to do whatever she wants just by catching the moment to dish out her cheese to them. Anyway, she gave me some tips on how to introduce Esme to Mitzi, who - as you know from her handbag visits - can be pretty yappy. And they worked."

"If it involves cheese, she could probably get me to jump through hoops for her," said the returning Drusilla as she studied her sandwich bulging with cheese, pickle and lettuce, perched precariously on top of a heap of chicken wings and sausage rolls. Who knew where the magazine had got to by now ... "Is this where you get your skills with the children, Tabitha? From treating them all as *puppies?*"

Tabitha smiled. "Actually, Melanie says I'm good with the children because I've naturally found out how to get the best from them - just as she does with her dogs." Feeling suddenly embarrassed at seeming to blow her own trumpet, she quickly changed the subject away from herself. "Did you see her on television the other day? They showed just a few seconds of her dancing with her collie on the local news. It was amazing! I don't mean like ballroom dancing," she laughed, as Gerard raised his eyebrows and made motions of clasping a partner in a waltz. "It's more of a routine where they reflect each other's moves - like ballet. And they manage to make everyone laugh at the same time."

"You should have that in one of your productions, Tabitha! The families would love it!" said Gerard, doubtless thinking of the joy he would see on the faces of his own young children, who Tabitha well knew he adored.

"Well, Shooting Stars is doing a piece which Esme will feature in. That's how I met Melanie. You see, I had no clue how to teach these tricks. I'm actually learning how to *dance* with my dog now!"

Gerard snorted into his coffee cup as he looked aghast. "You?! Last time I saw you dancing was Jeremy's party, years ago. Remember his place in Stafford Gardens?"

"Oh, please don't judge me on that!" laughed Tabitha. "Yes, what a grim place it was … But Jeremy could throw a mean party!" They both laughed, reminiscing together. "You see, one of the students at the children's group is a dancer, and she's teaching me the moves. It's important that the audience watch the dog without distraction! But it would be great to show off how a professional dog person does it. I'd love to see if Melanie and her wonderdog could be inveigled into a production here at the NDS." She paused while she thought of this.

"Planning to spend more of our budget, Tabitha?" asked Timothy as he joined the group, offering a big dish with what was left of the food. He smiled fondly on his new discovery. Tabitha loved that he felt vindicated in his plan to build his legacy to the drama world by founding the new Junior Academy. He'd told her that he'd fully expected her to take up the reins with enthusiasm and professionalism. With such strong support, she had surprised herself with her capability and grasp of the workings of such an Academy. And she knew that this meant that he trusted her to make the right decisions - although officially these decisions were made by him at their weekly meetings. Timothy wore the look of the cat that had got the cream, as he metaphorically preened his whiskers and happily swished his tail.

"Absolutely!" laughed Tabitha. "Though I know she wouldn't charge much. She'd be so thrilled to perform to a completely new audience. She really wants people to know that you don't have to be hard on dogs to get results. Just like me, really. That you don't have to browbeat kids to get them to be creative. You just have to take the lid off and let 'em at it!"

"Sounds very like us," said Timothy, "so keen to show people what we do and how it can change their lives. There's only a few actors who command the big figures the rest of the world seem to think we all get."

"Too right," mumbled Gerard, pretending to sound aggrieved. But Tabitha knew how much he loved his post at the NDS. Not for him the stresses and strains of the jobbing actor. A bit of security was what he needed for his beloved family.

And security was what Tabitha had found here, among friends. Her family was just little Esme, but she made no apologies for the fierceness of her love for her dog. At last she was able to express her true self, and she felt as if she were floating in a warm Mediterranean Sea, buoyed up by her self-belief, basking in the admiration she was at last receiving from her peers.

Her phone beeped. She glanced at it and slipped it back in her pocket. It was Angus. Again. Now was not the time to read his message.

The only fly in the ointment had been these endless texts and phone calls. It always jarred with her when she saw the notification on her phone, and it was with her heart heavy in her chest that she would open them, with thoughts of "What now?" But gradually even these messages were getting less frequent as he got involved with his travel and his new post. Fortunately his agent Philip was keeping him very busy with the plans for his new lectureship, coinciding with a US book tour for his latest book, which astonishingly he'd managed to complete amidst all this furore, and it was destined to bestseller status even before it was published. So while he still whinged and wailed, he'd eased back on the condemnations and insults and seemed to be moving into acceptance. This was such a relief to Tabitha, who hated conflict of any kind, and also hated the thought of upsetting anyone, even Angus. She still felt loyalty to him.

But some of Angus's friends were disappointed at how things had worked out, and Tabitha knew that they were working on him to "do the decent thing and share the spoils." Angus had mentioned it in one of his more rambly texts, that even his friends were turning against him. She wondered whether he'd got on top of his drinking yet. It really didn't sound like it sometimes. While she was content at Georgia's for now, she couldn't help thinking that just part of the proceeds of their big house would set her up for life, so she hoped that Angus would slowly become less bitter and fairness would prevail.

She realised that Drusilla had been telling one of her naughtier stories - this one about the leading man and leading lady being found in bed by her husband, the director.

".. So he said 'I do think you're taking method acting a bit far, Orlando'."

They all laughed uproariously, and Tabitha settled back into the group, content with her new world, her new home, and her new old friends.

# 34

The last of the autumn leaves were being swept up for bonfires by the dedicated old gardener. Tabitha had learnt that he rejoiced in the name Joe Bucket, and he had tipped his grimy flat cap at her from a distance, as he took the opportunity to lean on his rake. Tabitha waved to him as she and Esme came back into the house, Esme giving a most satisfying shake as Tabitha noisily breathed all the cold air out. The wind was biting and had brought a rosy hue to her cheeks. She slipped off her woolly hat and ruffled her hair to settle it. She still enjoyed the feel of her new hairstyle, representing, as it did, her freedom of choice and independence with money.

The post had arrived while she was out. She scooped up some of the envelopes from the mat, being careful to leave one for Esme to pick up and present to her - a task she performed with enthusiasm - then put them on the nearby windowsill. She used to restrict Esme to picking up junk mail as her early excitement at this trick resulted in a few wet and shredded envelopes, but now she was clean and efficient and didn't inflict any damage on even the thinnest letter.

"Here, Esme - let's be having you," she said as she grabbed the dog towel and got down to her little dog's feet and vigorously dried them and all her damp feathering - removing a few stray leaves from her tail - always a hard job when Esme was wagging so much that her whole body swayed and moved. As ever, the drying session ending with a slurpy kiss on the nose for the laughing Tabitha.

"*You're* done," she said as she straightened up, "off to your bed. Now for me," and as Esme circled and curled herself up in her bed by the sofa, Tabitha turned to fill the kettle and get something warm down her.

She had a day off today as she'd been working so many weekends in the run-up to the Christmas performance, just round the corner now. So she was making the best of it with a lie-in followed by a glorious walk in the grounds - she loved the rawness of winter weather. It seemed to reach right into her soul to clean out all the doubts and worries and leave it fresh and clean.

She was making the most of her day off by meeting Clare for lunch and having a training session booked with Melanie for the evening, preparing Esme for her first dancing competition. As Melanie's place was not that far from Maureen, she'd be dropping in there on her way. Maureen had been so thrilled to see her coming back to the full of her health, with the energy and enthusiasm that she had lost over the recent years - especially during the months of awfulness this year. She now felt able to give back in their relationship, after so much taking. But then, give and take - isn't that what friends are about?

She looked forward to all three of these events. As she poured her warming coffee, steaming in the cool room - must light the woodburner, she thought, reaching for the matches - she reflected on her new-found friends with whom she now spent plenty of time. And there was always something going on at the NDS. From being "Tabby-no-mates" to having a full social life was quite a jump, and she felt a lightening of her whole body when she thought of the activity and fun in her life now.

The amazing Maddie had cleared and laid the fire for her while she was out. She watched the flames licking the logs, adjusted the knobs and shut the door of the fire, already feeling the warmth on her face, and tossing the matches back into the log basket.

Clare was settling well into her new magazine role, getting herself a reputation for well-written, pithy articles with a new slant. Her article about Tabitha's move had prompted commissions from a couple of other editors, to write about change in people's lives. But she had proved more brittle than she'd first appeared when she arrived in the country. She missed the children more than she expected. And no matter how much she rationalised it - "They're grown up now, busy doing their own thing," - it still hurt her.

Tabitha hadn't had the joy of her own children so could only imagine the anguish of their absence. The nearest thing was her recent - but still painful - loss of Luigi. Her heart stopped for a moment as she remembered that awful day. Then she looked over to Esme, already fast asleep, and it brought a smile to her lips. But she was happy to keep Clare looking forward, keeping to the path she'd chosen. Now she was earning enough to buy her children plane tickets ("No budget airlines for this pair," she'd laughed), Clare was excitedly planning their visits just after Christmas. Clare wasn't made for a solo life, and it was no surprise to Tabitha that she had a number of boyfriends who were keen to get to know her rather better. For now she was happy to spread her favours - she was in no rush to jump into another relationship.

And Tabitha too had friends. But not boyfriends. She had had her fingers burnt by her marriage. And she knew that nothing could ever match the passion of her time with Jamie. He was truly her once-in-a-lifetime man. But gone.

She was always slightly surprised to find just how ok she was with this. She didn't seek another partner. For one who'd spent the majority of her life thinking she had to be of service to a man, she was glad to be feeling no desire whatever to try this again. She'd never enjoyed the comfy family life that Clare had had, nor the busy and noisy one that Maureen enjoyed, nor the quiet and structured life of Sally's warm family. Her home had for so long been a cold place, and her heart had not found a home at all. So the luxury of her little Summerhouse with Esme was perfection for her, and she had no wish to dilute it with an unknown new person.

"We're fine exactly as we are, aren't we, Es?" The sleepy dog slowly thudded her tail on her bed in response.

She grabbed the mail from the windowsill. The ones she had picked up were mostly junk mail and went straight into the bin, and there were a few Christmas cards. But Esme's letter, which displayed some light toothmarks and a slightly damp corner, had a handwritten envelope and ... a US university frank. She slowly returned the Christmas cards to the windowsill and walked across the room, gazing at the American letter.

Typical of Angus that even a private letter he put through the college office, to save himself the pennies on a stamp! But she dismissed such mean thoughts, settled on the sofa with her coffee - her toes toward the fire - and opened the letter, hoping not to find another whinge. She wondered why his staccato texts had more or less petered out a few weeks before, and why he'd now put pen to paper. She hadn't heard from him for a while, and had guessed he was busy with his new post. She truly hoped so. She really didn't like to feel she was still causing him suffering.

As she read the letter, though, her mouth fell slightly open and her face softened.

*My dear Tabitha,* she read.

*You were right. I think I was suffering some kind of mental breakdown. I've joined AA and haven't touched a drink in seven weeks. I feel I'm over the worst of it.*

*Life here is the best thing that could have happened to me. There's a huge amount of work involved with building the curriculum and designing the lectures I have to give. And I'd forgotten how very young and sweet students are. A bit like you when we first met.*

*I see now how I was at fault. I'm sorry, Tabitha. You did the right thing - you were a caged bird who needed to be freed. Philip's wife sent me the piece your friend wrote about you. I'm so glad you've found something that you're worth. Your success is well-deserved. I mean that.*

*The house is all but sold, and I'll be sending you half the money when it arrives with me. Try to spend it on yourself - a new home, perhaps - rather than sinking it into your school.*

*I won't trouble you again, Tabitha. You are right once more: I will never marry again. But you are still young and should you wish to, let me know and we can arrange things. But I will always be pleased to hear of your triumphs. If you ever cross the water you must look me up and I'll show you round.*

*Best wishes,*

*Angus*

Tabitha folded the letter carefully and laid it in her lap. Her cheeks were wet with what she knew were the last tears she would shed for her marriage, her thwarted hopes and dreams.

She had new dreams now, dreams that were being fulfilled. Dreams that fitted the energy she had to give to them. She wiped her face with her hands and gave a crumpled smile to Esme, who glanced up at her from her warm bed, quietly relaxing after her exciting romp in the bracing weather.

Tabitha took a sip of her coffee and was about to lean back and snuggle into the cushions when she heard a yawn and a whimper from the crate in the corner of the room. Her new puppy had awoken and required attention.

"Hiya, Cariad!" she said, as she scooped up the warm and wriggly little bundle, Esme jumped from her bed to come and nuzzle the puppy. Tabitha slipped a collar and lead onto the pup and they all headed out into the wind.

"You wait there, Esme," she said, motioning her to sit and wait at the door so as not to distract the puppy from the purpose of her outing. "Cariad has important business to attend to!"

They were soon back in the house to enjoy playtime and another meal for the puppy, followed by yet more puppy sleep.

"Time for her brain to grow, Esme," she explained as she popped her back in her crate with a favoured teddy bear to suckle. She had been teaching baby Cariad some tricks and essential doggy skills. "She's already a marvel at what she's learning. She'll be as clever as you soon!"

When Tabitha knew the time was right for another puppy, Melanie had been delighted to help her find just the right dog. She had loads of contacts and knew exactly what would suit Tabitha. Going puppy-shopping really was the best!

Without anyone else to please (save Georgia, who was bordering on delirious with delight at the prospect of a new puppy she could mind), Tabitha opted for a large dog. It was hard to know Cariad's parentage exactly, but her mother had had the look of a hairy lurcher, and judging by the thickset legs and large paws, Dad had been considerably bigger. Esme thought that all her Christmases had come at once, and would wait patiently for the puppy to wake from her endless sleeping to mother her and play with her.

An hour later Tabitha had settled her family, fed, watered, warm and dry, in their respective beds and was ready to go out to meet up with Clare. She tidied the room, turning her letter over again in her hands, before thoughtfully placing it at the back of a drawer in her desk.

Angus's letter had been the resolution she had needed. She was glad he'd written, and truly glad he was doing so well. They had for so long been pursuing the wrong course because of what they thought society expected of them. They'd both made a mistake. But now they had gone through the pain, acknowledged the truth, and were moving on. Tabitha no longer felt the need to fit in with others. She was her own woman, with her own plans and desires. She seemed to have everything she wanted. Everything she needed. For a moment she felt that old stab in her heart as she thought of Jamie. But the warmth and security of how she felt now washed it away. She could manage on her own, after all.

Life was indeed wonderful - could it get any better?

## THE END

Would you like to learn how Angus resolved his thoughts and feelings - and why he behaved as he did? Visit www.beverleycourtney.com/chapter for a free extra chapter where he reveals what he discovered about himself and his life with Tabitha, and you'll also get to hear when Tabitha and her friends will be back with you again.

# A Note from the Author

I've enjoyed a wonderfully varied life, and - simply by following my passion - helping thousands of people to improve their lives through my teaching, my articles, and my nine ever-popular how-to books, as a writer, coach, artist, and force-free dog trainer.

I have chosen to spend most of my life living in the countryside with my family and various animals - goats, sheep, chickens, donkeys, dogs, cats, an amazing parrot, and children (!) being chief among them.

Not afraid of handling difficult subjects, my accessible writing style with a dash of humour has already carried my often idiosyncratic ideas to many dog-owners. And this has continued into my first novel, where we live through Tabitha's struggles to discover her true path in life.

A common response from readers and students is, "It's so obvious when you put it like that!" In the same straightforward way I'm thrilled to be getting results for my clients in my coaching practice. If you are affected by any of the issues in this book, do visit www.beverleycourtney.com for ideas to get you unstuck.

If you got this far in the book, you must have some thoughts about it! It would be great if you could hop over to Amazon and leave a brief review. And I'd love to hear from you by email too, at beverley@beverleycourtney.com where I read every one.

Beverley Courtney
BA (Hons) CPC ELI-MP CBATI ABTC
Norfolk, England

# Acknowledgements

I wouldn't have got very far without some serious wisdom and cheerleading from the indefatigable Erin Lindsay McCabe, so – many thanks, Erin!

And thanks also to my children, for always keeping me driving onwards (whether they know it or not).

# Where can you find me?

www.beverleycourtney.com
www.brilliantfamilydog.com

My Author Page at Amazon:
www.beverleycourtney.com/author

Printed in Great Britain
by Amazon